Dark Mountain

Dark Mountain

Tales From The Dark Past Book 2

Helen Susan Swift

Published 2020 by Next Chapter
Cover art by Cover Mint

Foreword

I will relate events as they occurred and leave you, the reader of this journal to judge what is real and what is not. I cannot explain more than I write; perhaps you can understand things that I cannot, or maybe there is no explanation. I can only say what I saw, and what I heard and felt and experienced. I can do no more. Please, God that I did not do the things I may have done, or see the things I believe I saw.

I shall give you a little background before I properly begin so that you can slot me into the context of my story. I am an orphan. In 1896 somebody dumped me on the doorstep of an orphanage in Perthshire in Scotland, without a note or an explanation and only a scanty white cloth as covering. I knew nothing about that until I was eight years old when the good people who ran the orphanage took me aside and told me what little they knew about my life. I listened in silence and gave no hint of my feelings, for that was the way things were. I had already learned it was better to merge into the background than to step forward, and I knew how to sit on the sidelines while more important people took centre stage. I accepted the meagre facts of my life. I knew that nobody cared for me; I was a faceless, unwanted child, a burden on society and dependant on charity for my existence.

Perhaps my lack of worth explains why I have always been interested in the outdoors, in the wild spaces of Scotland. They provide an escape from the realities of modern life and allow me to think and contemplate and wonder who I am and from where I came. One can avoid people out there. One does not have to watch those fortunate enough to have friends and family and wish that life was different. One can be oneself.

However, I had never expected the spaces to be quite so wild as we found in those few days up in the Rough Quarter, the terrible peninsula of the *Ceathramh Garbh* in north-west Sutherland. Nor, God help me, did I expect the other events that happened on *An Cailleach,* the hill that people called The Dark Mountain. I can only hope and pray for my immortal soul, as the eagles soar above me.

Chapter One

Sutherland, Scotland, October 1921

'It's said to be haunted.'

We stood outside the remains of Dunalt Castle, with the wind tugging at the elder trees that strove to grow on the shattered stones and the smell of salt sea-spray strong in our nostrils.

'What rot!' Kate could still speak in the language of the schoolgirl she no longer was. 'It's no more haunted than I am.'

Rather than replying, Mary stepped closer to Dunalt and crept inside the gateway that gaped like the open jaw of a skull. I followed, resting my hand on the shattered stones as I entered. Despite the westerly wind, the stones retained the residual warmth of the autumn sun. Weeds and rubble choked the interior of the long-abandoned castle, yet the plan was distinct. The main keep dominated the north, soaring up from the sea-cliff-edge while the stables, kitchen and servants' quarters hugged the curtain walls.

I stood for a moment, trying to imagine what this place was like when it was all a-bustle with women and men, horses and children, and the proud standard flew over the keep. There would be the music of harp and pipes, the long tales of a sennachie and a flame-haired woman standing at an upstairs window, watching me, an intruder into her world. I could nearly hear the mutter of Gaelic and the clatter of iron-shod hooves on the ground, the batter from the blacksmith's forge and the soft lilt of a harp. I could also hear somebody's low moaning.

'There has been darkness here,' I said.

Mary gave me a sideways look. 'Now that's a strange thing to say.'

'I am a strange person,' I told her and she laughed uneasily.

'Oh, we all know that, Brenda Smith.' She stepped further away from me with the *clach gorm*, the blue stone crystal she wore for luck, swinging from her neck.

'Do you know this castle?' I asked.

'I know of it,' Mary said. 'It was a stronghold of the Mackays once, in the far-off days.' She pointed to the keep. 'There is said to be a *glaistig*, a green lady haunting that tower. She took a lover from the Gunns, the enemy of the clan and her father walled her into a tiny chamber until she starved to death.'

'Lovely fathering,' I said. *That explained the moaning.*

'Oh, there's worse than that in Sutherland,' Mary said. 'We have a history of clan feuds and massacres going back centuries.'

'Why is it a ruin?' I was aware that the others had crowded in behind us and stood in a chattering group, making inane comments and remarking about the romance of it all. I could not feel any romance in Dunalt. I could not feel much at all.

'There are two theories,' Mary had to raise her voice as Kate gave her views on Dunalt. 'One version of the story claims that there was a ball at the castle and the keeper ordered the blinds drawn, and the tongue ripped from the mouth of the cockerel so that the music and dancing would continue for days. In those days, you understand, there were no clocks so the cockerel would signal dawn. Naturally, there was whisky and wine.' Mary smiled, 'when the wine is in, the wit is out, and men and women began to argue about which music to play next.'

'Men and women don't need wine to argue about that,' Charlie said, loudly.

'No, they don't,' Mary agreed. 'In this case, the guests could not agree, so they wanted a neutral party to settle the dispute. Up here in

Sutherland, there were no neutrals, so they shouted for the devil to come and arbitrate.'

'Nonsense,' Kate scoffed.

We ignored her, which was what she deserved.

'When the devil arrived, he came with a burst of flames that set the castle alight and all the guests ran screaming away. The castle was abandoned and never occupied again.' Mary finished her story.

'Best not meddle with satanic powers,' I did not mock. 'What was the other theory?'

Mary ignored me, as I had expected.

'That was a good story,' Lorna said. 'You said there was another theory. How did that go?'

'Well, Lorna, the other theory is not so colourful. The owner abandoned the castle for a more modern house in a more convenient location.'

I nodded. 'I prefer the devil's story.'

'The first story was more entertaining,' Lorna said, exchanging glances with Mary when Kate gave a hoot of laughter.

'Some people are receptive to the atmosphere,' Mary murmured. She glanced at Kate. 'Others are not.'

I smiled and looked away. I am generally susceptible to the aura of a place, either good or bad. I could find neither in Dunalt. To me, it was merely a castle burdened with years. I felt neither ghost nor devil, only the sense of sadness that most abandoned buildings possess and a spirit of darkness from the deeds done there.

The voices that rose from the keep were neither devilish or from the past. I saw the gaggle of tinkers emerge from the battered doorway. They saw us at the same instant. There were six of them, three sprightly barefoot children, their parents and a dark-eyed woman with more than the wisdom of years in her glance. Her gaze passed over us until it rested on Christine. Her eyes widened, and she moved quickly to me. I saw her frown, hesitate and lift her chin.

I walked towards her, knowing she wished me to.

'Who are you?' She said.

'I am Brenda Smith,' I told her.

The lines on her forehead creased into the shape of a horseshoe. 'That is the name you call yourself,' she said, and added: 'you know.'

'What do I know?' I felt drawn to this unknown woman.

Her frown dissipated and the expression of her eyes altered to great sadness. 'You do not yet know that you know,' she said. 'Soon you will know.'

'What will I know?' I asked. 'I am afraid that I don't understand.'

'One of you understands,' the tinker woman said. 'One of you understands everything.'

'One of us?' I glanced around the company. Kate had led Christine and Lorna to examine the dungeon while Mary had interrupted a conversion with Charlie to glower at the tinkers. 'Which one of us?'

Mary stepped towards the tinkers. 'God between you and me, mother,' she said to the old woman.

'Oh, I'll not harm you,' the tinker woman said. 'You have bigger concerns closer to home. Be careful when you are safe from the big step.'

'You're talking in riddles, mother,' Mary shook her head.

'May God help you all,' the tinker woman made a strange sign with her thumb and forefinger, somewhat like a circle. Still watching me, she took hold of the youngest child and hurried away, with her family close behind.

'I wonder what that was all about.' I said.

'Strange people the tinkers,' Mary told me. 'They like to unsettle people by pretending knowledge they don't possess. Some say they are descended from the old broken clans. Others think they are far older, descendants of itinerant metalsmiths from pre-Christian days.'

'Is that so?' I wished I had the skill to keep the conversation flowing.

'Back then tinkers were sought after, skilled men. Now?' Mary shrugged. 'The women tell your fortunes, and the men fix broken kettles.'

'I didn't know the women told fortunes,' I said. 'The only tinkers I see in Edinburgh sell clothes pegs door-to-door.'

'Oh, yes they tell fortunes. Some are said to be able to see into the future. They claim second sight, that sort of thing.'

I was about to prolong the conversation when Kate decided to assert her leadership. 'We've had about enough of this place,' Kate said. 'Come on, girls!'

We followed her, as we always did, as everybody always did. Kate was like that; she was a natural leader. People may like her or loathe her, but they followed her. If she had been a man, she would have been an officer in the army, probably in the Brigade of Guards. I could imagine her leading a battalion over the top and advancing into enemy fire, winning the Victoria Cross and enduring fame. That was our Kate, forthright, domineering, thrusting and perennially successful.

Piling into our two cars, we roared away, leaving the tinkers alone in the castle. I could still feel that woman's eyes on me, and for a few moments, I wondered what she had meant. Then I forgot about her. More important things lay ahead.

Kate drove the leading vehicle of course; her Vauxhall Velox Tourer was a two-seater beauty that kicked up the dust that we in the second car had to drive through. Kate had Christine at her side while the remaining four of us squeezed into an ex-army Crossley 20/25 that had seen hard service in France even before Lorna brought it onto these twisting Highland roads.

'Poor Christine,' Mary said, 'sharing with Kate. She'll hardly get a word in edgeways.'

'They were at school together,' Lorna reminded. 'Christine will be used to her.'

'Poor Christine,' I echoed, but nobody replied. I relapsed into my habitual silence and wondered why I had come. As we headed west and then south through the most glorious scenery imaginable, we watched the magnificent mountains rise and envelop us with the grey-white mists that flowed over them.

'The Norse thought these hills were gods,' Mary nearly had to shout above the noise of the engine as it laboured on the rises.

'They look like gods,' Charlie spoke from behind me. 'Male gods, arrogant and domineering, thrusting themselves upon the landscape, bearded with mist, rough and pretty useless.'

We laughed and enjoyed the majesty of the scenery.

'I wonder what An Cailleach is like,' Lorna spoke from the driver's seat. 'Is it like Suilven? Is it jagged and rocky?'

'We'll soon find out,' I said.

'It's like none of these hills,' Mary said. 'An Cailleach is a hill unto itself. It's unique.'

'Have you seen it?' Charlie had her pencil poised above her notebook. 'Have you been there?'

'No and no,' Mary tossed her bobbed auburn hair. 'I have heard about it.' She was silent for a few moments before she added. 'Family stories passed down from generation to generation.'

I knew Mary did not wish to say more. Kate's Velox was pulling ahead, so Lorna double declutched, changed gear and stamped down on the accelerator, roaring us over the road and frightening a group of sheep that scampered into the surrounding heather.

'You'll never catch her,' Charlie had her notebook open and was sketching the tail of the Velox, as seen through a cloud of dust. 'She's far too fast.'

'I'm not trying to catch her,' Lorna shouted. 'I'm only trying to keep her in sight! It seems like the only proper thing to do as she knows where we're going!'

As we approached the Strathnasealg Inn, a thin smirr of mist eased over us, embracing the body of the car and smothering our view of the surrounding hills. Our headlights reflected back to us in a dim yellow glow, so even Kate was forced to slow to a modest forty miles an hour. To my imaginative mind, it seemed as if Sutherland was pressing down on us, trying to drive us away. We were southern intruders into this northern land, English speakers in the Gaeltacht, Lowland women with long skirts and lipstick in a land where hardiness was required even to survive. I kept my thoughts to myself and tried to appear cheerful.

'Come on girls,' I said. 'We're on holiday, and we're about to make history. Let's chase away the mist with a song.'

There was silence for a few moments until Mary said, 'how about some music, ladies?'

Somebody began with *It's a long way to Tipperary* until Lorna shuddered.

'Not that one,' she said. 'Not that one or *There's a Long Long Trail a-winding* either.'

'How about *Roaming in the Gloaming*?' Charlie asked and began singing. We all joined in right away, with *Roaming* followed by *I'm Forever Blowing Bubbles, A Good Man is Hard to Find, Swanee* and *Look for the Silver Lining.*

We were still singing when we rolled up outside the Strathnasealg Inn. Kate parked head on to the front door with the twin beams of her headlights boring into the windows, while Lorna turned neatly and reversed beside the Velox, ready to drive away. Only a pair of oystercatchers disturbed the sudden silence when both engines were cut.

'Well, here we are,' Charlie packed away her notebook and pencil. 'Let the great adventure begin.'

I had never been to the Strathnasealg Inn before so studied the building and its surroundings before I left the car. The Inn sat within a group of small fields, most of which had been recently harvested to leave stubble on bare brown earth. The Strathnasealg appeared to be a typical Highland hotel, a one-time shooting lodge built in late Victorian times in the Scottish Baronial style with dormer windows overlooking the views on all sides. More like a castle than an Inn, it shrugged off the mist that the westerly wind encouraged to drift across its splendid towers. Lights glowed inside, revealing a vast bar decorated with stags' heads and a gaudy tartan carpet.

'We're here!' Kate announced her arrival by hooting her car horn. 'Porters! We have luggage!'

'That will make us popular,' Mary murmured. 'For God's sake, shut up, Katie!'

A young freckle-faced man acted as porter, grinning as he lifted the first two bags of Katy's luggage and promising to return for the rest.

'I'll carry my own,' Charlie growled.

'Follow me, girls,' Kate commanded, and we trooped into the Inn.

A group of tweed-clad men in the bar turned to watch us enter. One muttered 'Good God' and turned away, while another gave us a friendly smile. His eyes were shrewd and shaded. I immediately knew that he had endured much.

Our rooms were small, decorated in the height of fashion perhaps twenty years previously and without plumbing, none of which mattered when we looked out of the window to see the most glorious vista of hills, sea and moors. I shared my room with Mary, while Lorna and Charlie were next door and Kate and Christine in the best room in the hotel.

'The bed's not bad,' Mary bounced experimentally. 'A bit creaky perhaps.'

'I've slept in worse, and it's only for one night.' I changed my travelling clothes into something less comfortable. 'Let's see what the food is like.'

'Probably vile,' Mary said. 'These Highland inns usually are.'

Mary was wrong. The Strathnasealg was noted for the quality of its seafood and had added venison and an excellent Aberdeen Angus beef to the locally caught salmon and haddock. I opted for the Cullen skink soup to go with my saddle of mutton and finished with a glass of what was meant to be a fine French wine. I was somewhat doubtful about both the adjective and the geographical origin but dutifully swallowed it down. I was not too happy about the quality of the bread either, although as nobody else complained, I kept my tongue still.

'Shall we repair to the lounge, ladies?' Kate invited. We all knew that ladies would not frequent such a place yet we liked to shock and followed Kate into that sacred domain of men.

The smell of expensive pipe tobacco and whisky wrapped around us the second we pushed open the double multi-paned doors. The carpet underfoot was faded Black Watch tartan, while glassy-eyed deer-heads stared at us from their position on the walls. As the Strathnasealg was a climbing inn, the company was mixed and exclusively masculine. As well as the hirsute locals with their ubiquitous black-and-white collie dogs and silent gazes there was a plethora of mountaineers and hill walkers all intent on maps and routes and serious discussions of past glories and future conquests. The advent of half a dozen of the fairer sex certainly unsettled their private little kingdom.

While Kate requisitioned a table and its attendant chairs, Charlie strolled to the bar. The eyes of every man in the room followed her, most disapproving, either of her very short hair or her presence in their world. The man who had smiled at us when we entered the Inn watched musingly, stroking his military moustache. His companions did not mute their comments.

'Good God, they've let women in here.'

'Don't they know this is a climbing inn?'

'They must be in the wrong place, surely.'

'It's bad enough granting them the vote without having to share the bar with them.'

Sudden blindness seemed to strike the barman when Charlie pinged the little brass bell for his attention.

'I say! Custom!' Charlie shouted until the barman shambled up as if reluctant to take her money. He stared at Charlie as she ordered a bottle of the house wine.

'We don't have wine,' he said.

'What do you stock?' Charlie kept her tone reasonable.

'Whisky.'

'Excuse me, ladies.' Kate pushed herself up from her seat at our table and sauntered to Charlie's side. 'The inn serves wine for meals,' she said. 'I am sure you could pop through and find some for your customers.' She presented the barman with her best smile. 'We'll wait here until you return.' Her voice hardened a fraction. 'Off you go now, Alan.'

The barman's face darkened as the noise in the bar quietened into a tense hush. 'I did not tell you my name.'

'You are Alan Finlay; you are 26 years old. You were a steward in the Royal Navy in the late war and took this position in June 1920.' Kate pointed to the back of the bar. 'The door there leads to the kitchen and the stairs down to the storeroom are on the left. I presume that's where the hotel holds the wine.'

Alan looked shaken. 'How do you know that?'

'My family owns this hotel,' Kate said. 'Off you go.' She turned away to talk to Charlie. The voice of authority had spoken.

I saw Mary's face darken. 'What's the matter, Mary?'

'Oh, nothing.' Mary's smile was forced. 'Nothing at all.'

The taller, saturnine man who came in Alan's place was apparently the manager. 'I did not know you had honoured us with your presence, your Ladyship.'

'That title belongs to my mother,' Kate said. 'I use the title The Honourable Miss Gordon.'

'Of course.' The manager gave a little bow and held out a hand. 'I am Maurice Nott. I do so apologise for my barman's inefficiency. Of course, we have wine, and it will be on the house.' His accent was southern English.

'Thank you, Mr Nott.' Kate accepted the complimentary wine with the ease of long habit.

'Of course, if I had realised that it was you, I would have served you in person.' Nott gave an obsequious smile that immediately repulsed me. 'Would you permit me to offer my apologies and honour the hotel by accepting my offer of providing free lunches tomorrow?'

Kate remained polite and aloof. 'Thank you, but we are going off to the hills tomorrow.'

'Then I shall arrange for a full packed lunch for all your party, Miss Gordon.'

'That will be acceptable,' Kate said. 'There are six of us, and we intend to be at least three days.'

Nott bowed again. 'I assure you will enjoy our packed lunches. We grow our own vegetables and grain here and have, I believe, the only rye bread made in Scotland.'

'Thank you.' Kate remained cool. 'One of my party has a fondness for marmalade.'

I smiled over at Kate, surprised that she knew my particular tastes.

'I shall ensure that one packed lunch contains marmalade sandwiches.'

'Thank you. Dundee marmalade if you have it, and if you could send over a couple of bottles of the house red, that would suit,' Kate said, 'and a couple of bottles of claret.' She returned to our table without a smile. Kate was used to having people jump to obey her.

'Are you ladies sightseeing?' The man who had smiled limped across to talk to us. About forty years old, with weather-battered features and a strong chin, he seated himself beside us and waved a dismissive hand toward the men in the lounge. 'Don't concern yourselves with them; they are just not used to seeing women in here.'

'We're the Edinburgh Ladies Mountaineer Club,' Kate told him. 'I am Kathleen Gordon.'

'Ah,' the man nodded. 'I am Graham Mackenzie. How do you do?' He shook hands with us one-by-one.

'Christine Brown.' Quiet Christine did not raise her eyes.

'Mary Ablach.' Direct and to the point, Mary held Mackenzie's gaze.

'Brenda Smith.' I found his handshake pleasantly firm.

'Brenda Smith.' Mackenzie gave me a level look. 'You're no stranger here.'

'I am,' I said. 'I've never been here in my life before.'

'No?' Mackenzie frowned. 'I'm certain I've seen you before.' He shrugged. 'You must have a twin sister.' His smile was apologetic as I wished that I did have a twin sister.

'Lorna Menzies.' Lorna opened her mouth as if to speak further and then closed it again.

'I am Charlie Gunn, Graham.' Charlie gripped Mackenzie's hand.

'Are you Major Graham Mackenzie who won the Military Cross at Passchendaele?' Lorna asked.

When Major Mackenzie nodded agreement without any further elaboration, my respect for him increased.

'You lost your left leg rescuing two of your wounded men,' Lorna said.

Mackenzie still did not pursue his heroism. 'Edinburgh Ladies Mountaineering Club?' He said, 'it must be the season for active ladies. Catriona, my wife, is sailing around the British Isles even as we speak.' His blue eyes twinkled. 'She should be hereabouts in a week.' I understood that he was informing us of his marital state to reassure us his intentions were innocent. 'We don't get many lady climbers in here. In fact, I think you are the only ladies we have ever had. Are you after a Munro?'

Sir Hugh Munro had died only two years previously. He was the most famous of Scottish mountaineers, having catalogued and climbed all the Scottish hills over 3000 feet. In respect, all Scottish hills over that height were known as Munros.

'Not this time,' Kate said. 'We're off on an expedition to conquer the most interesting hill in north-west Scotland.'

Mackenzie looked immediately interested. 'Tip top! Whither bound? Suilven? Canisp? Stac Polly?' He rattled off a list of the most famous local peaks.

'Each of these is well worth climbing,' Kate answered for us all. 'But we have a different hill in mind.'

'Ah, Ben More Assynt then,' Mackenzie nodded. 'A tremendous hill.'

'No,' Kate said. 'Not Ben More either.'

'Oh?' Mackenzie raised his bushy eyebrows. He sipped at his whisky, looking eager. 'Where then, if I am not too nosey?'

'An Cailleach,' Kate told him.

'An Cailleach? The hill known as the dark mountain?' Mackenzie's smile quickly faded. 'You understand that nobody has ever climbed that hill. It's not even a Munro.'

'We know,' Charlie said. 'It's only 2,995 feet high, and we don't know for sure that nobody has ever climbed it. There have been attempts.'

Mackenzie sipped at his whisky. 'As far as I know, Miss Gunn, every attempt failed, either through bad weather or some other reason. The last attempt was in '14.'

'The Mahoney expedition,' Charlie had her notebook and pencil ready.

'Exactly. Three men set off to conquer An Cailleach, and nothing was ever heard from them again. With the Great War starting, the news of their disappearance faded from the newspapers, and now they are forgotten.'

'They are not quite forgotten,' Charlie said. 'We remember them.' She glanced at Kate before she continued. 'Perhaps you could tell us what you know of the Mahoney expedition, Major Mackenzie?'

'I don't know much,' Mackenzie admitted. 'I was with the Cameron Highlanders at the time, waiting for the balloon to go up. Most of the local men were. I was one of the lucky ones; I came back.'

'What could you tell us, Major Mackenzie?' Charlie leaned forward in her chair. 'Any little snippet of information could be helpful.'

Mackenzie signalled for another whisky. 'There were three men in the party,' he said, 'Mike Mahoney was an experienced Irish climber. He learned his trade in Ireland and climbed all over the Alps so a wee Scottish ben should have been nothing more than an afternoon jaunt for him. Maybe he was too casual.'

'Do you think they fell?' I asked.

'They must have,' Mackenzie said. The *Ceathramh Garbh*, the Rough Quarter is a bad place for a fall, with no roads, no shepherds or even shooting parties. There's nothing out there except rock and bog, nearly perennial mist and the wind.'

'Tell me all you can, please,' Charlie asked.

Mackenzie smiled. 'Now don't go scaring yourselves, ladies, I'm sure you'll be fine. Mahoney had two companions whose names I have forgotten. They stayed here, at this inn, overnight some time at the end of July 1914, crossed over to the peninsula on which the dark mountain, An Cailleach, sits and were never seen again.'

'Has anybody tried to look for them?' Charlie had been scribbling notes in her small leather covered pad.

'Most of the local men were in the war, either in the Army or at sea,' Mackenzie said. 'The few that returned had other things on their minds, anyway by that time it was far too late.'

'Have there not been other climbing parties since the war?' Charlie asked.

Mackenzie shook his head. 'Not for An Cailleach. It's not popular with anybody and not worth the trouble to climb.'

'Why is that?'

Mackenzie nodded his thanks as the barman refilled his glass. 'It's an ugly lump of a hill with a bad reputation. The Mahoney party was only the latest of many attempts that were either beaten back by bad weather or had an accident. The eastern and southeastern face has bogland and mist while the western face is cliff rising sheer from the sea.' Mackenzie lifted his hand as an elderly man entered the room. 'Here's Duncan Og, young Duncan, he knows about the hill more than I do.'

Duncan Og looked about ninety with deep lines seaming his brown face and only the bright twinkle in his eyes revealing the spirit that still lay within. 'Oh, there are plenty stories about An Cailleach,' he confirmed. 'It's a hill better avoided than attempted and I don't know why you young ladies want to go there at all. I could tell you about broken legs and broken heads on that black hill, going back fifty years.'

'Has anybody ever climbed it?' Kate asked. 'I heard it was unconquered.'

'It is a virgin summit,' Duncan Og confirmed. 'Nobody has got to the top and nobody ever shall.'

'We'll be first,' Charlie said. 'An all-woman team will conquer Scotland's last unclimbed hill.'

It was then that I saw her. In a room where our climbing club was the only female presence, I saw another woman. I did not know who she was, or when she had entered. I only knew that she was standing in the midst of the men watching me.

'You may well conquer An Cailleach,' Duncan Og was drinking whisky from what looked to be a half pint tumbler. 'Or you may not.

An Cailleach has her own rules and chooses who she allows onto her flanks.'

'*Her* own rules?' Charlie hooked her claws on the sexuality of the word. 'An Cailleach is a mountain, a lump of rock. It is neither a he nor a she.'

Duncan Og smiled from beyond his glass. 'An Cailleach is more than a lump of rock, Miss Gunn. All mountains have a distinct personality. Some are friendly, and welcome visitors, others are unfriendly and do not wish to be disturbed. These are the hills you must treat with respect and ask their permission before you tread on them. An Cailleach is one of these hills, and she is undoubtedly a woman.'

'Why?' Charlie's voice cracked like a pistol. 'Are you saying An Cailleach is unfriendly so must be a woman?'

Duncan Og's smile did not falter. His eyes were diamond-bright as he examined Charlie. I wondered what sort of man he had been in his prime and thought of the old Highland warriors and mercenaries. 'I am not saying that at all, Miss Gunn. Now listen while I tell you the story of An Cailleach.'

I saw Kate fidget in her chair and guessed that she was about to chase this elderly man away. 'Yes, please Mr Og,' I intervened. 'I do like to hear a good story.' That other woman was gone. I had not seen her move, and nobody had commented on her presence. I wondered if I had imagined seeing her. She had been vaguely familiar, although from where I could not say.

Duncan Og glanced meaningfully at his glass and Mackenzie signalled the barman to have it refilled. 'Have you heard of the Badenoch witches?'

Rather than admit that I had, I solemnly shook my head. Encouraged, Duncan Og sipped at his recharged glass and continued.

'Away back when the world was young, Lord Walter Comyn was a wicked bad man. He owned the lands of Badenoch and had the power of pit and gallows over all the men and women who lived there. One autumn he had the idea that all the young women of Ruthven should be stark naked at the harvest.'

I looked over to Charlie, hiding my smile at her expected frown of disapproval. She shook her head, writing furiously in her notebook.

'I take it he paid for his lust,' I said.

Duncan Og chuckled. 'Oh, he paid all right. Naturally, the mothers of the young women were angry at Lord Walter's choice of entertainment.'

'I should say so,' Charlie said.

'If Lord Walter had known his tenants better, he would have known that the mothers of two of the girls were witches, who did not like their daughters to display their charms for a man, powerful landowner or not. The two mothers turned themselves into eagles and waited for Lord Walter. As he came to the ford over the River Tromie in Badenoch, they swooped on him, knocked him off his horse at *Leum na Feinne*, and ate him while he was still alive.'

Charlie nodded approval. 'Good. That's what the old lecher deserved.'

'Now,' Duncan Og chuckled and lifted a finger from his glass. 'The story of the Badenoch witches is well known. What happened afterwards is not known at all.'

I followed what was evidently a cue. 'What happened afterwards?'

Duncan Og took his time, as master storytellers do. 'The witches knew that killing Lord Walter would invoke revenge. They had to hide somewhere, so while one witch returned home to Badenoch, the other flew up here. Both became mountains and both were called An Cailleach.' Duncan Og leaned back in his seat.

We were all watching him, trying to reconcile our modern world with this ancient tale of witchcraft and folklore.

'Tell them what An Cailleach means,' Mary had been listening intently. 'And don't pretend it's Dark Mountain, that's just a nickname.'

'An Cailleach is Gaelic for the old woman or the hag,' Duncan Og was smiling over the lip of his glass. 'You may already know that a hag is another word for a witch.' His smile faded, and for a second I saw darkness in his bright old eyes. 'I'd advise you to ask An Cailleach's permission before you try to climb her. When I gave the Mahoney party that same advice, they laughed, and they have not been seen since.'

I heard Kate's sudden intake of breath, and for some reason, a shiver ran through me. Anybody who ventures onto the Scottish hills must be aware of the danger. The weather can change from summer to winter in a heartbeat and a slope that is dry and safe one minute could be a rushing torrent before one can blink. Yet I knew that Duncan Og was not warning us about the weather. That wise, wrinkled old man knew of more profound and darker dangers than mere gales and storms.

That other woman was back, invisible in plain sight as she stood among the unaware men. At her side stooped a white-haired man with a benevolent expression on his face and the most kindly eyes. When he gave me a very old-fashioned bow, I nodded back. Kate said something, I grunted my agreement, and when I turned to the old man, he was gone. Tomorrow we were going to An Cailleach. Tomorrow we were going to shake hands with the Hag. Some inner dread told me that we were not going alone.

Chapter Two

We gathered outside the Inn at six the next morning with the sun not yet up and a fresh westerly breeze bringing the tang of Atlantic salt. Our voices sounded hollow as we hoisted our rucksacks, stamped our boots on the gravel and tapped our sticks to hear the sound. Kate had one of our two maps and checked us all for equipment as if we were novices on our first trip to the hills.

'You all have your boots?' She looked downward. 'Well nailed and sturdy I hope? How about you, Christine, let me see.'

Christine dutifully lifted her boots while Kate inspected the soles and heels.

'The walker who essays a long hill walk without nailed boots is a fool,' Kate said. 'She doubles her fatigue and is putting herself in danger.' She looked at me and gave a grin that revealed something of her true self behind the swagger. 'I read that in a guidebook once, and I've been waiting to use it ever since.'

We laughed, although I am not sure why. Kate could do that to us. One moment she was hectoring and badgering, the next she was the finest friend you could ever have, and you knew she would do her very best for everybody.

'Head coverings, girls!' Kate continued. 'Something woollen and waterproof.'

We dutifully held up our assortment of hats and caps. I favoured a thick woollen cap comforter that I had bought in a pawn shop in

Edinburgh's Royal Mile. Khaki and warm, I supposed that some soldier had worn it in the trenches and pawned it when he returned from the fighting to find himself unemployed and unwanted. Kipling has the rights of it with his: 'special train for Atkins' in wartime and 'chuck him out, the brute' as soon as the guns fall silent. That goes for Jock, Paddy and Taff as well of course and no doubt Johnny Gurkha and the splendid Indian soldiers. Well, at least I had benefitted from the government's cynical disregard for the men who had fought for its existence.

'Sweaters?' Kate poked at us. 'You know that I recommend Shetland wool.'

I wore a heavy ribbed jumper I had knitted myself, in a fashionable shade of khaki to match my hat. Every wool shop in Edinburgh carried surplus khaki wool since the war ended. It was the cheapest buy imaginable.

Kate held up her hands. 'I wear mittens up the hills. Do we all have gloves?'

'Yes, Kate' we chorused, with Christine lifting hers in the air in proof.

'Ropes, pitons and hammers?'

We held up our climbing equipment.

Kate nodded. 'I can see the rucksacks and sticks. Does everyone have a compass in case we get lost?'

Some of us had a compass. I carried one, as did Lorna and Christine. Charlie and Mary did not.

'A compass is no good on An Cailleach,' Mary said. 'It is a magnetic hill and distorts the readings.'

'I didn't know that,' Lorna said.

'Nonsense!' Kate was more emphatic. 'You should always carry a compass.'

By that time, faces filled the windows as the other walkers and climbers watched us depart. A party of women going to the hills was not usual. We made the most of it, keeping our backs straight and laughing as if attempting An Cailleach was nothing to us. We all wore long tweed skirts except for Charlie, who scandalised the watchers with her male attire and short-cut hair. Charlie was like that; she loved to prove her equality to any man in every way possible.

Kate continued with her habitual lecture. 'The earlier we start, the better as every hour before noon is worth two in the afternoon. Walk at a steady pace, girls, and short rests. Rushing and resting lead to fatigue.'

'Yes, Kate,' we chorused.

'Has everybody got plenty of food?'

'Yes, Kate.' I felt like a school girl rather than a woman fast approaching twenty-five.

'We will eat little and often. Luckily the hotel has been generous in supplying us.' Kate looked at us, her girls. 'On we go then.' She lifted her staff in the air. 'Success to the Edinburgh Ladies Mountaineering Club!'

'Success to the Edinburgh Ladies Mountaineering Club!' We shouted, hoping to disturb the equanimity of the watching males.

With our preparations complete, we stomped away from the Inn and onto the rough road that led to the coast. Seagulls screamed overhead, and a pair of oystercatchers whistled to each other as they flew together.

'I like oystercatchers,' Mary said. 'They mate for life. In Gaelic, they are *Gillebridean*, the guides of St Bride.' She watched them fly past. 'They are the most beautiful birds.'

I agreed. I always had felt an affinity for birds and wildlife. It was another of the reasons I turned to the hills. 'How about you?' I pushed for a conversation.

'What do you mean, "how about me?" ' Mary looked confused; as well she might as she had not been privy to my thoughts.

'What draws you to the hills?'

We marched on as we spoke, with our boots echoing on the road and kicking up the occasional stone. Drystane dykes surrounded the small fields we passed, with shaggy cattle and equally rough black-faced sheep grazing the rough grass. One or two cows lifted their heads to watch us pass.

'I was never a city girl,' Mary said. 'Although I was born in Edinburgh, I never felt that I belonged there.' She lifted her head to the grey lagging dawn. 'Every chance I got, I was way up Arthur's Seat or some other open area. Oh, the trouble I got into for that!' She smiled across at me. 'I won't tell you what my mother said. You can guess!'

'I can guess,' I agreed. The sun peeped its head between a cleft in the hills behind us, welcoming a new day. I stopped to admire the view. After the confines of Edinburgh, the openness of the far North West spread before us, soothing with space, embracing with keen air.

'There's the sun, now.' Mary took off her headscarf and turned to the east. She mumbled something in Gaelic.

'What was that?' I asked.

'It's an old blessing my mother taught me,' Mary said. 'In English, it runs like this:

> Glory to thee
> Thou glorious sun
> glory to thee, thou sun
> Face of the God of life.'

I listened, 'that's lovely.'

'It's very old,' Mary stood on the road, allowing the sun to warm her. 'It predates Christianity.'

'Sun worship?' I asked.

'I imagine so,' Mary said. 'A lot of nonsense of course,' she laughed depreciatingly.

'I don't think it's nonsense,' I defended Mary from herself.

'It doesn't fit in modern life,' Mary sounded uncomfortable as if I had caught her out in some guilty secret. 'Not with motor cars and factories and railway trains. We've moved past all that sort of thing.'

I looked around at the emerging panorama of hills, sky and fields, and felt the hint of salt in the air from the nearby Atlantic Ocean. 'Have we?'

Mary looked sideways at me, opened her mouth as if to speak and closed it again.

'Come on, girls!' Kate's voice interrupted us. 'We'll change here!'

Kate had stopped in the shelter of a ruined cottage, with a single gable end still standing and the rest a rickle of stones that preserved the outline of what had once been somebody's home. We hurried to join her.

'Skirts off, trousers on and off we go!' Kate was jubilant as she stripped off her coat, unfastened her skirt and took off her boots. She stood in her underwear as she opened her rucksack to pull out a pair of tweed trousers. We followed her lead so for a few moments any passer-by would have the possibly delightful view of six young women standing bare-legged and partially undressed as we struggled into heavy trousers.

As I took off my boots, I felt the ground under my feet. It was friendly as if it welcomed me. Warm waves rose from the earth, through the soles of my feet and up my legs to spread through my entire body. I had never experienced anything quite like it before.

'Can you feel that?' I asked Mary.

'Can I feel what?' Mary looked confused.

'A warmth,' I tried to explain. 'It's like a wave of heat coming up from the ground.'

Mary shook her head. 'I can't feel anything.' Bending over, she placed the palm of her hand on the bare earth. 'It's cold if anything.'

I noticed Charlie watching us, her eyes fixed on Mary. 'I must be mistaken,' I said.

Mary threw me a curious look as she straightened up. 'Yes, you must. It's freezing.'

Charlie was still watching Mary, narrow-eyed and lips pursed.

'You'd better get your trousers on,' I said, 'before you catch your death.'

'Pack your skirts, girls,' Kate ordered. 'We'll need them when we return to the Inn as the first people to conquer An Cailleach.'

'This expedition is your idea, isn't it?' Charlie asked Kate as we pulled on our rucksacks and headed down the final stretch of road toward the ford. 'Why are you so interested in this particular hill, Kate?'

For the first time in the two years I had known her, Kate looked uneasy. 'Is this for your magazine article, Charlotte?'

'Writing is my job,' Charlie said. 'When you told the club about your plans for this expedition I asked my editor if he was interested in an article. He agreed.'

We continued to walk along the increasingly rough track. The fields on either side gave way to a belt of open moorland, dotted with patches of reeds that revealed peat bog. A whaup passed overhead, its curved beak down-pointing. Behind us, the Sutherland Hills were freeing themselves from the mists of dawn. Ahead was the scent of damp heather and seaweed, the surge of the sea and the sound of seabirds.

'My editor would be interested in your motivation for this particular mountain.' Charlie continued.

'My reasons are my own concern,' Kate was unusually curt.

'Well, my reasons are transparent. I'm coming here to write an article,' Charlie said. 'And, just as importantly, I want to be part of an all-woman expedition to achieve something that men have failed to do.'

'You suffragette, you,' I tried to install humour into what could develop into an ugly confrontation.

'Rightly and proudly,' Charlie turned her attention to me.

'I won't argue with that,' I gave her my brightest smile as she produced her notebook.

'As Kate is reluctant, Brenda, tell me why you joined this expedition.'

'I like hill-walking,' I told part of the truth. 'And I like the wild places.' I also sought friendship, but she was not writing that into an article.

'Are you proud to be attempting a hill that no male has climbed?' Charlie pursued her theme.

'I did not know that we would be first until yesterday,' I confessed. 'It will be good to be first up a new summit.'

'Would you agree that conquering An Cailleach will add proof that women are every bit as good as men?' Charlie asked.

I shook my head, deliberately provocative. 'Not in the slightest,' I said as Charlie looked up, pencil poised above her notebook and a frown developing on her face. I allowed her a few moments to consider my answer. 'We don't need proof for something that should be self-evident.' I gave her meat for her article. 'During the Great War, women stepped into men's roles, worked in factories, gave the Glasgow landlords the right-about-turn, won the right to vote, drove ambulances, looked after farms and still brought up families.' I saw Charlie's frown change into a much more attractive smile. 'Tell me any man that could produce a child and I will agree that they are equal to us.'

The track curved and dipped, with puddles of muddy water underfoot and the sound of rushing water increasing.

'We're nearing the ford,' Kate said. 'Now everybody gather round, and I'll give you a geography lesson.'

We dutifully obeyed. Mary winked at Charlie, who kept her notebook to hand, Lorna appeared to be in a trance, as if her mind was many miles away, while Christine did as she was told.

'I've told you all this before,' Kate unfolded her map and pinned down the corners with rocks. 'We are here,' she stabbed down with her finger, 'and An Cailleach is here.' She stabbed again. 'As you see, An Cailleach dominates an empty peninsula, the very one we will see once this early morning mist lifts.'

We laughed at that, as Kate had intended.

'The sea is on three sides, and there is only a tiny neck of land connecting the peninsula to the mainland. Even that neck is mostly underwater, with an extensive bog stretching across most and a river running through the bog.'

We looked closer at the map, trying to get our tongues around the Gaelic names.

'*Allt an loin*,' Lorna said. 'I wonder what that means.'

'Burn of the marsh,' Mary said at once. 'Most Gaelic place names are very descriptive. They tell things as they are.'

'Allt an loin,' Kate said. 'It starts here,' she pointed to a point high inland, 'and gushes down to the low country, and then gets a bit lost in the bog.'

'It's not lost,' Mary said. 'It's there all right, but the peat hags and high bankings will hide it. People used to call the peninsula *Ceathramh Garbh*, the Rough Quarter or the Rough Bounds.' She tapped her stick on a nearby rock. 'It has small areas of great fertility and other areas that are bleak and bare and stark beyond imagination.'

'Have you been here before?' Kate's voice was sharp.

'No,' Mary shook her head.

'Well then, you know less than me. I have studied this area.' Kate's look would have shattered glass.

'Oh, do carry on, Kathleen.' Sarcasm laced Mary's voice.

'There is no bridge across Allt an loin,' Kate's voice was edged, 'but there is a ford at the end of this track.' She looked around to ensure we were all paying attention. 'There used to be a Fordswoman there, somebody who carried travellers across. Nowadays we are left to our own devices, and Shank's Pony must suffice.'

I envisaged a woman waiting at the ford, hitching up her plaid and carrying people one at a time. I could see her face, red-skinned with exposure, and feel the strength of her brawny arms.

'Once we are across,' Kate interrupted my reverie, 'we have a few miles to tramp before we reach the hill itself.' She glanced upward. 'Hopefully, the sun will burn off this mist and then we will see our route better.'

I studied the map, not for the first time. 'An Cailleach seems quite a straightforward climb,' I said. 'I'm surprised that nobody has conquered it before.'

'It's the weather,' Kate spoke with authority. 'It can change in minutes here.'

Lorna peered into the shredding mist. 'Does anybody live over there?'

'Not now,' Mary said. 'There used to be a *clachan* and summer shielings.'

'I'm not surprised they left,' Charlie said. 'There's nothing here.'

'People lived there for hundreds, perhaps thousands of years,' Mary continued as if Charlie had not spoken. 'Until the Clearances.'

I heard the resentment in Mary's voice and decided not to probe further. We were here to climb a hill, not to recount bitter history. 'Well, we're here now,' I kept my voice deliberately bright. 'Or we will be once we cross the ford.'

'We'll cross the ford to the peninsula today,' Kate told us, 'tramp up the foothills and we'll shelter at the base of An Cailleach. There's a place called *Clach Dhion*, the Shelter Stone or Shelter Rock.' She graced us with her smile, daring Mary to challenge.

'Look,' Lorna the practical pointed ahead. 'The mist is lifting.'

We all looked up. Usually, mist dissipates slowly, either blown away by the wind or burned off by the sun. This mist was different. One minute it smothered the peninsula and the next if swept upwards as if an invisible hand was hauling it to heaven. An Cailleach revealed herself to us.

I do not know what I expected, perhaps something as spectacular as Suilven, as graceful as Schiehallion or as majestic as Ben Nevis. An Cailleach was neither of these. She was a great, graceless lump of a hill with neither shape nor form, yet she dominated the peninsula and glowered at the world as if challenging everybody and everything. She was indeed like an old witch, I thought, secure in her own power and ready to strike at all who opposed her. *She?* I realised that I had personified the hills and accepted Duncan Og's opinion of her femininity.

'That is an ugly hill.' Lorna sounded disappointed. 'No wonder it's not on the main climbing menu.'

'We'll be the first to conquer her.' Kate had not lost any of her enthusiasm. 'Our names will be known in the climbing world.'

I stared at An Cailleach. There was something about her that other hills did not have. I could not put my finger on it. I just knew that this hill was different. 'I don't know if she is ugly,' I said. 'There's something there.'

Christine looked sideways at me as Mary repeated my word: 'Something?'

'Yes,' I said. 'There is an appeal as if this hill is inviting us to come over, or perhaps daring us to try. Shall we seek her permission, as Duncan Og suggested?'

Charlie tapped her stick on the ground. 'Don't be daft, Brenda. Anyway, a hill named after a woman will want women to climb it,' she said and laughed. 'Come on ladies!'

I lagged behind a little until Kate led the rest in a boot thumping advance, and then bent my head toward An Cailleach. I don't know what possessed me as I mumbled. 'I crave your permission to climb you, An Cailleach.'

Naturally, the hill did not reply. Great humps of granite do not respond to a silly request, and only Christine noticed what I had done. She gave me a small, quiet smile as I re-joined the others. I did not mind Christine observing my idiosyncrasies for she would not say anything and even if she did, Kate would soon blast her into silence.

We were quite cheerful as we strode on, with Kate humming some American jazz tune and Mary singing a Gaelic air. 'Kisimuil's Galley,' she said, fingering the blue crystal stone around her neck as she translated the words into English for our benefit.

> 'High from the Ben a Hayich
> On a day of days
> Seaward I gaz'd,
> Watching Kishmul's galley sailing.
> O hio huo faluo!'

'Written by a woman, bard to MacNeil of Barra,' Charlie said at once. 'There's the ford, ladies!'

The track wound down to a level area where the burn spread out in rippling water. A pair of rowan trees marked the start of the ford on this side, while across the water a large rock, surprisingly smooth, indicated the other side.

'That's the Bore Stone' Mary said. 'I don't know why it carries that name.'

'The ford looks easy enough,' Christine glanced at Kate before speaking and then pointed with her stick. 'There's somebody already there.'

'It's an old woman,' Lorna said.

'That'll be the witch.' Christine gave a short laugh and stopped when Kate threw her a look.

'She's doing her washing,' Charlie shook her head. 'Aye, send out the woman to wash in the wee small hours. I bet her husband is still lying in bed.'

'Oh,' Mary stepped back, suddenly pale. 'A washerwoman at the ford.'

'Yes,' I said.

'Don't you know what that means?' Mary asked.

'It means that her clothes are dirty.' Lorna said.

'No,' Mary looked shaken. 'I wish it did. I have to see.'

I accompanied Mary as she hurried across a belt of splashing moorland to where the woman knelt by the side of the burn, banging the clothes on a rock and squeezing them dry. As she worked she chanted in Gaelic: '*Si do leine, 'si do leine ta mi migheadh.*'

Mary clutched my arm. 'Brenda!'

'What is it, Mary?' Even although she wore antique Highland clothing that covered her from head to foot, I could see the woman was ancient and so thin she was gaunt, nearly skeletal. She did not look up as she continued to squeeze and pound her washing. 'This woman scares you.'

'Yes,' Mary said. 'Look at the washing. What is that woman washing?'

I did as Mary asked. 'Nothing I have seen before. Lengths of white linen.'

'Shrouds.' Mary stepped away. 'Do you know what the woman is saying?'

'I don't speak Gaelic,' I said.

'She is saying: "Tis thy shroud, tis thy shroud that I am washing." '

'Shrouds?' I was slow-thinking that morning. 'I don't understand. Shroud for what?'

Mary's voice was strained. 'Shrouds such as are used for the dead. Grave shrouds.'

'Oh, I see.' I said without understanding. 'There are five shrouds.'

'Five of us will die.' Mary took a deep breath. 'There is a shroud for five of us. That woman is the *Bean-nighe*, the Washer at the Ford. People who are about to die meet her washing their shrouds.'

I laughed. I could do nothing else. 'That's nonsense. That is ancient superstitious nonsense Mary, and you know it as well as I do. We are modern women in the 20th century for goodness sake. This is 1921, not 921. We don't believe that sort of thing now.' I gave her a hug. 'It's only a woman washing clothes.'

I felt her shaking. 'Take a deep breath, Mary.'

'You're right of course.' Mary's smile was weak. 'It's only an old lady doing her washing.' We ignored the washerwoman's chanting and joined the others at the ford, with the water rippling at the roots of the rowan trees and sparkling under the morning sun. I looked over to the washerwoman. She was no longer there. I had not seen her move.

'I love these trees,' Christine said. 'These berries are so red!'

'It's a rowan,' Mary was speaking to tear her mind away from the washerwoman. 'In the olden days, people believed that rowan trees kept away fairies and witches. They used to hang rowan branches above barns, wear necklaces of red rowan berries and carry rowan crosses.'

I deliberately laughed. 'What strange ideas people used to have back in the old days. Here,' reaching up, I broke off a small branch. 'Here's some rowan wood.' My scarf was of Royal Stuart tartan, all bright colours. Unravelling a length of red wool, I snapped the twig into two unequal lengths and tied it in the shape of a small cross. 'There you are, Mary. You can pretend that you believe in that sort of thing.'

Although Mary laughed with me, I saw her place the cross inside her rucksack and touch the blue stone that hung around her neck. She had not yet recovered from her superstitious scare with the washerwoman.

'I hate walking in wet boots,' Kate had been too preoccupied with being Kate to notice anything else. 'I'd advise we all wade across the ford barefoot.'

When I dipped my hand in the ford, the water was only a few degrees above freezing. We removed our boots and stockings and rolled up our trouser legs. 'This is where skirts score over trousers,' Lorna said. 'They are much easier to hitch up.'

'First to cross the ford,' Kate shouted as she plunged in. 'By George it's cold!' Her voice seemed to echo in the suddenly still air as if somebody had repeated them. I looked around, wondering if the washerwoman had returned. There was nobody else there.

I am imagining things, I told myself. That's Mary's ghost stories getting to me. All the same, I touched the rowan tree for luck. On an impulse, I broke off a small twig and stuffed it inside my rucksack. I knew I was being silly, but sometimes circumstances circumvent one's rational thoughts.

Up ahead, An Cailleach waited, with a mantle of grey mist hiding her face.

Chapter Three

We were laughing again as we waded thigh deep through the ford. Kate was first across, with Lorna second and then Charlie. I would have been next but stopped to help Mary, who stumbled over a loose stone, recovered and scrambled ashore at the Bore Stone, with Christine at her side. In the event, I was last, padding ashore on the mud as a gust of wind rocked a circling buzzard high above.

'Here we are,' Kate balanced against the Bore Stone to dry her feet and put on her stockings and boots. 'We've reached the *ceathramh garbh*.' Her Gaelic pronunciation was perfect, being Kate.

'We have,' Lorna agreed.

'It feels as if we're on the edge of the world,' Charlie said.

I did not agree. I thought the peninsula was quite welcoming, with that same sensation of warmth as soon as I placed my bare feet on the thin soil. An Cailleach dominated the entire area, with the sun speckling the east-facing slope, revealing deep gulleys down which gushed the white thread of burns. Nearer to us, the ground was surprisingly fertile, with some lush pastures running in long strips and a scattering of nettles, which is always a sign of good soil.

'I like it here,' I said. I did not expect a reply.

'No time to waste. I want to reach the Shelter Rock and get all settled in by evening, ready for an early start.' Kate gave her usual infectious grin. 'I want to be on the summit at noon tomorrow and back down to the Shelter Rock before dark.'

'Why that route?' Lorna asked. 'We could go up the west face, it is steeper but nothing we haven't done before. We could be up and back in one day rather than two.'

'I chose this route,' Kate's smile immediately dropped. 'It's the one we will follow.'

Lorna jerked a thumb over her shoulder. 'Look behind you.'

We all looked. Two men were splashing over the ford with a third a few yards behind.

'They won't go the slow route,' Lorna said. 'They'll go straight up the west face and get to the summit first.'

'They're heading into foul weather,' Charlie nodded to the black clouds that gathered behind us. 'I don't know where that came from.'

'The weather here makes up its own mind,' Mary said. 'It's uncanny.' I was glad to see her smile after her scare with the washerwoman. 'This area has its own climate.'

'It's only the combination of sea and mountains,' Lorna said. 'Here are these two men coming up now.'

The leading men waved their sticks to us, striding over the rough track. I could not see the third man.

'Don't wave back,' Kate ordered. 'Come on. Walk away.' She led on without another word, long-legged as she left the track and headed for the north-east face. As always, we hurried after her. I looked back. Two men were watching us. The third must have lagged behind.

This relatively level area of the peninsula had once been cultivated, with traces of the old field boundaries and dense patches of nettles. As Kate stormed ahead, Mary was looking around with a frown on her face. I saw her mouth working, and twice she dashed the back of her hand across her eyes as though to wipe away a tear.

'Brenda,' Christine's voice was so low I had to strain to hear her.

'Hello, Christine.'

'Do you believe that old man's story about the witches?'

'Not a bit of it,' I said.

Christine was quiet for a few minutes as our boots thumped rhythmically on the ground.

'Have you ever heard of the Reverend Robert Kirk?'

'No,' I gave my brightest smile. 'That question came out of the blue. Should I have heard of him? Who was he?'

'He was a Gaelic scholar and a bit of an eccentric,' Christine said.

'Christine!' Kate shouted. 'Come here!'

'Excuse me,' Christine gave an apologetic nod of her head. 'We'll talk later.' She scurried away, leaving me wondering what on earth she had been talking about. I plodded on, with my rucksack and attendant gear weighing heavily on my back.

Half an hour after we left the ford, the rain arrived. It started as a drizzle, a grey misery that seeped across the desolate landscape and gradually increased to a steady rain. Bracken had encroached on what track there had once been, and we pushed through the dripping fronds, grumbling at the wet. We slowed down as the ground steepened and then levelled out to a small plateau. This late in the season, the bloom on the heather had faded, but I the yellow blink of a small tormentil flower was a cheering sight, and the pink blossom heads of lousewort reminded that summer was not long past.

Head down against the rain, Kate stumbled over something, recovered and stumbled again. She looked down, cleared away a shrub of heather. 'There's been a building here,' she said.

I looked around, wondering why anybody should wish to live in the middle of a moor. With the rain now pelting down, obscuring most of An Cailleach and already hiding the mainland beyond the ford, we seemed cut off from civilisation. My earlier good feelings had entirely vanished.

'They called this clachan Penrioch,' Mary spoke slowly as if to herself. 'Nobody knows how old it was or who founded it. It was certainly here before the Norse came and it survived the wars and upsets of the middle ages.'

I looked at her curiously, wondering how she knew such things. Kate said something, I don't know what. I was more interested in Mary's tone and words.

'What happened to it?' Christine sounded upset.

'The landowner happened to it,' Mary said. 'In August 1818 an Improver from the English Midlands married the daughter of the local landowner, who soon inherited the land. The Englishmen adopted his wife's name and moved north to live in one of her mansions. One year later they began to extend the husband's Improvements to their Scottish Highland estates.'

Only Kate was not listening as Mary continued. 'Do you know what the term Improvements means?'

'Making things better?' Christine hazarded.

'You would think so,' Mary said. 'However, to people like the landowner and her husband, improvements meant increasing their already immense wealth at the cost of those who struggled merely to survive. Their actions improved the landowner's bank balance by removing the people from their homes and bringing in more profitable sheep.'

I saw Kate shuffling uneasily. The rest of us listened to Mary's increasingly impassioned words. 'The landowner hired Christopher Grant, who had worked with Patrick Seller, the infamous factor who worked for the Marquis of Stafford to clear thousands of people from Sutherland. Grant came along with his bully-boys, his hired thugs and on the 13th October, just before the autumnal storms, he cleared Penrioch.'

That woman was back. I saw her standing amidst the sodden green mounds that marked where the cottages had once stood. She was about my height, with a traditional Highland plaid wrapped around her and her feet and ankles bare. Her eyes were intense as she gazed at me, although I could not make out her features.

'Can you imagine this clachan bright with laughter and busy with families, men and women working in the fields, cattle lowing and the old black houses with heather thatch?'

I could not. I was more interested in that woman. The others nodded, drinking in Mary's words.

'They came in the pre-dawn dark, Grant and his thugs. They banged on the doors and set fire to the thatch, so the inhabitants had no choice but to leave. Bewildered, still half-asleep, the occupants stumbled out, driven by smoke, flames, fear and the hoarse shouts of Grant's bully boys. Women were in their shifts, children in night-shirts or nothing at all, while old men with long grey beards tried to control the yapping of collie dogs. Above the crackling of the flames, there were the screams of an old woman as her house burned around her. Irene Mackay was ninety. She did not survive.'

Even I was listening now. Only Kate seemed unconcerned. In fact, she deliberately walked away.

'Christopher Grant and his bullies hustled the people away, pushing them down to the church. The people did not enter, for they were religious and believed the church was for services, not shelter. One elderly woman died that night. Long before dawn the next morning, Grant pushed the people through the ford despite the dark and the wet. Three children died in the water. Two more died of cold and shock that night as they were shuffled to a boat that took them to Canada. Twenty died of typhus on the voyage.'

Although I listened, I could not picture the scene. It was all just words to me. It was a horror story that concerned strangers, and I could not get myself emotionally involved.

'One family slipped away before the rest were hustled onto the ship. They hid in the hills and eventually headed south to Edinburgh. They were my great-grandparents.' Mary raised her voice, standing in the pelting rain with her hair smeared to her head and water dripping from her coat to form puddles around her boots.

'Oh, Mary, I'm so sorry.' Tears glistened in Christine's eyes.

'My father told me the story, and he got it from his father, and he from his.' Mary spoke quietly. 'I have no brothers and no sisters. Until I marry and have children, I am the last of the Ablachs from Penrioch.' Tossing the rain from her face, she looked towards Kate. 'My father, and no doubt his grandfather blamed only two people for the clearance of Penrioch. One was Christopher Grant, and the other was the landowner, Lady Catherine Gordon.'

At the name, Kate turned around. 'That would be my great-grandmother.'

'I know.' Mary said. 'Your family turned mine out of their home.'

'You can't hold Kate responsible for what her distant ancestor did,' Lorna acted the peacemaker.

I felt the tension build as Kate and Mary faced each other.

'It was a long time ago,' I am sure I heard guilt in Kate's voice, 'and my family were doing what they thought was right.' She gestured at the sodden moor that spread around us. 'The people would have a better life in Canada than they could ever manage, scraping a living out of this wasteland.'

'It was not a wasteland then,' Mary's voice was deceptively quiet. 'It was productive farmland. Your ancestors made it into a wilderness when they perpetrated genocide, mass evictions, turning old people out in the blast of autumn.' Mary's voice was bitterer than anything I had heard before. 'How can anybody think that was right?'

'What was the alternative?' Kate stepped towards Mary. 'Leaving the people to live in destitution and starvation? If the landowners had not helped them move to better circumstances what would have happened to them? When the potato famine came in the 1840s, we would have had an Irish situation in the Highlands.'

'These people were evicted from their homes so the landowner, your ancestors, could make more money from sheep! It was a heartless, cruel, uncaring act.' Mary's voice rose. 'You should pay for your ancestor's cruelty.'

'Don't be silly, Mary,' Kate said. 'It was an economic necessity. It happened a hundred years ago, and the tenants would have a better life elsewhere than in this sodden moor.'

'I hate your whole family,' Mary said. 'They still hold the land they stole. They should be eradicated from the country.'

'That's enough!' Lorna stepped between them. 'We're not here to argue about something that happened a hundred years ago. We're here to climb a mountain.' She glared from one to the other. 'Have we not had enough of suffering and hate? We just lived through four years of horror, and personally, I've seen enough fighting to last me a hundred lifetimes.' She lowered her voice. 'Come on, ladies, we're all friends here.'

'We're here to prove that women are at least as good as men,' Charlie put a hand on Kate's shoulder. 'Come along Kate.'

'Kate's right,' Christine said. 'The landowner was doing what she thought was best.'

I spoke for the first time. 'Let's forget what our ancient ancestors did,' I tried to smile.

'What would you know about that?' Kate asked. 'At least Mary and I know who our ancestors were!'

It felt as if somebody had slapped me across the face. 'It's hardly my fault that I'm an orphan,' I immediately became defensive.

'Are you an orphan?' Kate altered the direction of her attack from Mary to me. 'We don't know that, and neither do you. You were left at the door of an orphanage, or so you told us.'

'And what do you mean by that?' I felt my temper rise and rose to Kate's challenge.

'I mean maybe your mother had one look at your dismal face and decided she did not want you.'

I stepped forward, ready to do battle.

'Enough!' Lorna pushed me back. 'No more squabbling.'

I was not yet prepared to withdraw. 'You mind your mouth, Kate,' I glared at her with years of resentment coming to the fore. Kate's words had re-opened wounds that were always sufficiently raw to bring tears behind my anger.

'Who's that?' Mary's voice was shrill.

We all stopped to look. I don't know what I expected, but the tone of Mary's voice made the small hairs on the back of my neck stand erect.

'Who's what?' Lorna peered into the rain. 'I can't see anybody.'

'These people,' Mary waved her hand. 'They're all around us.'

'Stop kidding,' Charlie said. 'There's nobody here except us.'

'Maybe these three men we saw have joined us,' I said. I knew Charlie was correct. There was nobody here except us.

'There were only two men,' Kate said curtly, 'and they've gone a different route. It's only Mary playing silly buggers.' She gave her sudden, infectious grin. 'Lorna's right, of course. Here we are arguing and bickering about something that happened hundreds of years ago when we should be planning for tomorrow's ascent.'

'I wasn't playing silly buggers,' Mary said. 'I thought I saw something. I thought I saw people here, walking around and shouting.'

'What were they shouting?' Lorna asked.

'I don't know. I could not hear what they were saying. I only saw their mouths working.' Mary looked away. 'I saw them though.'

'I believe you,' Lorna said. 'In the war, we saw all sorts of things that did not make sense. If your ancestors were here, you might have caught their memories or something.' She shrugged. 'I don't know, Mary.'

'You mean Mary saw ghosts? There's no such thing.' Charlie snorted. 'Tell me about this eviction though. I can maybe add it to my article. This cruel Christopher Grant evicted women and children.'

'And men,' Mary said softly. 'My great-grandfather among them.'

'The Improving landowner, what was his name? He must have been a swine. Sorry, Kate, I know he was your great-grandfather or some such, but he must have been a pig.'

'I believe he was,' Kate said. 'His wife was worse though.' Her smile included Mary. 'She was a horror who dominated her husband and terrorised her children and tenants. She would have been a suffragette, Charlie, if the term had been invented then, although her cry would not have been "votes for women", it would have been "Isabel Gordon for prime minister!" '

That was another thing about Kate. She could forgive as quickly as she attacked and expected others to be as accommodating.

'Come on, Mary, I'm sorry for what my distant ancestor did to your distant ancestor. I could not stop her, you know, as I was not born at the time.'

'Well said, Kate,' Lorna nodded. 'Now shake hands, kiss and make up.'

'What?' Mary glanced at Lorna and then at Kate. Both women were smiling. 'Oh, all right.' Mary extended her hand.

'That's better.' Lorna approved. 'You too now Brenda, it's the proper thing to do.'

I remained stubbornly unrepentant.

'I am sorry, Brenda. I should not have mentioned your childhood. Can you forgive me?' When Kate gave her apology and her smile, a woman with a heart of granite would forgive her.

'Of course,' I was not used to handshakes and kisses, but I pecked her cheek, she pecked mine, and we parted if no friendlier than before then at least without increased animosity. I stood in the rain, feeling isolated and wishing I had never come.

'The rain is getting heavier,' Kate said. 'I think we should stop for something to eat. There's a ruined house over there.' She pointed to a two-storey structure half a mile away.

'That's *Tigh-na-Beiste*,' Mary translated for us. 'The House of the monster.'

'The house of the monster?' Christine repeated. 'What a strange name! What was the monster?'

'It was not a what. It was a who.' Mary said. 'After he cleared the peninsula, Christopher Grant the factor took over the land as a farm and introduced sheep. He knocked down the old church, built himself a house lived here from time to time when he was not evicting other families.'

I was surprised that the walls of Tigh-na-Beiste still stood, together with most of the slated roof. We hurried in to escape the still-increasing rain, with Kate leading and Mary dragging in the rear. The second I stepped inside, I wished I had not as the force of evil enveloped me.

Those words are very glib, the phrase 'force of evil' slides off the tongue like jelly off a slab of ice, yet I actually gasped as I entered Tigh-na-Beiste. Of all the women present, I suppose that Lorna had the most experience of true horror as she was a nurse during the War and would have seen sights that most people would never see in their lifetime. Yet the horror affected me most, more even than Mary, whose blood had flowed through the people that the occupier of Tigh-na-Beiste had victimised.

How does one define a force of evil? It was not like the Gothic horror stories. No black-cloaked undead or great lumbering demi-humans were waiting to attack me. It was far worse, more of a psychological and emotional attack that drained all the pleasure and hope from one's life. I felt a sudden depression as if somebody or something had wrapped my soul in a blanket of hopelessness. I felt the utter frustration of life as if there was no point in continuing with anything and a desire to curl up on the stained wooden floorboards. The air was dull and damp and chill, and I saw things as through a veil. What is true evil? The absence of all hope, the desolation of uncertainty, the disability to make decisions, the aching agony of ageless loneliness, are all signs of evil. One can be in pain and know that one is loved and find comfort. Solitary hopelessness is evil, and that spirit reigned in Tigh-nan-Beiste.

As I entered that house, I was aware that none of my companions liked me and therefore I had no motivation to like any of them.

Kate, our leader, I knew to be a woman who lived for her own ego, a grasping, loud-voiced individual who relied on her parent's money and position to see her through life.

Mary was a whining creature who resented the past.

Lorna ran away to the war and had never recovered. She thought herself too good for the rest of us who had not taken part in such glory.

Charlie? I doubted she cared as much for women's rights as she claimed. More likely she liked to push herself forward as a successful woman in a man's world. Her short, cropped hair and habit of wearing male clothing indicated she was headed in another direction from the rest of us.

Christine was a little mouse, too scared to do anything unless Kate allowed it.

And that left me, Brenda the foundling, Brenda the unwanted, Brenda the ugly, awkward child with neither family nor prospects.

'Are you all right, Bren?' Mary pretended to look concerned as she touched my arm.

'I'm fine,' I said as the evil from Tigh-na-Beiste coiled around and entered each of us. For a second I saw Mary as she would have looked if she had lived a century or more ago, barefooted and in shabby Highland dress, with short, dirty fingernails and the smell of peat smoke permeating everything she wore.

Relics of the last occupant littered the interior of the house, with wallpaper peeling from the walls, a stained table in the centre of the first room that we entered and a broken, three-legged desk against the far wall. Chairs lay at all angles and cobwebs hung silver from a ceiling that had lost much of its plaster.

'We'll get a fire going,' Kate decided, 'dry off and then head out when the rain stops.'

'That will be next April,' I was not at my best yet.

'Oh, listen to the optimist,' Mary tried to cheer me up. 'Our April showers last for days and don't have breaks. It will be May at least.'

'These two men will be halfway up the west face by now,' Charlie said. 'We should just crack on and ignore the rain. It's not the end of the world.'

'It won't be the end of the world if we get dry either,' Lorna said. 'I'm with Kate on this. Why suffer when we don't have to?'

I could not tell these vibrant women that I felt the presence of evil in that house. I could only give a weak smile and help as Kate kindled a fire in the grate and the others broke up some of the smaller pieces of furniture for fuel. Oh, we all knew that the furniture did not belong to us, but we were young and carefree and set on a big adventure. Anyway, as Kate said: 'My father owns all this land, so he is the owner of this house. If the last tenant wants his broken furniture back, he can ask my father for compensation.'

Even Mary laughed at that. We set to work with gusto, keeping the chairs and table for ourselves and smashing up whatever else we could find to feed Kate's fire that sparked and smoked in the fireplace.

'There's more smoke than fire here,' Lorna coughed in the sooty blue haze. 'I think something's stuck up the chimney. Be careful we don't set the lum up.'

'Who cares if we do?' Charlie laughed.

I agreed. 'The best thing that could happen would be for this house to burn down,' I said. 'Fire may cure the evil in it.'

'The evil?' Mary fixed on my choice of words. I knew she was still troubled by whatever she had seen at Penrioch and at the ford.

I laughed as if I had been joking. 'If Christopher Grant lived her he must have left something of himself behind.'

'I see,' Mary's laugh was as unconvincing as mine had been.

'Here,' Charlie had found an old birch-broom in a cupboard of cobwebs and mouse droppings. 'Poke this up the lum and see if you can clear it. No, I'll do it.' Kneeling at the fireplace, she thrust the handle of the broom up the flue as far as she could. 'Yes,' she coughed in the smoke. 'There's some sort of obstruction.'

'It's a man,' Kate said. 'He heard you were coming and hid himself up the lum.'

I did not smile.

Charlie poked harder. 'Here it comes!'

The thing landed in the middle of Kate's fire, showering sparks and soot.

'It's only a birds' nest,' Mary said.

'What did you expect?' Kate jeered, 'a crock of gold?'

Mary glanced at me and away again. We both had expected something sinister. I was glad it had only been a bird's nest.

'Now build a fire up,' Kate ordered. 'The fireplace is big enough to roast an ox.'

There was something satisfyingly liberating about breaking up a stranger's old furniture and throwing the fragments of wood on the fire. Flames roared up the flue, with the occasional lump of blazing soot coming in return.

'The lum's up.' Lorna said.

'Good.' Kate laughed.

Once again, I could only agree. I faked my laughter to try and fit in.

Despite the house being old, it heated quickly. Kate was first to take off her coat, with the rest of us following suit.

'Should we not be on our way?' Charlie glanced out of the window. 'We can still make the Shelter Stone before dark.'

'I'm just getting comfortable,' Kate said.

'I thought you wanted to be first up An Cailleach,' Charlie said.

'I do.'

'The longer we stay here, the more chance these men have of reaching the summit first.'

'They won't get there.' I do not know from where the words came. I spoke without thought as if somebody momentarily took control of my mouth.

'What makes you think that?' Mary looked curiously at me.

'I did not think that,' I was sincere. 'I just know.'

'You're strange, Brenda.' Kate's smile did nothing to ease the sting of the words.

'I know,' I tried to turn an insult into a joke, as I had done so often before. 'It's a gift.'

Lorna laughed uneasily as Kate grinned. Christine glanced at Kate before she gave a half-smile while the others merely stared at me.

'As we seem to be making ourselves comfortable,' Lorna said, 'we may as well eat as well. The hotel gave us plenty of food.'

'The more we eat, the less we have to carry,' I tried humour again without success.

Lorna glanced outside as rain rattled the window panes. 'I'll have a look upstairs,' she said. 'I might get a look at An Cailleach from up there.'

I heard Lorna's footsteps, hollow on the wooden floorboards. 'One of the doors up here is locked,' she shouted down. 'This one's open though.'

'It might be better not to disturb anything,' I said.

'Why's that, Brenda? Will the previous tenant complain?' Kate mocked me again.

I closed my mouth, resolved to say no more to these women.

'What's this?' Lorna hammered down the stairs. 'I found this in the study, or whatever room it was.'

Kate looked up. 'What's that?' She extended her hand. 'Give it here.'

'It's a notebook,' Ignoring Kate, Lorna perched on one of the chairs, leaning the back against the wall. Blowing off a film of dust, she opened the front page. 'That fellow Mahoney's name's on the inside cover.'

'Give it to me.' Kate stepped across the floor. 'Please, Lorna.'

Lorna looked up. 'Did you know this was here?'

Snatching the notebook, Kate hurried back to her place beside the fire. 'No, how could I?'

'I would like to see that,' Charlie said. 'It might help my article.'

'Maybe later,' Kate held the slim green volume as though it was the crown jewels. She opened the book and bowed her head low.

'Kate?' I saw Kate beginning to shake. 'Kate? Are you all right?' I sat beside her and read aloud over her shoulder.

'*Mike Mahoney led us through the ford and up as far as the Shelter Stone. The weather turned foul, and we thought it best to return to Tigh-na-Beiste for the night.*'

Charlie was scribbling in her notebook, looking up and writing again. 'Carry on, Brenda.'

I paused as Kate looked into the fire. 'Wait until Kate is ready.'

'The Mahoney expedition was here then.' Charlie said. 'They might have sat around this very fireside.'

Kate nodded and returned her attention to the notebook.

I read on. '*Bill again said he had seen a woman watching us, although this peninsula has no resident population and no woman had stayed in the hotel for months. The only woman we have seen was the old washerwoman as we crossed the ford.*'

Mary gasped and looked at me. 'The washerwoman at the ford.'

I stopped reading as Kate frowned.

'What do you mean, Mary?' Kate asked.

'Brenda and I saw an old woman washing at the ford. There is an old Gaelic tale that people see the washerwoman shortly before they die.'

'Nonsense,' Kate said. 'Utter rot.' She took over the reading, following the words with her finger so that I could see where she had reached.

'*The atmosphere in Tigh-na-Beiste was horrible. We argued about trivial matters, discussed the forthcoming war in Europe and finished a bottle of whisky. Adam...*' Kate stopped there, looked up and took a deep breath.

'Bill was William Gilchrist,' Kate's voice was calm. 'He was an experienced climber. Adam was my brother, Adam Gordon.'

Only the crackle of the fire broke the sudden silence in that room.

'I'm sorry, Kate. I didn't know,' Charlie was first to speak.

'None of us knew,' I touched Kate's shoulder with all previous animosity gone. The loss of a loved one was more important than any petty misunderstanding.

'Well, now you do.' Kate looked around the circle of faces. 'Adam was a high-level climber. He had climbed in the Alps and had conquered most of the Munros. Coming here was meant to be a simple little jaunt before the much sterner test of war.'

Kate spoke mechanically as if reciting something she had learned years ago. 'Adam was commissioned in the Gordon Highlanders and was to join his regiment the following Tuesday.' Her face twisted into a frown. 'He never got there. As you know, Adam and the entire party disappeared.'

'Is that why you are here?' Charlie asked.

'That's why I am here,' Kate said. 'I'm trying to trace his footsteps to see what might have happened to him. I knew his planned route.' Taking an old and much-creased Batholomew map from her rucksack she opened it on the floor at our feet. The map showed An Cailleach as a brown splurge, with a dotted line marked in faded pencil.

'He discussed the trip with me the day before he left. Adam, Mike Mahoney and Bill Gilchrist stayed at our house at Brora before he set off and Adam showed me their intended route.' Kate put her finger on the Shelter Stone. 'As you see, Adam intended to head for the Shelter Stone and then up this secondary peak, Bein a Ghlo and across the saddle to An Cailleach. That's why I am following this route and not the more direct west face.' She smiled. 'Sorry, Charlie, we might not beat the men to the summit after all.'

'We might not.' Charlie agreed without rancour. 'Read on, Kate.'

I stepped back and joined the others. It was better that Kate read about her brother.

'I will,' Kate returned to the pencilled notes. '*Our night in Tigh-na-Beiste was disturbed by some animal howling outside. Bill thought it was a vixen, Adam some night hunting bird. I do not know what it was, but the noisy beggar certainly kept us awake.*' Kate gave a little smile.

'They had a rough time,' I said.

'So it seems,' Kate said and continued. '*The next morning was as bright as could be and quite lifted our spirits. We breakfasted on cold bacon sandwiches the inn had provided and blithely set off to the Shelter Stone. Adam hoped to complete the entire climb to An Cailleach in one day while Bill and I were more circumspect.*'

Kate looked up again. 'That's just typical of Adam,' she said. 'He would charge at things like a bull at a gate.'

'Not like his cautious sister, then,' I said with a smile.

'It must be a family trait,' Kate agreed. 'I will carry on. "*After an adventure with a pair of eagles on what we called the Wall of Death we found crossing the saddle more tricky than expected. Once again Bill said he saw a woman. He set out to speak to her without luck. Bill said that she vanished like smoke on a misty day, but not until she studied him carefully. We no sooner reached the Saddle than the weather turned into a full gale, and we were forced back here again. Tomorrow we will try again.*"'

Kate put down the notebook. 'That's the last entry,' she said. 'They must have come back here and tried again.'

We were silent for a few moments.

'Do you wish to continue?' I asked. 'You've found out what happened to your brother, or at least part of it.'

'How about you girls?' It was the first time I had ever heard Kate ask our opinion on anything. 'Shall we carry on?'

'Adam was your brother,' Lorna said. 'I think you should decide and we will all respect your decision.'

'Vote,' Kate glanced at Charlie. 'After all, women have the vote now; let's settle this in a democratic manner.'

'Quite right,' Charlie said. 'Let's all use our vote. Secret ballot or open?'

'Open,' Lorna said. 'There are too many secrets in this place without us adding to them. We are all friends, and nobody will harbour a grudge if we don't all agree.'

'Open it is then,' Kate said. 'You first, Lorna. You are the most sensible and mature of us.'

'Why thank you, ma'am.' Lorna gave a short curtsey. 'I say we go on. We are climbers after all, so it's the proper thing to do.'

'Charlie?'

'We go on,' Charlie said. 'I need this job, and it will be a scoop for women as well as for the paper.' She paused for a moment. 'I hope they did not make it. I hope we are first to the summit.'

Surprisingly, Kate did not respond. 'Brenda?'

I shook my head. There had been too many mysterious happenings for me to feel comfortable here. 'I say we should return. Something is not right here.'

Mary nodded to me. 'I agree with Bren. I know my ancestors came from this place, but I don't like it.'

'Christine?'

Christine looked at Kate and then at Lorna. 'I don't know. What do you think, Kate?'

'I think that you're old enough to make your own decisions.' Kate scolded. 'You'll have the vote when you are 30. Practise now. What do you think we should do?'

We waited as Christine tried to make up her mind. Eventually, after an imploring look at Kate, she whispered. 'I think we should go home.'

'That's three to go and two to climb An Cailleach,' Kate said. 'Well, I say we should continue and conquer this blasted mountain.'

'That's three votes each then,' I said. 'How do we decide?'

'We toss for it,' Kate said. 'Who has a penny?'

'I have,' Charlie produced a stained copper penny, with Queen Victoria's image worn nearly smooth with age. 'It's my lucky penny, dated 1895, the year I was born.'

'Ready girls?' Kate asked. 'Heads we carry on, tails we turn tail. Agreed?'

We agreed.

Charlie balanced the penny on her forefinger and flicked her thumb. The brown penny spun up and descended to land on the dirty floorboards. Queen Victoria's imperious head was uppermost.

'That's that then,' Kate said. 'We go on.'

I looked out of the window and saw only darkness.

Chapter Four

'We'll stay the night here,' Kate decided. 'There's not much point in going anywhere at this time. Tomorrow we'll rise early and get to the Shelter Stone.'

'We might get all the way to the summit,' Charlie said.

'Even if we do,' Lorna pointed out, 'these two men we saw will be well on their way by now.'

Nobody except me had seen the third man. I was beginning to doubt that he had existed. Perhaps that strange woman had accompanied the men across the ford. Maybe she was merely another climber. I remembered that Bill Gilchrist had also seen a mysterious woman and wondered if it was the same one. There were too many ifs and maybes here.

Even with the blazing fire, I still felt it chilling in that room. Kate led the way in preparing for bed with laughter and high spirits, joking and laughing and playing little-girl tricks on one another.

'We'll all sleep in the one room,' Kate said. 'It's fine and warm in here, and the smoke will keep any midges away.'

Nobody argued. Maybe the others agreed because of the warmth. I agreed because I had no desire to spend a night alone in any room of Tigh-na-Beiste. I would have preferred the rain outside to whatever lurked in that place.

'Have we all brought Euklisia Rugs?' Kate seemed to have recovered from finding the journal as she strove to control every detail of our lives.

'Of course, we have,' I replied. 'We're not your little juniors at school, Kate.'

'Christine is,' Kate said. 'Aren't you, Chrissie?'

Christine gave a shaky smile and looked away. 'Yes, Kate.'

'Oh, tell her to go away, Christine,' I advised. 'You're twenty-one now, an adult.' I thought there was gratitude in her glance.

We heaped wood on the fire as the light outside faded and stripped for bed, leaving our clothes for the fire to warm.

'Now there's a familiar sight!' Kate pointed as Christine stood in her underwear, ready for bed. We watched in some embarrassment at Kate flicked at Christine with her towel, catching her a stinging crack on the bottom.

Christine yelped and clutched at herself. 'Stop it, Kate!'

'Can you remember when you were my study servant, Chrissy?'

Christine rubbed at her bottom, saying nothing.

'Take your hand away, Chrissie or I'll give you extra.' Kate flicked again as Christine obeyed.

'Leave her alone, for goodness sake,' I said as Kate aimed a third time.

Chrissie yelped louder as the shot hit its mark. She rubbed furiously at herself, wriggling.

'It's fun, isn't it, Chrissie? It brings back old memories.' Kate was laughing.

'I see the family blood runs true,' Mary said. 'Bullying the weak, like your ancestors did when they evicted their tenants.'

Lorna and Charlie were watching, saying nothing as Kate landed a ferocious shot.

Chrissie gave a loud squeak and forced a grin. 'It's all right,' she said, clutched at her backside.

'See?' Kate said. 'She enjoys it. Go on, Chrissie, bend over and give me a better target.'

'No.' I stepped between them. 'That's enough fun and frolics.' I could see tears gleaming in Christine's eyes, but whether of pain or humiliation, I did not know. 'We've got a long day tomorrow.'

'We have, and that wasn't fair.' Charlie put a hand on Christine's shoulder. 'That must have hurt, Christine. I could rub some cream on.'

'No, I'm fine.'

Kate laughed again and turned away as Christine crept into her Euklisia Rug. I stood until she was settled and lay in my own uncomfortable rug. Ever since they were invented, climbers, campers and soldiers have blessed these sleeping bags that are so much more convenient than carrying even the lightest of beds.

The incident of the flicking towel, minor though it was, left a bad taste in my mouth. I don't like bullying of any sort, and my heart went out to Christine. I had thought that she was friends with Kate. Now I wondered if perhaps there was a completely different, unhealthy, relationship between them.

'I hate her,' Christine murmured into the dark. 'I hate her.'

I said nothing, hoping that nobody else had heard.

'Did you hear me, Kathleen?' Christine raised her voice. 'I said I hate you.'

'Go to sleep Chrissie,' Kate ordered. 'And stop talking nonsense. 'You know that you'll feel better in the morning. She does that, you know, girls. She always talks like that when she is over-tired.'

'I'm not over-tired, Kathleen, I am hardly tired at all. I hate you, and I'll still hate you in the morning. I want to kill you.'

'There will be no killing,' Lorna said. 'Now will you both shut up, get to sleep and let us get to sleep. This is meant to be an all-women's expedition to prove that we are at least equal to the men. We won't prove anything if we fall out on our first night in the hills.'

'Lorna's right,' Charlie said. 'Go to sleep for Goodness sake. Kate, stop bullying Christine, you're not a school prefect now and Christine, stop talking nonsense.'

I lay still, feeling the cold sweat of fear engulf me. I wondered if I could survive the night in this place of evil. Taking a deep breath, I closed my eyes. This house brought out the worst in some of us. I closed my eyes, seeing once more that washerwoman at the ford and repeating the words of Mahoney's journal. I had always been susceptible to atmosphere, either in old places or in rooms full of people. I had no doubt about the evil in this house, whether it had affected the factor or if it had come from him to infest the place. I did not wish to imbibe the evil; I did not want it to affect me. I was scared. I clenched my fists so tightly that my nails dug into the palms of my hands.

God help me in this terrible place.

Shuffling onto my side, I could see Christine lying watching me. Her eyes were huge. I winked at her and stuck out my tongue. I saw a flicker from her left eyelid and just a hint of her pink tongue protruding from between her lips. That tiny gesture cheered me immensely.

I watched the fire slowly fade with the embers altering from bright red to a dull orange. I wished it to last until I was sleeping, and then I wanted not to increase my vulnerability by falling asleep. An unconscious body is only an invitation for invasion. Yet if I did not sleep, I would be stupidly tired on the morrow, which was not an ideal condition when ascending a Scottish mountain.

No, I told myself, the house did not bring out the worst; it enhanced what was already there in the most harmful way. That was the form of this evil; that was why Kate reverted to the school bully and Christine to the scared little girl. And me? I did not even know who I was.

The scream exploded inside my head. I woke with a start, sitting up on my rug and wondering where I was.

'Did you hear that?' I looked around the room, seeing dark shapes of people by the fading light of the fire.

It came again, louder than before and I got up. 'What's happening?'

We were all up now, peering into the dark. Somebody, Charlie I think, had the sense to light a candle, and the yellow glow pooled over our circle of faces.

'It's Lorna,' Charlie said.

Of us all, only Lorna remained in her rug, tossing and turning, so her limbs thrashed around her and her hair a tangled mess around her face.

'Lorna.' Charlie knelt at her side. 'Lorna!'

I joined her, shaking Lorna's shoulder to wake her. 'Lorna!'

Lorna woke with a start and screamed again, wordless, inarticulate. Charlie slapped her face, left to right and then right to left. 'Lorna!'

'What?' Lorna looked around, lifted a hand to her face and stared at us. Sweat beaded her forehead. 'Was I screaming?'

'Yes,' I said. 'Did you have a nightmare?' I found a cloth to clean her face.

Lorna nodded. 'Old memories.' She tried to smile. 'Did I wake you?'

'Very effectively,' I said.

'I'm sorry, I'm sorry,' Lorna was still gasping.

I held her shoulders. 'Do you have nightmares a lot?'

'No.' Lorna shook her head. 'Sometimes the memories come back, after a bad experience.'

'Or in a bad place,' I said. 'This house is a bad place.' It had enhanced Lorna's war memories. Tigh-na-Beiste had explored Lorna and found her weakness.

'Was it the war?' Mary understood at once.

'It was the war,' Lorna said.

'Do you want to talk about it?' Charlie was surprisingly sympathetic.

'No,' Lorna shook her head. 'It was too horrid.' She closed her eyes. 'These poor men, hundreds and thousands of poor men, some no more than boys, broken, blinded, mutilated, torn to pieces and all trying to be so brave.' She shook her head as if to chase away retained memories. 'We could not save them all.'

I could only imagine the horror. 'You were an ambulance driver weren't you?'

'I was out with the very first lot, the First Aid Nursing Yeomanry,' Lorna said. 'Fany for short. Grace McDougall tried to get the government to have us with the British Army. The government turned that down, so we worked with the Belgians for a couple of years.'

'You must have seen some sights,' I said.

Lorna was shaking. 'Yes,' she said. 'Horrible, horrible things.' She managed a weak smile. 'I'm sorry to bother you, ladies. I'll try not to have any more nightmares.' Her eyes were mobile, haunted within deep-sunk sockets.

'You have nothing to apologise for,' Kate told her.

'I think we should sleep outside,' I said.

'I am quite comfortable here, thank you.' Charlie said. 'I'm not sleeping in the rain if I don't have to.'

I wondered which aspect of Charlie's character the evil would enhance, or if Charlie was immune to such intrusion. Perhaps her hard-bitten persona radiated from an inner core of such resilience that it could repel even the force inhabiting this place. I checked my watch. It was one in the morning. There were many dark hours remaining, many hours to suffer and wait for the next manifestation of whatever was here.

How would it affect me?

I did not know.

Perhaps it already had, I told myself. Maybe my quaking fear was the evil working on me, intensifying my doubts.

'Get back to bed, ladies,' Lorna said. 'I doubt that I'll wake you again. These dreams only come every so often and never twice in one night.'

We left her and returned to our rugs. Christine gave me a small half- smile and brushed her hand against my arm in passing. It looked accidental, but I knew it was a continuation from our earlier shared wink. I felt a faint stirring of hope and wondered if I had found a friend. *No,* I told myself. *You've thought that too often in the past, Brenda Smith. Don't create false hopes that lead to profound disappointment. People such as I don't get friends.*

'Who am I?' I spoke out loud. 'I wish I knew who I was.'

'Go and find out.' The answer came as clearly as if a friend had spoken.

'Who said that?' I sat up from my rug. 'Who is there?'

Although I spoke loudly, I knew that nobody heard. I could see the sleeping forms of all my companions, lying recumbent on the floor. Kate lay on her back with her hands behind her head. Christine faced me in a foetal ball, smiling faintly in her sleep, Mary had one arm free of her blankets, and her hand grasped the blue crystal she wore around her neck. I could see a faint light around her, based on the rowan cross that she had removed from her rucksack and placed beside her rug. Lorna was whimpering in another nightmare while Charlie's face was set like Biblical flint.

I looked around that room. The woman sat on the table, hands grasping the edge and her face invisible in the dark. 'I said that,' she said in a familiar voice that I could not place.

'Who are you?' I asked.

'Who are you?' she echoed.

'Were you at the Inn earlier?' I attempted to peer through the dark.

'I was at the Inn,' the woman confirmed.

'Was that you I saw at the ford?' I tried to stand, but the bedding tangled maddeningly around my ankles.

'I was there if you were there,' the woman said.

'What does that mean?' Freeing myself from the rug, I stumbled towards her. The floorboards were cold and gritty under my feet. I gasped as the menace coursing up my legs, through my thighs and thrusting inside me like an intrusive physical presence.

'Who are you?' I reached out to her and touched nothing. I had not seen her move yet she now stood where I had laid, an ethereal being amidst my sleeping companions. I could not make out her features yet her eyes never strayed from my face.

'Who are you?' Her question touched the very core of me.

'I don't know,' I said. 'I don't know who I am.'

'Then how can I know who I am?' The woman's answer was more perplexing than her presence.

'What do you mean?' I asked. 'Why are you here?'

'Why are you here?' The woman asked.

'To climb a mountain.'

'Which mountain are you here to climb?' The woman asked. 'Will you climb the physical mountain of An Cailleach or the spiritual mountain of your ignorance, the actual or the metaphoric?'

'What does that mean? Tell me!'

'You will only know when you know.'

She was gone. I was standing by the table in a room full of sleeping women with an evil thing crawling about inside me. I could feel it infesting me, expanding from my womb to flow with my blood into my heart and then being pumped into my liver, my kidneys, my spleen, my brain and into every fibre of me from the tips of my toes to the frazzled ends of my hair. I could not fight it although I wished to claw the skin from my body to rid myself of this unwelcome intrusion.

'Get out!' I could feel the loathsome creature taking control of my body, the evilness of doubt and depression and fear infesting me like some spiritual disease.

Gasping, I stumbled outside where a blanket of cold rain welcomed me. I shivered, turned my face to the heavens and saw a sickle moon through a rent in the storm wrack. I do not know from where the words came, yet I mouthed them. I spoke in Gaelic, a language I did not know and understood the meaning without thought.

'When I see the new moon
It becomes me to lift mine eye
It becomes me to bend my knee
It becomes me to bow my head.'

I stepped away from the doorway of Tigh-na-Beiste and onto the thin soil of the peninsula.

'Oh, sweet Lord!'

I felt the change immediately as my bare feet touched the earth. There was warmth rising from the ground through the soles of my feet and into me. It was the opposite of the oppressive chill of Tigh-na-Beiste, a welcoming, gentle acceptance that soothed away the evil. I stood in the faint light of the moon as the two entities battled within me, the coldness of sin and the warmth of the earth. I was the vessel in which they operated, and I could do nothing to assist or resist. I could only exist and receive both forces as they spread within me.

The moon was a mouth, the crescent a smile and the whiteness its teeth. I looked up, fully aware that moonlight was only the reflected warmth of the sun. I accepted that, as I knew the celestial orb was merely a chunk of rock many thousands of miles away. I also knew that the moon affected the tides and the growing of crops, which in turn meant food and therefore life and death for every woman, man and child on this planet. I observed the wonder of the sky, not worshipping the moon but aware of its place within the cosmos and the power it exerted. I wondered if my ancient ancestors had shared that knowledge; I wondered if the time-worn stone circles had indeed been created to worship the moon and stars, or if they only acknowledged the power these distant creations represented in the vast cosmos in which we lived.

I felt the evil depart from me as if it was a physical rather than a spiritual force. It left with a jolt that made me gasp and then I was free. The rain was cleansing, the moon bathing and the soil nourishing.

'Who am I?' I asked myself, or perhaps I asked the moon, as a representative of a far greater entity.

And then I saw them. Twenty men a-marching with torches, guns and axes, their feet silent on the ground, their voices guttural, not speaking in the Gaelic that was native to this place. I watched without acting as they approached the friendly clachan of Penrioch, where the cattle clustered in the closest fields and the drift of peat-smoke perfumed the night air.

I saw the torches flare and heard the fierce laughter. I saw the heather thatch spark and burn and smoke. I saw the roof-trees smoulder and collapse inward to the people inside.

The voices sounded harsh in the night air, the language English, the accent Lowland Scots. 'Damn her, the auld bitch, she has lived too long – let her burn.' I heard the wild screams of an old woman and the panicked squeals of children. I saw old bearded men stumble into the night to face the attackers and fall under the swing of cudgels and iron-shod boots. I heard the frantic barking of dogs turning to high-pitched squeals as men beat them with sticks. I heard the wails of women. I could feel the terror and despair, the sense of disbelief from the people of the clachan and the cruel joy of the interlopers. There was evil here, raw and unharnessed, backed by legality without compassion; there was savagery without mercy and despair without depth.

I knew it was not happening. I knew I was witnessing events that had occurred a century ago, and yet I felt the same grief and shock and shame that I could not help. I could see the evil, like a foul black cloud, suspended above Tigh-na-Beiste, and the same darkness was in the men who had committed the evictions. As I watched, I saw the darkness surrounding each man like smoke, with baleful eyes and talons that thrust into hearts and souls.

'Oh, dear God,' I said.

At my words, the images vanished, and I was alone outside that house with the rain hissing around me and my hair hanging in sodden serpents on my shoulders. I was not cold. Despite the rain, I felt an inner warmth that repelled any chill. Looking over my shoulder, I knew that I was safer out here with the good earth under my feet than I would be closeted within Tigh-na- Beiste. The rain was natural, it belonged here as much as the wind and the soil and the solid granite; it would not hurt.

Stepping further away from that house, I found a handy rock and sat beside it, leaned back and closed my eyes. I could feel An Cailleach's presence, watching me, watching us, as easily as I could feel the wind and rain. She was tangible, substantial and she was waiting.

Chapter Five

'Brenda?' When I opened my eyes, Mary was staring at me. 'What on earth are you doing out here? You'll catch your death!'

I smiled at her. 'No, it's perfectly all right.' I rose, shook the water from my hair and laughed as she backed away. 'It's only rainwater, Mary. It won't bite.'

'The fire's on, and we have bacon sizzling,' Mary invited. 'We've been looking for you for ages. I thought you had wandered off somewhere and got lost.'

'Thank you, Mary,' I said. 'I've not been far away.'

The women were all dressing for the climb, testing boots and ropes, looking at the map, discussing the route and acting as though the events of the previous night had never taken place. Kate was talking animatedly to Christine, and Charlie was scribbling notes while Lorna tended the bacon.

'You'd better get dried,' Mary said.

I stripped and towelled myself dry, wondering if Kate would try her towel nonsense with me and knowing I would retaliate far more forcibly than Christine ever had. I felt incipient anger bubbling inside me and knew it came from the fabric of the house.

'Let's eat outside,' I said, 'it's a beautiful morning.' In the few moments since I had come inside, the rain had stopped. Dawn brought the sun, the call of the golden plover and the bubbling trill of the whaup.

''Put some clothes on first,' Lorna advised. 'These two men may be around, and we don't want them getting any interesting notions.'

'Men!' Charlie spat out the words as if it were a curse. 'If only we could invent a way of getting babies without their help this world would be a far better place.'

'Much less fun, though,' Kate said, and most of us laughed. Charlie did not.

The evil in Tigh-na-Beiste had discovered Charlie's enthusiastic support for suffrage and warped it into a dislike of men. As women we would all welcome equal rights; as rational, warm-blooded human beings, we did not pretend to despise or demonise half the human race.

'Come on, ladies,' I dressed hurriedly and led them outside. The contrast to only an hour ago was astonishing. The rain had vanished, the air was crisp and invigorating, and the hill slopes invited us up.

'It's exactly like Mahoney's journal,' Lorna breathed deeply. 'It's absolutely gorgeous today.'

'Could not be better,' I agreed. Seabirds were wheeling, screaming in the air and a pair of oystercatchers arrowed past, piping to each other to praise the glory of the morning.

We ate at the rock where I had spent the night, enthusiastically gobbling bacon sandwiches and gulping down hot sweet tea as we surveyed the route ahead.

'Ready girls?' Kate was herself again, enthusiastic, vibrant and cheerful. She stamped her boots on the ground. 'On we go! To the Shelter Stone!'

'To the Shelter Stone!' We repeated her words, waving our sticks in the air as we made final adjustments to our rucksacks and packs and followed her. All the tension of the previous day had vanished, we were one unit again, we were the Edinburgh Ladies Mountaineer Club, and we were going to conquer An Cailleach, come what may. It is strange what a little sleep and a gleam of sunshine can do to lift the spirits.

As usual in the Scottish Highlands, the view was immense. Out to sea was a panorama of islets and islands, with the blue smear of the

Outer Hebrides sweetening the far horizon. To the east, the mountains of Sutherland and Ross offered range upon range of shapely hills interspersed with delightful green glens and the mottled brown of heather moors. It was scenery to gladden the heart, a vista of which Sir Walter Scott would have been proud and a slap in the face to those warmongering politicians whose ambition sought domination through war.

Immediately outside the clachan the ground was level and had once been tended. Nettles and small bushes marked the memory of fields, and I could nearly hear the clink of agricultural tools and the low voices of long-gone people. Beyond that, between us and the first true rise of the hills, the ground sunk in a depression marked by patches of peat hag and pools of dark water.

'This is not marked on the map.' Kate stopped at the end of this bogland as we crowded behind her. She tested the depth with her stick. 'It's deep, with a soft bottom. We won't be wading through that.'

'There must be a way through,' Charlie said. 'The people who lived here must have got through.'

'Not necessarily,' Lorna also poked in her stick. 'Maybe it formed after the landowner cleared Penrioch. What do you say, Mary, you're the local expert.'

'The bog was always here,' Mary said. 'It's fed by the burns running off the hillside. 'I remember my granny telling me about it. She said the folk had a causeway through the burn so they could drive the cattle to the summer shieling up the hill.'

'That'll be long gone now.' I said.

'Maybe not.' Christine surprised me by giving an opinion without waiting for Kate. 'Some of the old castles were built in lochs, and they had causeways going to them. The causeways were slightly under the surface of the water, so only the defenders knew where they were. The causeway may still be there, but the water level will have risen with time.'

'Oh listen to the professor,' Kate jeered. When did you get so clever?'

I smiled encouragement to Christine. 'We'll look for the causeway then.'

'Yes, well done, Christine.' Charlie rubbed her arm.

Spreading out, we walked along the fringes of the bog, thrusting our sticks into the mud. After a few minutes, Lorna called out. 'It's shallower over here.'

The ground was firmer underneath an inch and a half of peaty water. Lorna stepped gingerly into the bog and tapped with her stick. 'It seems to continue on,' she took another few baby-steps. 'Yes, we've found it.'

'Christine should lead us,' Charlie gave Christine a wide smile. 'She should have the honour.'

I was not surprised when Kate decried that suggestion and pushed forward. 'It could be dangerous,' she said. 'I'll go first.'

'Yes, Kate,' Christine stepped aside so Kate could take the lead. We followed one by one onto the causeway.

'My granny told me that the foundations were floated on bundles of heather sunk in the bog,' Mary said. 'And there was a wee hut halfway across in case of bad weather.'

'I can't see a hut,' Kate said.

'It's probably got blown away, or sunk into the peat,' Mary said.

'As long as we don't get sunk in the peat,' Charlie kept rigorously to the centre of the causeway. 'What a horrible way to die.'

Despite the early hour, midges rose in clouds as we slowly negotiated the bog. Kate poked into the peaty morass before taking any step, and we followed her lead, enjoying the scenery even as we swatted at the midges.

'This is a desolate place,' Charlie looked around. 'I love the austerity of the mountains, I love the bustle of Edinburgh, and I love the fertility of agricultural land. This useless moorland is just a waste. It's horrid. What do you think, Christine?'

'It ends soon,' Christine said. 'The ground rises over there,' she pointed with her stick. 'Actually, I rather like the loneliness of the bogland.'

'Trust you to be contrary,' Kate called from in front. 'Wait now, girls!' She held up her stick. 'The path ends here.'

'It'll be there somewhere,' Mary said. 'Poke around.'

We stood on the causeway with the water lapping at our boots and the midges clustering to feed on our blood.

'There's nothing here,' Kate said. 'We'll have to swim.'

Nobody laughed at Kate's weak joke.

'Let me try.' Squeezing past us, Mary joined Kate. She widened the search, prodding her stick into the mud in a circle. 'Here!' She jabbed the stick down harder. 'There's something there,' she indicated a spot well to the right of Kate and a full five feet in front. 'Maybe this part of the causeway collapsed, or the Penrioch folk put in a bend.'

'What a stupid thing to do,' Kate said.

'The old castles often had gaps and bends as well,' Christine said.

'Did they,' Kate's tone indicated that she had no interest in Christine's opinion or in old time castles.

'It's a bit of a step across,' Mary said. 'We'll have to jump or make a bridge.'

'If the causeway's set on heather bundles,' Lorna said, 'it might not hold if we jumped on it. Six full-grown women thumping down! It will have to be the bridge.'

'I don't know about you,' Charlie said, 'but I don't carry a bridge in my rucksack.'

'Plenty bits of furniture left in the house,' Lorna the practical said. 'Come on, Brenda, you and I will find something.'

Frustrated at the delay, we returned to Tigh-na-Beiste. The best we could find was the table which was luckily of deal and not too heavy to carry. It took us nearly an hour there and back, and my temper was beginning to fray when we arrived back at the bog to see Kate munching on a sandwich and Charlie sketching the view in her notebook.

'Thank you for your help,' I said. Only Christine had the grace to look guilty.

'Too many cooks would have spoiled the broth,' Lorna eased any tension. 'We're lucky we had not gone far.'

The table was not quite long enough to bridge the gap, so we positioned it in the middle and had to take long strides on either side before we could continue. Our makeshift bridge swung alarmingly under our boots but held as we crossed one by one and continued on the causeway.

'Those rowans will mark the other end,' Mary pointed to a small clump of rowan trees. 'My people used them for all sorts of reasons.'

'Now we're on our way,' Kate spoke with some satisfaction as we passed the trees and thumped onto what passed for dry land in the peninsula.

'I'm glad to get out of the bog,' Charlie waved her hand in a weak attempt to chase away the midges. 'I hate bogs and moorland. The idea of drowning in mud! I can't think of anything worse.'

Lorna nodded. 'We saw plenty of that at Passchendaele,' she said. 'The soldiers feared that as much as they feared gas.' She wrestled with silent memories. 'Horrible. Like these midges.'

'We'll lose the midges when the wind rises,' Mary nodded to the slope ahead. 'Looking at the way the bushes are growing, the wind here is pretty steady from the west.'

We walked slowly and steadily, for to rush and stop is far more tiring, and we were all experienced in the hills. The first part of the climb was only a long slog through the rough grazing of the foothills, where grass gave way to patches of peat and then the granite skeleton of the mountain thrust through the purple-brown heather. I paused for a moment to view a stag and his harem of hinds feeding on a sheltered ledge above us. The stag was restless, pacing back and forth.

'Rutting season,' Mary said. 'Best give the stag a wide berth.'

Charlie snorted. I half expected her to bracket male stags into her dislike of men, but she refrained. As the hill grew steeper, we plodded on, passing the circular foundations of the summer shielings and the marks of old peat cuttings.

'Now we're beyond human reach,' Mary looked around, where quietness brooded over the rough ground and rocks protruded from patches of struggling heather. 'This land is the true wilderness.'

'We are on the outstretched hand of An Cailleach.' Although I intended to speak only to myself, Christine threw me a small smile. We walked on with the wind cutting at our faces and the views immense.

I thought of the crowded streets of Edinburgh with trams and omnibuses and people crammed into dark streets of tenements, living between tedious jobs and damp-roomed houses. Only a century before or less they had lived in this vast space; the lives of thousands altered on the whim of a landowner. I thought of the scene I had witnessed, the brutality of forced eviction. Was life intended to be so unfair? There must be something better for the majority.

'She's not the little innocent you think she is,' Kate stepped beside me.

I had to refocus my mind from the visions of the previous night. 'Who?' I asked.

'Young Christine,' Kate said. 'I said: she's not the little innocent she appears to be.'

'She's a full grown woman,' I said. 'She's not a little girl anymore.' I was careful not to criticise.

Kate was silent for a few moments as we trudged upwards, gasping to gain our second wind. 'Don't let her fool you,' she said.

'Why you do treat her as you do?' I could not restrain myself any longer.

Kate held my eye for longer than I liked. 'To keep her in her place,' she said. 'Believe me, Brenda; you don't want that woman to be in charge.'

'I don't think she has ever been in charge,' I said. 'Not the way you bully her.'

'You only see part of it,' Kate was almost pleading with me. 'I'm not the monster you seem to think I am.'

An eagle circled above, its wings outspread as it rose higher on some current of air. I heard its harsh call and thought how puny and slow we must appear.

'Kate,' Christine hurried up, 'are we going all the way to the top today?'

I slowed down a little to allow Christine and Kate to be alone. What had Kate meant with her: 'don't let her fool you'? I watched as Christine edged closer to Kate, eager to be recognised, desperate for attention.

The slope steepened so we had to lean forward. My rucksack was heavy on my back, the straps cut into my shoulders, and the nails in my boots scraped on the rocky ground beneath. I looked up, where the hill stretched before us, undulating into a series of heather-and-rock ridges that seemingly extended forever.

From this angle, An Cailleach did not appear formidable in the slightest, a long, tiresome slog and nothing much else. I could not understand why nobody had climbed it.

'I see Kate and Christine have made up,' Mary panted to me.

'It appears so,' I said, and abruptly changed the subject. 'I saw your people last night.'

'Which people?' Mary looked at me sideways with the sun catching the blue crystal that hung from her neck and the rowan cross pinned to her breast.

'The people of Penrioch,' I said.

Mary's eyes narrowed for a moment as if she suspected mockery. 'Oh them!' She gave a high-pitched laugh. 'I was only joking,' she denied her previous experiences. 'Besides you would see nothing in the dark.'

I should have known better than to expose myself to ridicule. I closed my mind. 'I must have been dreaming, then,' I walked on, every step one pace deeper into the peninsula, every yard further from civilisation and nearer to An Cailleach.

'That must be it,' Mary matched me step for step. 'There is a lot of dreaming in the Highlands. A lot of scheming, too.'

Kate was well in front, tapping her stick on the ground as she ploughed ahead with Christine struggling to keep up with her.

'That was awkward last night with these two,' I nodded to Kate.

Mary shrugged. 'It was only a squabble,' she said. 'It's all blown over now. They've known each other for years.'

'Since school at least,' I said. It seemed that Mary was not keen to pursue the objects that interested me. I closed my mouth and struggled on.

There was no path up the steadily increasing slope, so we each chose whatever route seemed best as we panted and slogged upward to the first ridge. We stopped there to catch our breath and look around at the expansive view.

I had initially believed that An Cailleach stood alone, a single peak on this peninsula. However, the shoulders of An Cailleach hid another, lesser height that hugged the hill to the east. I saw the pair now, like a mother hill and its daughter, an ill-matched pair of unyielding granite, partially seen through a haze of cloud.

'That is Bein a Ghlo,' Mary said, 'Hill of the Mist, and you can see why.'

Grey-white and slowly shifting, mist shrouded the top third of Bein a Ghlo and hid the gap between the two hills. I love watching mist drift across a mountain, now concealing, now revealing and always evocative. I said nothing for a good three minutes, wondering who had stood here before us and what An Cailleach thought of us watching her across a sea of mist.

'He was here,' Lorna said.

'Who?' Kate asked, too sharply.

'Your brother.' Lorna spoke quietly. 'You were thinking of him.'

Kate frowned and looked away. 'We have to ascend Bein a Ghlo first and then cross the saddle between the two peaks to conquer An Cailleach. All the other approaches are up precipitous cliffs. We have at least one sheer cliff on this route as it is.'

'Let's get going then,' Charlie had been examining the route. 'I can't see any sign of these two men we saw yesterday. They've probably got the summit of An Cailleach, celebrated and returned to the inn to boast how they beat the women once again.'

'They aren't back at the Inn,' I spoke without thought. 'They wouldn't be able to cross the ford last night. With all that rain it would be too deep. It might be passable later today.'

I felt Kate's eyes on me. 'How would you know that? You haven't been here before.'

'It's pretty obvious,' I told her. 'It was thigh deep when we crossed, and the rain was continuous after that. The burn will be swollen, and so the ford will be deeper.'

Kate frowned and moved on. Christine scampered after her, and we followed to begin the first serious piece of climbing that we had undertaken on this expedition. Bein a Ghlo was not a significant height, being about two thousand three hundred feet in height, yet it posed particular challenges. The direct way up was inaccessible, being sheer cliffs of a thousand feet, but there was an easier ascent up a steep gulley topped by a cliff of three hundred feet with a perilous overhang.

'Are we going up there?' Christine was the least experienced climber among us.

'Oh, don't be such a baby!' Kate snapped. 'Just follow the rest of us.'

'It's all right, Christine,' Lorna said. 'We'll all be roped together so if anybody slips, the others will hold her. We won't let you fall.'

'I don't wish to be roped,' Charlie said.

'I know its constricting,' Lorna allowed, 'but it's also safer. It's the only proper thing to do.'

I traced the route we had to take, taking in every obstacle before we began the ascent. I had seen worse, but it could be tricky climbing. Christine was also staring at the cliff, with her breathing fast and shallow.

'It's not as bad as it seems,' I whispered. 'There are always more hand-holds than one can see from a distance.'

'I hope so,' Christine gave a watery smile. 'I don't want to let anybody down.'

'You won't let anybody down,' I said. 'Trust yourself.'

Christine rewarded me with a shy smile.

We tied the ropes around our waists, checking each knot for strength, reassuring Christine that we had all done such things before, giving little laughs. The Mahoney expedition may have come this way before, we did not know. We may have been the first to attempt the climb, which excited Charlie more than anything. It was not the ascent that played on my nerves, but the words from Mahoney's journal and the strange happenings that plagued us on this expedition.

There was that woman that nobody else had seen in the inn and at the ford. There was the washerwoman at the ford and the sickening atmosphere at Tigh-na-Beiste, and there was the scene between Kate and Christine, plus my vision of the Clearance ghosts at Penrioch. Any of these things would be unnerving on their own but taken together they scared me. Lastly, and most disturbing, was the woman who had appeared in Tigh-na-Beiste last night. Was she the same person who I had seen at the inn and at the ford?

I knew she was not real. I must have imagined her, yet she was vaguely familiar although I had never seen her face. The fact that we held a conversation was the most unsettling of all for not only had I seen her, she had also seen me.

'Ready, girls?' Kate scraped her right foot on the ground, with the nails in her boots raising bright sparks.

'Ready,' we replied in unison.

After the rain of the previous day, the scree within the gully was damp and slippery, so we slithered upward, using our hands nearly as often as our feet. Kate set a fast pace, throwing herself upward as if it was a race although by that time only Charlie was concerned about beating the two men to the summit, or even thought about the men at all. After Mahoney's journal, I felt that any ascent of An Cailleach would count as a notable success. Twice I gasped as my ankles turned on the scree and I blessed my stout boots. I wondered how the old Highlanders had lived in this environment dressed in the great plaid and only brogues on their feet. They must have been an active, fit race of women and men.

Little spiders ran hither and yon among the scree, racing away from these monsters that had invaded their territory. I wondered vaguely if they had stories of strange giant creatures as they gathered together in their webs, or if it was only humanity who harboured such imaginative fancies.

The scree ended in a stretch of heather-and –glacial rocks that was much easier to ascend. There were patches of brilliant green bog between the rocks, and the hum of insects that clouded around us, seeking blood or salt or whatever it is that these biting creatures feed on.

'Blasted midges,' Lorna flapped her hands around in a vain attempt to free herself from the increasing hordes.

'Scotland's last line of defence,' Mary said. 'My father told me that when the Ninth Legion of Romans came here, the midges got under their armour and they were so itchy they all jumped into a loch and drowned.'

'I can see why!' Lorna said. 'We should have used midges against the Huns rather than poison gas. It's more effective.'

'Look!' Christine pointed upwards. 'Is that an eagle?'

'Two eagles,' Charlie said. 'They're circling us.'

Although the birds were high up, it was evident that they were huge. They circled Bein a Ghlo and descended, still flying in spirals, until we had a clear view of them.

'Mahoney's journal mentioned that he saw eagles,' Lorna said.

'I remember,' Kate was short. 'They won't bother us.'

A slight wind rose from the west, strong enough to drive away the midges and dry our perspiration without being in the slightest bit uncomfortable. We moved on, with the eagles circling closer until we could make out the individual feathers and the predatory eyes. Every time I had seen eagles before, they had been tiny specks in the distance. Only now did I see how large they were, and how dangerous they looked.

'Do you remember that story Duncan Og told us in the inn?' I asked.

'Who?' Charlie was paying more attention to the eagles than to me. 'Oh, that old man. I remember.'

'He told us about two witches that turned into eagles.'

'Do you think these two are witches?' Charlie grinned. 'I thought witches flew on broomsticks and had pointed hats.'

I thought of the happenings of last night. 'No,' I said. 'I don't think these two are witches. I just think it's a bit of a coincidence that Duncan Og mentioned two eagles and here we have two eagles.'

'One flew to Badenoch,' Charlie said. 'So they wouldn't both be here.'

Mary was beside us, fingering her rowan cross as she watched the eagles. 'I've never known eagles to come so near to people,' she said. 'I don't like them at the best of times.'

We halted at the base of the cliff, looking for the best ascent. 'Normally one has a named route to follow,' Kate said. 'Here we must make our own.'

'All the better,' Charlie tapped the rock. 'We'll name it Suffrage Ascension.'

'That's a bit of a mouthful,' Mary said. 'How about Women's Success?'

'Let's get up first,' Kate said. 'We can play with names later.'

'Over here,' Lorna shouted. 'There's a rope up the face.'

'We're not first then,' Charlie did not hide her disappointment.

The ropes stretched from the foot of the cliff to the top of the overhang, secured by a series of eye bolts that had been fastened into the rock.

'These two men have already been here.' Kate said.

'No.' Lorna tugged at the double rope. 'This line has been here for some time. It's worn and jaded. I would not trust it.'

'The two men did not come this way,' I reminded. 'They headed to the West face. I would guess that the Mahoney expedition left this rope. We know they came this way.'

I pictured the scene, Mahoney, Bill and Adam standing where we stood, hammering in the eye bolts, attaching the rope and launching themselves up this cliff. I could nearly hear the clink of hammer on steel and smell the sweet tobacco of their pipes. I touched Kate on the arm. 'Are you all right?'

'Of course,' Kate laughed. 'How secure are the pitons?'

'They're pure steel,' Lorna pulled at the first two. 'As solid as they were the day they were put in.'

'We'll trust them then,' Kate said.

'We'll use our own ropes, though,' Lorna decided for us. 'These old ropes are frayed and dangerous.' She cut through the original line, attached one of ours and pulled it through the eye bolts. 'These lads knew their business,' she said.

'I'll go up first,' Kate announced.

Nobody argued. Kate was following her brother's footsteps. Kate was our leader; Kate had the right to lead. She started slowly until she was sure of the stability of the pitons.

'They're perfectly secure,' Kate called out and swarmed up without looking down, eased herself over the overhang and vanished from our view.

'Easy as pie,' Kate called down. 'Who's next?'

'Me,' Charlie tested the rope first and pulled herself up, finding hand and footholds that soon had her beside Kate.

'You go next,' I said to Christine.

'I've never gone up a rope,' Christine whispered.

'You hold the rope and walk up the cliff,' I said. 'I'll come with you.' I hoped that the rope would sustain our combined weight.

'Yes, Brenda.' Christine said quietly. I tried to jolly her along.

'On the count of three; one, two, and three and off we go.'

Christine took hold of the rope in hands that appeared far too white and delicate for such an operation. Throwing me a nervous smile over her shoulder, she began to climb. I gave her a head start and followed.

She walked herself up, gasping and hesitant but without major difficulty until she reached the overhang, where she stopped. I felt the drop pulling at us, enticing us downward.

'On you go,' I encouraged. 'We're roped together, so there is no danger.'

'Yes, Brenda,' Christine said.

I watched as she hauled herself up, following the moment she reached the most critical section of the climb when she was momentarily semi-horizontal with a void behind her. She stopped, gasping, as she hung over the drop, so I came behind her. I have no love for overhangs myself. I took a deep breath.

'One more effort,' I tried to sound as cheerful as I could, and then Lorna was pulling Christine up, I scrambled over, and we were on a spacious ledge with the wind caressing the sweat from our faces and the hills of the Rough Bounds rising before us. I saw the shoulder of An Cailleach, with mist hiding her profile like the veil of a bride on her wedding day.

'That wasn't so bad,' Lorna said as Christine took deep breaths to control her nerves.

'Maybe not for you,' I viewed the next stage in our assault on An Cailleach. The slopes of Bein a Ghlo rose rocky and steep to a sharp, skyward thrusting pinnacle. Even as I watched, mist formed, blotting the summit from view. Closer to hand a tiny alpine willow somehow braved the ever-present wind.

Christine knelt beside it. '*Salix herbacea*,' she breathed. 'Isn't it lovely?'

Kate frowned. 'We've no time for flowers. We've got a hill to climb.'

Christine stood up as we studied the route ahead. As quickly as it had arrived, the summit mist dissipated, giving us an open view of our initial destination. An Cailleach taunted us, showing us herself in part, daring us to approach and drawing her misty mask so we could not see everything, a teasing virgin on her wedding night, offering herself and pulling back again.

'All we have to do is scramble up this hill and cross the saddle between Bein a Ghlo and An Cailleach,' Kate said. 'We can rest at the Shelter Stone and then it's a wee climb, and we're there. All Sir Garnet, as Adam used to say.'

Charlie was standing on the ledge, drawing us all with her forehead wrinkled in concentration. 'When you're ready, ladies, we'll be on our way.'

Kate stamped her boots on the ground. 'Follow me, girls!'

The summit of Bein a Ghlo was a bit of a disappointment, an ice-smoothed ridge with a pinnacle of rock that was less impressive close-up than it had seemed from a distance. With An Cailleach waiting for us, we did not feel any elation, only a sensation that the real challenge lay ahead. The old folk knew their stuff when naming hills, for mist surrounded us, slow swirling to obscure anything except the most slender of views.

To the west, the mist rose and fell, revealing a glimmer of gold as the afternoon sun illuminated the fringes of the cloud. I did not feel the breath of wind that parted the mist to unexpectedly show us our route. The saddle stretched between Bein a Ghlo and An Cailleach in a knife-edge, curving ridge with chunks of broken granite littering the top and patches of mist drifting this way and that as the wind gusted and faded. One persistent cloud hovered halfway across, where the curve of the saddle was most pronounced. Beyond that, it sloped downward so we would lose height and have to climb all over again.

'That doesn't look too bad,' Lorna gave her opinion. 'All we have to do is hold our nerves and don't fall.'

Charlie tapped her stick on the ridge. 'It's secure as the Castle Rock. This has been an easy climb so far.'

I looked across the saddle, with mist boiling and writhing in the hidden vastness below. An Cailleach was showing her face, beckoning us onward. As Charlie had said, it had been easy so far. I still did not understand why nobody had ever conquered the old hag.

'Follow me, girls,' Kate stepped boldly forward, stamped her feet to prove the ground was firm and strode on. She dislodged a tiny flake of granite that fell into the mist without a sound.

'You next, Charlie,' Lorna said, 'then Mary and Christine. Brenda and I will be the backmarkers.' Christine was in the middle, the safest place, with experienced women in front to trail-blaze the route, and behind to ensure she did not get into trouble. Lorna was looking after the youngest member of our party.

By the time I stepped onto the saddle, Kate was a good thirty yards in front and making good progress. The ridge sloped slightly on the western side, where the ocean wind had eroded the surface, so I kept to the very top, careful that I did not slip into the unseen depths below. I say unseen because a dense mist concealed the valley beneath us on either side. It felt as though we were walking along a stone bridge above a shifting grey mass of cloud.

'This isn't too bad,' Christine spoke over her shoulder, echoing my earlier thoughts. 'I don't know why An Cailleach hasn't been climbed before.'

With every hill in Scotland conquered, and women and men scaling the Alpine peaks as if they were mere lumps on the countryside, An Cailleach should present no problem. I shrugged; perhaps it was because it was so easy that the climbers had not bothered. There was no challenge to serious mountaineers, and An Cailleach was too difficult to access for the casual day wanderer.

'We're not there yet,' Lorna warned. 'You pay attention where you put your feet, Christine. Take it one step at a time.'

'Yes, Lorna,' Christine obeyed. I heard the scream of an eagle echoing through the mist. There was no other sound except the steady thump of our boots and the irregular tapping of our staffs. On one occasion, a drift of the wind brought us the rush of a burn or a waterfall from far below.

Up ahead, Kate vanished into the bank of perpetual mist. Charlie followed, and then Mary. I saw Christine hesitate.

'I'm right behind you, Christine.' I kept my voice cheerful.

We entered the mist together with the cold clamminess enfolding us like a mother's arms, distorting sound, diminishing vision and reducing the temperature. I could see Christine as a dim figure shuffling ahead, and had a very vague view of Mary, while the two women in front had entirely vanished in that shockingly dense mist.

'Mary, Brenda…' Christine's voice wavered. 'Are you there?'

'We're still here,' I called out in false jollity. I fought my desire to reach out and touch Christine's shoulder, knowing that she might start. I had a terrifying vision of her sliding over the edge and vanishing into the mist.

We were moving slower now, feeling our way along that treacherous ridge with the hellish drop on either side.

'Stop!' Kate's voice called out, clarion-clear from the front. 'There's a gap here. We can't go any further.'

Chapter Six

I felt Charlie's dismay. 'I'm not giving up,' she said.

'We must if Kate says so.' Christine did not sound too disappointed.

'Let me see.' Lorna had caught up with me. 'Stand aside ladies, and I'll squeeze past you.'

I did as Lorna asked; although how she managed to inch past on that narrow ridge I will never know. Lorna was like that; she remained at the background until times of need and then she was there, quiet and competent. She stepped to the front, and I joined them, although Charlie was far more experienced in the hills than I was.

The ridge curved ahead for another ten yards and then abruptly fell away in a great cleft, as though one of the Norse Gods had taken his axe and cloven the solid rock with a single mighty chop. With the mist so thick, we could not see how far the gap extended. Somewhere above us, the eagle screamed again as if in mockery.

'That's awkward,' Lorna said. 'Maybe we could climb down and up the other side.'

We craned our necks to look. The ridge fell away in a vertical drop, smooth as glass until it vanished into the mist. Grey-white tendrils snaked around us, writhing and coiling at our feet.

'I can't see a single hold,' Kate said. 'Does anybody have any ideas?'

I kept silent. If experienced climbers such as Lorna and Kate were baffled, I had nothing to contribute. Lorna got down on her hands and knees. 'If only this mist would clear,' she said. 'Wait now! Just look down there.'

We looked where Lorna indicated. Set into the rock was a sturdy pair of pitons, both holding a length of rope that stretched across the gap into the unknown.

'How on earth did we miss that?' Kate asked.

'Goodness knows,' Lorna got to her feet. 'One minute I saw nothing and the next it seemed to appear. The mist must have hidden it.'

'What is it?' Christine asked.

'A rope bridge, silly,' Kate said. 'Adam and I used to make them between trees in the grounds of the house.'

'Oh how I wish we had grounds like that,' Mary said. 'On land stolen from the peasants, no doubt.'

'Shoosh, Mary,' Lorna threw her a frown. 'Carry on, Kate.'

'One has to balance on one's hands and knees and drag oneself over,' Kate ignored Mary's comments.

'I don't fancy that much,' Charlie peered into the mist. 'I can't even see how far it goes.'

'Oh, it's easy enough,' Kate said. 'Once you have your balance you just carry on. The only thing is, don't look down.' She smiled. 'Adam and I used to throw stones at each other when we were in the middle.'

'I can imagine that,' Mary said.

'You two were close, weren't you?' Charlie asked.

Kate shrugged and said nothing.

'How secure is that rope?' Lorna asked. Before we could reply she had slid down to the nearest piton and taken told of the line. 'It's in surprisingly good condition,' Lorna said. 'The rope is hardly worn at all.'

The vision came unbidden. I saw three men working away, one hammering in the pitons and the others attaching the rope. They were laughing, enjoying themselves as they worked. The tallest man wore a tweed jacket and had a pipe at the side of his mouth, around which he gave cheerful orders.

'The Mahoney expedition,' I said.

'It could be nobody else,' Kate agreed. 'If Adam secured it, then it will stay secure, and the rope will be of the finest quality.'

'Of course,' Mary said.

Charlie took out her notebook and began to sketch the slender rope bridge. 'This will bring more drama to my article.'

'Oh, hang your article,' Mary said.

Lorna stared across the void. 'I think I can see the far side. It's not too far away.'

'Let me see,' Kate scrambled to her side. 'Oh. Yes,' she said and threw us a massive grin. 'Nothing ventured, nothing gained, girls!' Pushing her stick through the straps of her rucksack and without another word, she crouched on the twin ropes, pushed herself forward and began to crawl along. 'This is like the old days!'

'Be careful,' Lorna shouted as we watched her vanish into the mist.

'We're lucky there's no wind,' Lorna said. 'I'd hate to try this in a gale.'

'Thank God for small mercies,' Mary said. 'I can't even see Kate now.'

We waited for Kate to cross, holding our breaths and biting our lips. I am sure that Christine's mouth moved in silent prayer, although for what outcome I was not sure. After what seemed like hours but was probably only five or ten minutes, Kate's voice sounded.

'It's safe as houses, girls! About forty yards and you're on the far side, and the saddle continues. Who's next?'

'Me,' Charlie said at once, tucking away her notebook.

'If I were a giant I would cross in a single step,' Christine said.

'Maybe these old witches made this to keep An Cailleach secure,' Mary said. 'Now there's a name for it, the Witch's Step.'

'Good name,' Lorna approved. 'As far as I know, it's not on the map, so let's call it that.'

And so the Witch's Step was named, the first feature in the Rough Bounds to be named by female climbers from Edinburgh.

We crossed one by one, with even Christine managing the double rope bridge with hardly a qualm and only minimal fuss. Once across, the saddle continued in a smooth curve that eased toward the veiled bulk of An Cailleach.

'We're getting lower all the time,' Lorna pointed out.

She was correct. The saddle sloped downward, now gentle, now reasonably steep, so we were losing hundreds of feet as we continued.

'Now we have to climb upward again.' I said. 'All that effort wasted. No wonder nobody comes to this hill.'

'It's a bit disheartening,' Charlie said. 'On the other hand, it makes the final conquest all the more worthwhile.'

The saddle descended at least fifteen hundred feet, so we were only a few hundred feet above sea level when it merged with the bulk of An Cailleach. As we stepped onto the ribbed granite, a sudden cold blast from the sea greeted us, ruffling our hair and forcing Christine to pull her jacket tighter.

'Is that it? We've arrived on the dark mountain?' Charlie had stopped to face the direction in which we had come. She drew a quick sketch of the saddle, with mist shrouding the Witch's Step, and then added another sketch that showed Kate crawling along the fragile bridge with her pack balanced on her back. 'Is this finally An Cailleach?'

'It is,' Lorna confirmed.

We stood on the granite flanks with mist slithering and fraying around us and the peak itself capped by white cloud. I fought my sudden urge to remove my boots and socks and feel the ground under my bare feet. There was a voice inside my head, the words formless. I was not afraid.

'I can hear the sea,' Christine lifted her head, smiling. 'Listen.'

'It's not surprising,' Kate growled at her. 'We're on a peninsula that sticks out into the Atlantic.'

'I hear it as well,' Lorna said. 'Look.'

A slight breeze was fragmenting the mist to permit us a glimpse of a horseshoe-shaped beach of glorious white sand, where wavelets washed the shore in near pristine clarity.

'That's beautiful,' Charlie said. 'I must draw it. Is that on the map?'

Lorna shook her head. 'Not as such. If this beach were near Edinburgh or Glasgow, day trippers would flock to it, and here we have it all to ourselves.'

'That's something else for my article,' Charlie said. 'If only we had the time to spare to investigate properly.'

'Why don't we?' Christine asked. 'It looks lovely.'

'Come on, girls,' Kate had to lead the way as we trundled down what proved to be a gentle slope to the shore.

Backed by patches of wind-twisted bramble, the beach was of soft sand and outcrops of seaweed- encrusted rock with a tinge of sunshine made more welcome by its unexpectedness. A single palm tree stood slightly apart as if aware it was an alien intruder in this harsh northern coast.

'Well, this is lovely,' Lorna said. 'It's a taste of paradise after the trials of the hills. What a contrast!'

I could only agree. My boots sunk into soft sand as the sun glittered on gentle surf. 'Why is the sea so serene?' I looked further out, 'oh, I see.' A line of skerries broke the force of the North Atlantic rollers. Surf surged in serried silver ranks, the regular boom echoing from the flanks of An Cailleach. 'It's like a lagoon,' I said, 'a Scottish lagoon. Pure paradise.'

Kate laughed. 'I'll have to get my father to blast a road through,' she said. 'It would bring in money for the estate.'

'And that's all the estate cares about,' Mary bit at her. 'More wealth.'

'More wealth and more jobs,' Kate retaliated. 'With the post-war recession and the huge toll of unemployed I'm surprised you don't agree with anything that brings jobs to people or are you more concerned about reliving things that happened a hundred years ago?'

'That's enough, you two,' Lorna said. 'Rather than argue, why don't we all enjoy this beautiful place?'

'We have a mountain to climb,' Charlie seemed to regret her decision to visit. 'We're wasting time.'

'I don't care,' Kate said. 'I've never been here before, and this is a delightful surprise.'

'There used to be a *ceasg* here, a mermaid.' Mary said. 'She sat on these skerries there, either as a harbinger of storms or singing to entice seamen to their deaths.'

'Mermaids, monsters and things that go bump in the night,' Kate laughed. 'You know that these stories are all nonsense.'

I looked again at the skerries, picturing a long-haired mermaid sitting on top amongst the bursting spray and spindrift. All at once I felt a slight uneasiness, some indefinable dread, as though the mist from An Cailleach had slithered over Edinburgh's Botanic Garden on a bright April morning. I shivered and shook away the image.

'Did the locals not fish from here?' Charlie asked.

'No.' Mary shook her head. 'The skerries stop access. No boat could pass through them.'

'Well, I for one think we deserve a break,' Lorna said, 'and what better place to take one?'

With my disquiet banished, I could only agree. The atmosphere was unlike any other part of the peninsula. This soft beach was a suntrap, and we removed our rucksacks and piled them under the palm tree. I would not have been surprised to see coconuts and exotic birds chattering under the fronds.

'How did a palm tree get here?' Kate asked.

'It's a *Cordyline australis* or cabbage palm,' Christine spoke quietly, as though ashamed of her knowledge. 'The skerries will shelter the bay from the prevailing winds while the Gulf Stream warms the sea and brings in seeds from the tropics.'

'All right, clever clogs,' Kate said. 'I knew I should have caned you more at school.'

I felt an immediate rush of anger toward Kate. I was not sure whether it was a general dislike of bullying or a desire to protect elfin little Christine. Either way, I called out, 'I didn't know that, Christine. Thank you for telling me. Never mind Kate; she is just jealous.'

Ignoring Kate's evil look, I walked over to examine the cabbage palm. It was warm to the touch, a lonely stranger. 'I know how you feel,' I whispered.

'First in the sea!' Lorna said. 'Come on ladies!'

'No!' Charlie yelled. 'We're not here to have fun!'

'I am!' Lorna said. 'Come on Charlotte!'

I could not help laughing at the expression on Charlie's face as Lorna plumped herself onto the sand, unfastened her boots and then tore off her clothes. Naked as the day she was born, she scampered down the beach and plunged into the sea.

'It's hardly even cold!' She yelled. 'Come on in!'

'Me next,' Mary said, following Lorna's example.

'We've got a hill to climb.' Charlie said. 'We have to beat the men, remember?'

We ignored Charlie's protests as one by one we stripped and ran to the water's edge. Perhaps because of the influence of the Gulf Stream, the water was warmer than I expected and certainly far warmer than the North Sea on the opposite coast. My feet sank into soft sand as I walked up to my thighs and then ducked under to swim half way to the offshore skerries. Lorna waved to me, smiling, turned and swam away. Mary and Kate raced as far as the skerries and returned. We were all laughing and shouting, and eventually, even Charlie joined us.

'Glad you could make it,' Lorna laughed.

'Glad I did,' Charlie said. For all her severe suffragettism – is there such a word? Well, there is now – for all her severe suffragettism, Charlie could be good fun when she relaxed. Like Kate, she never bore a grudge, except to men, of course. She dived under the water, surfaced beside Lorna and ducked her under. Within a few minutes, we were capering like schoolgirls, with only Christine not venturing far from the shore.

'Come on Christine!' I shouted, 'out you come! The water's lovely.'

'I can't swim,' Christine said. 'I'm fine here.'

'I'm not a strong swimmer either,' I said. 'It's safe in here.'

'Chrissy can't swim,' Kate mocked. 'Little Chrissy never did learn to swim. Come here Chrissy, and we'll look after you.'

Splashing across to Christine, Kate took her by the arm and propelled her into deeper water.

'No, please Kate.'

'She's scared,' Lorna said. 'Leave her alone, Kate.'

'It's for her own good,' Kate was laughing as she pulled Christine into ever deeper water, first to her waist, then her breasts. 'Come along Chrissie, time you learned!'

We watched as Kate put a hand on Christine's head and pushed her under, laughing as Christine struggled to escape. 'Go on, little Chrissie, learn to swim.'

The image slid into my mind, a group of schoolgirls at a swimming bath with the tiles white and the voices echoing. A youthful Kate and another girl I did not know were swinging Christine by her arms and legs, 'one, two, three' and tossing her into the water, laughing as their victim screamed. I could read the panic in Christine's face and the pleasure in the features of her tormentors.

'I think it's no longer funny.' Stepping forward, I gripped Kate's forearm. 'Best leave Christine alone now. I know you are only in fun.'

Kate stared at me as if trying to work out who I was. 'She's fine.'

'She's scared,' I retained my hold on Kate's arm, gradually raising it so Christine could resurface. 'Are you all right, Christine?'

'Yes, thank you.' Gasping for breath, Christine wiped water from her eyes. She was white-faced and shaken.

'Kate was only playing,' I tried to keep the peace between the two.

'I know,' Christine said. 'We were at school together.' She forced a smile. 'Kate used to play all the time there.'

I wondered what sort of playing Kate had done at school. I could imagine her as the boisterous school bully or the officious prefect picking on the younger and weaker pupils. For a second I imagined how she would react if I took hold of her and ducked her under the water.

No, that was not how I acted. I cannot cure a bully by bullying.

'Maybe we'd best get back to the hill,' I said. What had been a magical place only a few moments ago was now tainted by childish cruelty.

'No, it's all right, really,' Christine said. 'We're best friends.'

Christine was lying. The desperation in her eyes did not stem from friendship.

'I know that,' I said.

'What's that over there?' Lorna had been an interested observer. Now she pointed to the furthest corner of our little queendom. 'Something is floating in the water.'

I watched as she splashed toward it. Lorna was a picture of innocence, a young woman on a sublime beach with afternoon sunshine gleaming from her naked shoulders and along the swell of her hips. For one minute I imagined her as a nymph in Arcadia, fresh and wholesome. The artist William Adolphe Bouguereau could not have created a more evocative image than we presented on that secluded Hebridean beach. Charlie must have had the same idea for she had retreated to the beach to perch on a rounded rock and sketch our antics.

'You'd best come here, ladies.' The tone of Lorna's voice warned us that all was not perfect in paradise. 'Not you, Christine. You stay there.'

'Why not me?' Naturally, the command to remain only heightened Christine's curiosity and she ran through the water, raising great splashes that rose high and sparkled diamond bright before falling again.

'No, Christine.' Lorna shook her head. 'Brenda, can you hold her back, please?'

As well could Canute try to stem the tide than I could try to restrain a curious woman. Christine was first to reach Lorna, and we all followed, eager to see what she had found.

Our eagerness did not last. The two bodies floated on the surface of the water, one face up and the other face down, roped together in death as they had been in life. Neither man could have been older than thirty.

'That's the two men who were attempting An Cailleach,' Kate said.

Mary nodded. 'The mountain got them.'

'That's a strange thing to say.' I did not say that I thought the same thing.

Mary shrugged. 'It's true. Poor chaps. They must have fallen off.'

No, I thought. *An Cailleach threw them off.*

'Obviously!' Kate said.

I looked upward where the cliffs and steep slopes of An Cailleach merged with the ever-present mist. 'I thought they were going up the western face, not the southern.'

'They must have changed their mind.' Kate put me down with a withering look. She had not forgiven me for stopping her little game with Christine.

With the offshore skerries trapping them in the bay, the two men bobbed on tiny waves. Used to witnessing death, Lorna began to drag them to shore. Kate and I helped, with Christine keeping back and Charlie sketching furiously.

'Their rope is frayed,' Lorna held up the trailing end. 'It must have caught on a sharp rock.'

'Maybe it was poor quality,' Kate said. 'They might not have taken An Cailleach seriously as it's not even a Munro.'

'Wartime economies,' Lorna shook her head. 'It is a reminder what a dangerous sport we have chosen.'

Mary touched her rowan cross and the blue crystal she had worn even in the water. 'Maybe it was the death of these men that the Watcher by the Ford warned us about,' she said. 'Maybe we are safe now.'

About to blast her for superstitious nonsense, I changed my mind and my words. 'That will be it,' Mary. 'The woman at the ford was warning these poor chaps, not us.' Given my recent experiences, I could hardly condemn anybody for supernatural beliefs. *That is two shrouds less; two out of the five.*

Charlie completed her rough sketch and came to help. 'Look on the bright side, ladies. We will be the first to conquer the hill. We'll still beat the men.'

'That's hardly important now,' Lorna said. 'Any death is a tragedy, and these men's lives were every bit as valuable as any woman's.'

Shrugging, Charlie looked away. 'If you say so.'

We dragged the men up the sand and laid them side by side under the cabbage palm. They looked quiet there, two handsome young men in that place of terrible beauty.

'We should go back to the Inn and report their deaths,' Lorna said.

'Why?' Kate responded. 'Would that bring them back? They're dead, and that's an end to it.'

'We came to conquer An Cailleach, and that's what we'll do,' Charlie said. 'In a way, this makes our expedition ever better. Imagine the headlines when a party of women return, not only as the first to ascent the dark mountain but also the discoverers of the men who failed.'

'We'd best go back,' Mary said. 'She's warned us how dangerous she can be.'

'Who has warned us?' Kate asked.

'She has,' Mary nodded to the hill. 'An Cailleach, the old woman.'

'It's only a hill,' Kate said, 'not a living being. You are really stupid sometimes, Mary.'

I kept quiet, not wishing to share my thoughts. I felt An Cailleach watching and knew she was inside my head.

'Maybe Mary's right,' Lorna said. 'We'd best return. It's not proper that we should find these men and carry on as if nothing has happened.'

'We've come this far,' Kate said. 'We're over the worst with that saddle and the Witch's Step. The deaths of these men prove that this hill is not easy, so let's carry on. Let's get up there and back down, let's show the world what women can do.'

'I'm with you, Kate,' Charlie agreed at once.

'You agree, don't you, Christine?' Kate said.

'Yes,' Christine looked at her feet as if ashamed of her decision.

'I don't know,' Lorna looked up at the granite bulk of An Cailleach, just as a slant of wind shifted the mist. For one glorious minute, the hill revealed herself to us, squat, moody, with impressive multi-coloured cliffs veined with pink granite through dark Lewisian Gneiss. The sun touched on the last of the summer's wildflowers, sea pinks, primula scotia and others I did not know, brilliant life on stark granite. Deep dark gulleys seamed An Cailleach's flanks, the marks of dignified old age. I could feel her presence, I could feel her watching us, and nearly hear her inner voice.

Gin ye daur, An Cailleach whispered to me. *If you dare.*

It was a direct personal challenge. I lifted my chin in response. I had done nothing with my life. I had no idea who my parents were, and my attempts to find out had foundered on the rock of ignorance. I did not know where to begin to look, and nobody else cared enough to help. I had wandered through my childhood, eased through education and spent more time day-dreaming than planning for the future. Lorna had been an ambulance driver and had saved lives in the war. Mary spoke two languages. Kate was heir to vast lands. Charlie was a self-made woman, a reporter and journalist who had been active for the suffragette cause. Christine? I did not know much about Christine. She seemed to be Kate's follower and a target for Kate's ill humour and sadistic streak.

I was the least of them all, and now An Cailleach had challenged me.

Gin ye daur.

I looked up at the hill again, wondering about the appeal of this tremendous magnetic chunk of gneiss and granite that lowered over the Rough Quarter. In the sunshine, she seemed like any other hill, not as dramatic as the more famous Sutherland peaks, not as dominating as Ben Nevis, not as shapely as Schiehallion, just a high hill on the edge of the sea. Why was she avoided and why did she attract me like no other?

I looked down at the two bodies underneath the palm tree. An Cailleach had flicked them from her body as if they were nothing. She had sucked in the Mahoney party and kept them from the ken of Man, and now she was waiting for us, mocking as we pondered whether we should continue or not.

'Brenda?' Kate was looking at me. 'Don't tell me that you're scared.'

'I'm not scared,' I said. 'I think we should continue.'

'That's a majority to continue,' Kate said.

I looked up at An Cailleach just as a cloud blotted out the sun. My vote had been decisive. From now on I could take the praise for any success we had, or accept the blame for any disasters. An Cailleach had issued her challenge with a smiling face. I had accepted, and she had closed up again. I had dared.

Chapter Seven

Rain swept in from the sea, propelling us up the slope we had come down in such happy curiosity, dampening the leaves of the lonely palm, and beading on the dead bodies of the men we left behind.

'The domination of men has passed,' Charlie said. 'The time for women is about to begin.'

'Now there's a good quote for your article,' Lorna was tackling the slope long-strided with her rucksack high on her back, her climbing rope looped at her waist and her boots clacking on the stony ground.

However energetic Lorna may have been, Kate was well in front, marching up the hill with her hips and shoulders swaying and her head out-thrust. Without a doubt, she was the most determined woman I had ever met.

I watched Kate for a while, wondering what made her as she was. Perhaps she had inherited her drive from generations of achieving ancestors, with the ruthlessness necessary to rise up the social scale, grab tens of thousands of acres of land and hold onto it through the roller-coaster of history. Maybe it was merely part of her personality, forcing her on, proving herself or testing herself. I did not know.

I did know that I admired her, whatever her faults. I also knew that we were not alone on that hillside. I had accepted An Cailleach's challenge, and now she beckoned me on. That woman was in front of Kate, matching her pace for pace and occasionally looking over her shoulder, holding me with her gaze, enticing me onward and upward.

'Who are you?' I mouthed the question, knowing that she would hear me.

The woman gave a small, enigmatic smile, turned her head away and drifted into the increasingly heavy rain. Although I had a clear view of her face, the second she turned away I forgot it. I could not describe a single feature except the dark intensity of her eyes.

'We should not have delayed so long at the beach,' Lorna had to raise her voice above the hammer of the rain.

'If we hadn't' I said, 'we would not have found these men and An Cailleach would have another mystery.' Strangely I was not upset about finding the dead climbers. Unlike Charlie I was not overly concerned about being first up the mountain, so had no feeling of triumph to tamper any true sorrow over a death. I just accepted the fact that these two men had been alive and now they were dead. I had not known them, I would not mourn them, and I did not think their deaths made my journey any more perilous.

Does that sound terribly selfish of me? I think it does, but I am resolved to write the truth and so I shall.

'Come on, girls!' Kate stopped to encourage us. I will never forget that image of her, standing on a prominent rock above us with her legs apart and the wind tossing her raven-black hair. Ignoring the rain that dripped from her bare head and the ends of her jacket, she leaned on her long stick and smiled down on us, like an elder sister or a benevolent Girl Guide leader. That was the best side of Kate, our leader.

'We're coming.' Lorna said.

'We're going to the Shelter Stone,' Kate told us.

'We would be faster going directly up the hill,' Charlie said.

'There's no need for speed,' Kate said. 'We're the only people here.' She lowered her voice. 'We're the only people left and better to go slow and get there in one piece than rush and end up like these men we left under the palm.' Kate glanced at Christine. 'Under the *cabbage* palm.'

The reminder sobered us.

'Besides, I wish to visit the Shelter Stone,' Kate said. 'We might never be here again, and it would be a shame not to see all we can.'

'I've already seen enough of this mountain,' Lorna said softly. 'It kills people.'

Nobody else dissented. Kate had that effect on people. We followed her like religious devotees, trudging up an increasingly steep slope with the wind now howling around outcrops of broken rock, driving rain against our backs and blowing our hair into mad tangles over our eyes.

'It's over here!' Kate still strode ahead, her boots crunching on the fragmented stone and her stick clicking rhythmically. 'Here we are, girls,' she shouted. Her voice echoed hollowly on that grim slope. 'In we go.'

The Shelter Stone suited its name. It was little more than a shelf of granite leaning at an angle from the face of the mountain, with space beneath which a dozen people could sit in relative comfort.

We followed Kate under the stone, touching the cold granite and searching for a comfortable place to sit. 'This is cosy,' Lorna said as she slid down at the furthest corner.

The stone did its job, immediately stopping the blast of wind and rain. I took off my cap comforter and wrung out the water. Pushing aside the memory of the two dead climbers, I grinned to Lorna.

'Somebody's been here before us.' Mary kicked at an empty bottle that lay on the ground.

'Probably an earlier climbing expedition,' Lorna said. 'Another one that failed or they would have told the world that they defeated An Cailleach.'

'They've left their mark on the wall,' Mary pointed to a spot directly above her head. 'You'd better see this Kate.'

The names were beautifully carved into the granite. *Mike. Bill. Adam.*

Kate joined Mary. She traced Adam's name with her finger. 'They got this far.' She said.

'We're following their footsteps,' I agreed as Charlie scribbled notes down.

'I wonder,' Kate spoke so quietly that I could hardly make her out. 'I wonder if maybe he's still alive somehow. Maybe trapped here or living as a hermit.'

'Not after this length of time,' Charlie said. 'This is Scotland, not the far Pacific or Africa or somewhere. Robinson Crusoe was only a story.'

'You're right,' Kate said. 'I was being a silly, and that's Chrissie's job.'

I caught the anger in Christine's glance. 'Are we staying here all night?' I had no desire to hear Kate reminisce about perfect Adam, 'or shall we push on for the summit.'

'I say we push on,' Charlie said. 'It's only three o'clock. There's plenty of daylight left, and we're over the worst. We can be up and back here before it's fully dark.'

'It's been easy so far,' Lorna said. 'The only slightly awkward parts were the cliff face with the overhang and the Witch's Step, and we managed both without any drama. I can't understand why nobody's done this before.'

'Maybe somebody has,' I decided to be provocative. 'Maybe they just didn't talk about it.'

Charlie looked daggers at me. 'We'll be the first to scale An Cailleach and return to talk about it,' she said. 'People will name this route after us. Women's Triumph, we'll call it, and show the world that we are equal to any man.'

'How about Suffragette's Success,' Lorna said. 'Or simply, Kate Gordon's Route. After all, Katie is the mainspring here so naming it after her is the only proper thing to do.'

I intercepted Kate's smile. *Well said, Lorna*, I thought. It must have been a shock for Kate to see her brother's name carved into the rock.

'We'll have to get back soon,' I said. 'I've only got half a dozen sandwiches left, and I get cranky when I don't get my marmalade.'

'Oh, we can't have you without marmalade,' Lorna was laughing. 'Now we will definitely have to crack on.'

'No.' Kate said. 'We've done enough for one day.'

'You want to stay where Adam was,' I felt as if I could read Kate's thoughts, or was it her feelings? My powers of empathy had increased since we crossed the ford.

'I'm only thinking of the group,' Kate said. I knew she was lying. 'Chrissie got a fright climbing that cliff. I think she needs to rest for a while.'

'Resting is fine but how about our food supplies? How about poor Brenda's marmalade?' Lorna asked.

'We've plenty for tonight,' Kate said. 'If we get going early tomorrow we can get up and back. It will be a long day, but knowing we've conquered An Cailleach will buoy us up.'

'Or girl us up,' Charlie smiled to hide her disappointment. 'We will still be first to conquer An Cailleach.'

'Adam might have been first,' Kate reminded quickly. 'We know he got this far and I can't think of any reason why he would turn back. He was not the sort of man to give up.'

'Well either he did, or he died,' Charlie said. 'Either way, we'll be first to conquer An Cailleach and return to claim the hill, It's a big success for women, Kate and you should be proud to be part of it, rather than bleating about some man who happens to share your biological parents.'

I heard Kate's sharp intake of breath and wondered if she would slap Charlie. I would have.

I tried to like Charlie, I really did. I certainly admired her for her thrust and determination, for her desire to be successful in a career dominated by men. But I did not like her. I found her constant anti-male tirades tiresome and her refusal to grant any man credit pointless.

'Are you scared of men, Charlie?' I regretted the words as soon as they left my lips.

Charlie stiffened. Her look was poisonous. 'No, Brenda. I want to make men scared of me.'

'Why?' I knew I was damaging any chance of friendship with Charlie, but some perverse streak within me insisted that I continue. Besides, my interference gave Kate time to plan her retaliation.

Charlie was ready with a quick reply. 'I want to pay them back for centuries of male oppression. Men have enslaved us for too long. It's our turn now.'

'I don't want to enslave any man, or anybody else,' I said. 'I doubt that Lorna does, either, or Mary or Christine.' I winked at little Christine to show I was not insulting her. 'I'm not sure about Kate though.' I gave a slow smile as if I had intended to be humorous all along.

'Oh, I'd love a man as a slave,' Kate deliberately turned her shoulder to Charlie. 'Imagine what fun I would have with him.' She gave a big grin that made me smile and brought colour to Christine's face.

'And here's me thinking that Christine was your only slave,' Lorna said.

'Oh, no, Chrissie and I are the best of friends,' Kate said. 'If anything, I am her slave, always helping her through life when she can't cope.'

I added no more to this conversation that I had started. Christine looked down at the ground until Lorna touched her shoulder.

'It's all right, Christine,' Lorna said. 'We know you're not a slave driver.'

'You don't know her as well as I do,' Kate jeered.

I was watching closely as poor Christine shook her head. At that minute I wanted to give her a hug. She seemed as friendless as I was myself.

'Come on, Brenda,' Mary took me by the arm. 'Let's leave these women to their silly games. I want to see something of this An Cailleach. After all, my family should still live here.'

Wondering if there would be bloodshed in my absence, I allowed Mary to take me outside. The rain had eased to a succession of drizzly showers, leaving the ground sodden and running with excess water through which we splashed. As so often happens in the west, the rain cleared abruptly so I could see the Shelter Stone in its own context. We were part way up a gradually steepening slope, with what appeared to a vertical cliff between us and the summit and half Scotland spread out below.

Drifting on vibrating wings, a whaup called, the sound enhancing the feeling of desolation more profound than anything I can describe. I took a deep breath, started when I saw a pair of wild goats observing us from a ledge a hundred feet above and wished I were somewhere else. I had never felt more unsettled than I did at that moment.

'This is an uncanny place.' I said.

'What do you mean?' Mary looked sharply at me.

'I did not like Tigh-na-Beiste.' I said. 'And this place,' I hesitated, 'there's something very wrong here.'

'I like it here,' Mary said. 'I belong here.'

'I'm not sure that I do.' I habitually sought out the wild places. I preferred them to urban centres where I was a stranger among groups of friends. In the desolation of the hills, nobody cares about a solitary walker yet here, the atmosphere was wrong. I could not say why; there was not the malevolence of Tigh-na-Beiste, there was no sense of oppression, it just felt out of kilter as if it did not belong to the rest of Scotland or even to the rest of the world. An Cailleach was as out of place as I was myself. Can a hill be a stranger?

'Even you can't deny that the views are spectacular,' Mary pointed downward. 'That is utter beauty.'

I had not noticed the small loch before. It lay in a corrie, shadowed by the surrounding stony slopes and lonely under the rain-laden autumnal sky. Flurries of wind lifted ripples across the surface. Impressive it certainly was, but at that moment I did not see any beauty.

'I cannot deny the drama,' I agreed. 'There is an amazing majesty here.'

'You see?' Mary was prepared to be magnanimous now that I had agreed one point with her. 'It's not so bad.'

'What do they call this place?' I looked down at the *lochan*, the small loch, with the gushing outflow that gurgled down the rocky slope to the dark depths below.

'*Poll nan ban*,' Mary spoke without consulting any map. 'It means Pool of the Women, so it suits us.'

'It's very inviting,' I said. *From where had that come?* I had no inclination to venture to that forbidding place.

'Oh, you like it now?' I was not sure if Mary was sarcastic or genuine. There seemed to be two Marys here, the modern woman who I had known in Edinburgh and the woman who reverted to speaking and possibly thinking in Gaelic.

I studied the lochan. From up here, it appeared innocent, virgin water surrounded by slender beaches of either white sand or small pebbles, I could not be sure. Yet there was something wrong. I did not know what. 'I don't think I would like to go there.'

'Don't worry, you won't have to,' Mary said sharply. 'It's not on our route. The old folk, before the Clearances, avoided it as well.'

Mary walked away. For one minute she was silhouetted against the dying sun, a long-haired woman with the pride and long memory of the Gael. Seen like that, Mary was timeless, only her mode of dress belonged to this 20th century. Her attitude and appearance would fit into any age.

That strange woman returned, standing between Mary and me. She turned to face me, fixed me with those intense eyes and then stepped back.

I saw Mary falling into space, falling toward greyness. I heard her scream and stretched forward to help. I could not reach her. Mary was falling, falling forever into a damp abyss. I could not move. I could not help. I could only stand and watch. The strange woman reappeared, and Mary was back on the skyline, safe as if she was walking in her own front room, which in a way she was.

What was happening to me?

I heard the sound twice before it registered and even then I was not afraid. 'Did you hear that too?' Mary called out to me.

'I did,' I said. 'Like somebody crying.'

'It was that,' Mary's accent had altered over the last few days. She always had a twist of Gaelic within her words. Now it was pronounced.

'We'd better go and see,' I walked across to Mary, wondering if that strange woman was responsible for the weeping.

'We'd better not!' Mary took hold of my arm. 'That sound was nothing human.'

For some reason, Mary's words did not surprise me. There were too many mysteries here, too many unexplained events that pulled at my reason. 'What do you think it was? Was it a vixen perhaps?'

'It was a *caoineag*, what the Irish know as a banshee.'

'I've heard of banshees,' I said. 'I thought they were only in tales.'

'You thought that about the washerwoman at the ford as well,' Mary said.

'I think there is too much happening in this little peninsula.' I said. 'I'll be glad to get back to reality.' Yet at the same time, I wanted to unravel the secrets and find out what was happening here. In particular, I wished to know who that mysterious woman was and if she, the washerwoman and the *caoneag* were one and the same.

'We know the *caoneag* as the weeping one,' Mary said. 'She wails and cries on the hillside through the hours of darkness.'

The cry came again, a low, long-drawn-out howl that ended in a bout of bitter sobbing.

'I have to look,' I stepped away from Mary with my curiosity overcoming my unease. The rational side of me denied any possibility of a caoneag, as it shied away from the washerwoman at the ford. Yet I had seen the image of the Clearance victims and that strange woman who slipped in and out of my life or my mind. *From where had that wailing come?*

A thousand stars accompanied the scimitar moon, reflecting on Poll nan Ban far below and spreading faint light across the rugged landscape. I followed our route of the previous day and looked forward to the climb we faced on the morrow. An Cailleach loomed over us, her bulk more impressive now we were sitting on her lap, so to speak.

The *caoneag* wailed again, the sound seemingly wrenched from a soul in torment. The hairs on the back of my head stood up in sympathy, yet now I was not afraid. I knew that this creature, whatever it was, meant no harm to me.

'Who are you?' I called. 'What do you want?'

There was no reply. I had not expected a reply.

'Is there anything I can do to help?' I did not shout the words but allowed the wind to carry them to their destination. 'You sound upset.'

The wailing sounded again. Long drawn out and low, it bubbled across the desolate hills and from the lochan far below.

'Come back in,' Mary had followed me. 'It's not wise to search for the *caoneag*.'

'I don't think it will harm us,' I said.

'I have not heard of anybody ever looking for it,' Mary took hold of my sleeve. 'It's a creature of the night, something supernatural, rather like a vampire or such like. It's best to leave these things alone.' She lowered her voice. 'Please Brenda, leave it alone.'

Mary was so sincere I could only assent. 'All right then, Mary.' I looked around the landscape. Clouds now obscured the moon, so only faint starlight reflected on the lochan far below. Looking down, I shivered. 'Now I am not sure if I really like this place,' I said, 'or if I really dislike it.' Something had happened to me during the last ten minutes. I did not know what it was.

'My blood is here,' Mary took hold of my arm. 'Or at least my blood is in Penrioch. Generation after generation of my family farmed and lived here.' She took a deep breath. 'My grandmother asked permission to be buried here when she died. The landowner refused.'

'That was unkind,' I said.

'I thought so, too.' Mary took a deep breath. 'I want to die here,' she said. 'I want to die where I should live, where my ancestors lived for centuries.'

'You're too young to even think about dying,' I said. 'By the time that comes, you might have made enough money to purchase this place and bring it back to life.'

Mary snorted. 'The Gael should purchase most of the Highlands and bring them back to life,' she said. 'Somebody once said the Highlands are the mere playground of idle sportocracy. It is terrible that so much of our country is only used for the wealthy to kill things.'

'It will change,' I said. 'Time changes everything. Maybe now that women have the vote we can make things better.'

'Maybe,' Mary said. 'And maybe women such as Kate Gordon will ensure things remain just as they are.'

'She's not all bad,' I said.

'Her type should be removed from the earth forever so only their memory survives as a reminder of how cruel humans can be.' Mary's voice was low and passionate.

I was strangely relieved when the *caoneag* wailed again, as if in mourning for the desolation of the Highlands. I turned around. That strange woman was twenty paces away, watching me through intense eyes. 'Who are you?' I shouted.

'The *caoneag* won't reply,' Mary said. 'Come back to the Shelter Stone.'

'Please, tell me who you are!' I shouted again. The only reply came from the wind although for a second I also saw a man watching me. I had seen him before, standing beside the strange woman back at the inn. I followed Mary to the Shelter Stone with a score of images crammed into my head and confusion in my heart.

The other women were sleeping, with Kate on her back with both hands behind her head and Christine snuggled up close to her. I could not kill my jealousy. I wished I had a friend who cared for me to that extent. I wished I had a friend.

Chapter Eight

Dawn flushed the eastern sky with diffused pink light, silhouetting the tumbled hills of west Sutherland and Ross in a glorious panorama of peaks. As we watched, the last of the morning mists were rising from the tops to dissipate in the keen air.

'Once we've done An Cailleach,' Charlie said, 'I think we should go further afield.' Sitting with her legs splayed in front of her, she scratched at her head. 'What do you think, ladies? How about we try a more ambitious peak than just a wee Scottish hill?'

'Where do you have in mind?' I wondered.

'The North Face of the Eiger,' Charlie said, 'or cross the Atlantic to Mount Moran or the Devil's Tower in the Rockies maybe, they've never been scaled. Nor has Annapurna or Everest.'

Lorna led the laughter. 'Now you are over-optimistic,' she said. 'The Eiger North Face is probably the hardest climb in Europe. It's hardly to be compared with An Cailleach. Everest? That's so high up that aircraft can't fly over it, let alone climbers scale it.'

'Exactly my point!' Charlie said. 'Who says it is impossible? *Men* say it is impossible.' She looked around in triumph. 'Imagine how they would feel if a party of weak women achieve what they won't even dare!'

Although Kate laughed, Lorna lifted her head. 'I've seen men at their worst and their best,' she bit into an apple and spoke through a mouthful of half-masticated fruit. 'They don't despise women, Charlie, whatever you may think. When they are dying, the youngest wanted their mothers, and the married men often asked me to let them hold a picture of their wives.'

We were silent. Lorna had never spoken of her experiences in the war until this expedition.

'Some just wanted a woman's company,' Lorna's eyes were far away. She was back in the nightmare of Flanders with the mud and mustard gas and agony.

'Typical,' Charlie said. 'They ignore women until they need them.'

Lorna continued. 'I don't know how many men held my hand as they died. Broken men, horribly disfigured men, men torn to shreds. They all wanted the same thing, not to die alone. They were all so terribly grateful for even the smallest sign of affection.'

Not to die alone. I can understand that.

'Sometimes,' Lorna said, 'sometimes we could not help them.' Her voice dropped to little more than a whisper. 'Sometimes they did die alone. Alone and ignored in the hands of the enemy.'

When Lorna stopped talking, the only sound was the faint whine of the wind at the edges of the Shelter Stone and the distant scream of an eagle.

I inched closer to Lorna. 'You can't help everybody all the time,' I said.

'No,' Christine took hold of Lorna's hand. 'There's only so much that even you can do.'

We sat like that for a moment while the echoes of the eagle's scream faded and Lorna shook away her momentary disheartenment.

'You are right in a degree though Charlie. I agree some men won't like women to be first at anything,' Lorna said. 'I met plenty who did not want women in uniform at all. Many men thought that war was men's work. They were wrong. War is not men's work; it nobody's work. War is a tool of the devil.'

'I don't believe in the devil,' Charlie said. 'Or in God or heaven or hell or any of that religious nonsense. It's all a device of men to keep women in their place.'

'I believe in the devil,' Lorna said. 'And in hell, and I saw enough selfless kindness and generosity to believe in angels as well. Battlefields bring out the best and the worst in people.' She lowered her voice to a whisper. 'They brought out the worst in me.'

Christine patted the back of Lorna's hand in wordless sympathy.

'Maybe they did, Lorna,' Kate said. 'But we're not in a battlefield. We're on a mountain. Are you all still game to try for the summit?'

'Yes,' I said at once. I wanted to stand on the summit of An Cailleach and try to solve some of her mysteries. If I left now, the memories would haunt me for the rest of my life.

'Of course,' Charlie said. 'We must defeat the men.'

'We've come this far,' Lorna said, while Mary nodded. We all knew that Christine would do whatever Kate wished.

'Adam will have got there,' Kate traced his name with her forefinger. 'Adam never gave up in anything he attempted.'

I had a sudden vision of the Mahoney party standing in triumph on the summit of An Cailleach. Mahoney was in the centre, smiling happily, while Adam was on his left, his freckled face creased in a grin and saturnine Bill on his right. They stood arm in arm, laughing as dark storm clouds gathered behind them.

'Did Adam have freckles?' I asked.

'Yes, how did you know that?' Kate looked at me with sudden curiosity. 'I don't believe you met him and there were no photographs of the expedition.'

'Maybe I saw a picture in the newspapers or something.' I kept my answer deliberately vague.

'There weren't any.' Kate's voice was flat.

I shrugged. 'I don't know then.'

The Mahoney party had reached the summit of An Cailleach. I knew that. I had seen them there, although I could not explain how.

'We go on,' Kate said. 'We'll take another fifteen minutes to get ourselves ready and then set out.'

The wind had increased when we stepped away from the Shelter Stone. I looked upward, where the slope grew ever steeper before merging with the drifting mist. There was no skill to this section of the climb, only a grim determination and the endurance to withstand the damp and wind. Things would get tougher further up the hill. We entered the mist within half an hour and stopped to rope ourselves together.

'Is it dangerous?' Christine asked.

'The rope is only a precaution,' Lorna reassured her. 'The map only shows the contour lines, nothing else. We don't know what's underfoot. Remember the Witch's Step? That was not on the map so we don't know what other surprises there might be.'

After we were roped, we climbed in silence, saving our breath for the hard labour of taking each step, testing the solidity of the rock and making another. As the slope steepened, I began to count my steps, one to a hundred and then stopping for the count of ten to catch my breath.

Lorna had said that battlefields bring out the best and the worst in people. This peninsula was a battlefield that enhanced the worst and the best in us. All our negative traits were coming out, one by one, and being exposed to the others. I had seen Kate's bullying, Christine's fear, and Charlie's dislike of men, Lorna's terrible memories and Mary's bitterness over the Clearances. *How about me? What aspect of my character or personality was being revealed?* I did not know.

'Stop!' Kate's voice called out, clear in the mist. I saw her like a haze, although she was only a few yards away. 'Are we all here? Call out your names.'

We did so, one by one.

'Keep together,' Kate ordered. 'We can't see a thing in this muck.'

I staggered over a loose stone, recovered with a jerk and slogged on. After another ten minutes, we were using our hands to scramble upwards.

'How far is the summit?' Christine's voice floated through the mist.

'I don't know, carry on!'

The ground steepened further, so we were no longer walking or scrambling, we were climbing, searching for handholds and footholds on ground that slithered away from us. I pushed on, realised that I could see nobody in front and stopped.

'Where are you all?'

The shapes were indistinct in the mist. Only when they moved could I tell the difference between a woman and the rocks that surrounded us. I counted, one, two three, four five six.

Six.

Including me, that made seven. We were only six strong. Had that strange woman joined our group?

'Who's all there?'

Standing still, I identified my companions as they reached my position and inched past. There was Kate, annoyed that I had somehow overtaken her, Lorna, silent with her thoughts, Mary, humming a Gaelic air I did not recognise, Charlie, intent on being part of the all-woman ascent and Christine, lagging behind with the final and mysterious member of the group.

'Christine,' I called. 'Who is that beside you?'

'You are,' Christine shouted back. 'What a silly question.'

'I'm up here,' I said.

'Stop playing silly tricks,' Christine said. 'I can see you.'

The damp chill that ran down my spine had nothing to do with the mist. 'Look up Christine,' I said.

I saw Christine's face as a white blur through the mist.

'Brenda,' she said. 'I thought you were behind me.'

'It must have been a trick of the mist,' I said. 'Some sort of projection that fooled us both.'

'That would be it,' Christine accepted my explanation with relief. 'The mist plays tricks on us all.'

I looked down. The other figure had vanished. I knew that it had been the same woman I met in Tigh-na-Beiste. I wanted to complete our expedition and get as far away from this peninsula as possible. I vowed never to return. However alluring it was, however much I wished to solve the mysteries, there was too much unease her.

There were only six of us, Christine was at my side, and we were contemplating the next stage of the ascent. I had not expected the summit to be so steep. Most Scottish hills are reasonably easy to climb, with the most severe challenges being a long, arduous walk combined with changeable weather. There are cliffs and pinnacles of course, while the Cuillin ridge in Skye poses problems. Other hills have difficult routes that have yet to be conquered. As it was virtually unknown, An Cailleach's routes were unnamed and unexplored. Now we were facing an unexpected climb to reach the top.

The mist had thickened if anything, so we could hardly see each other.

'I don't know how far we have to go,' Kate admitted. 'We'll just have to climb into the mist.'

The first part was more of a scramble than a climb although we needed our hands as much as our feet. After a quarter of an hour, we rested on a ledge and looked upwards. We were at the foot of a vertical wall that ascended as far as I could see.

'Look,' Lorna pointed to a piton thrust into the face. 'Your brother must have been here.'

'So he got this far,' Kate said.

I saw the quick frown disfigure Charlie's face. 'It's all right Charlie,' I said. 'We will be the first team to reach the top and return safely, and what a scoop for your newspaper.'

'Are there more pitons in the cliff-face?' Using the first piton as a foothold, Lorna pulled herself up. 'Yes,' she said. 'We can stretch up a rope, or climb one at a time with only the eye-bolts.'

'We'd be safer with a rope,' Christine gave a rare opinion.

'We'll use the pitons,' Kate decided. 'It'll be quicker. Down you come, Lorna, so I can start. I'm the leader so I must face the danger first.'

That could have been Second-lieutenant Adam Gordon of the Gordon Highlanders talking, I thought. Leadership ran in the blood.

'Up you go then, Kate.' Lorna jumped down with the clatter of nailed boots. 'We'll follow.'

We were lucky that Mike Mahoney had not been overly tall, so the pitons were within easy reach without stretching. The granite was slippery-smooth with moisture, but there were miniature ledges and numerable handholds to ease our passage. I was fifth up, immediately behind Christine, with Lorna, probably our best climber, taking a position in the rear. Held in the cold embrace of grey-white mist, I could hardly see Christine above me, although I heard the scrape of her boots on rock and her irregular harsh breathing. The mist consumed all other sounds so I could have been alone in a clammy world, just me, my thoughts and my fears.

'I can't go any further!' Christine's voice suddenly quavered above me. 'I can't.'

I looked up as a fortuitous breath of wind rent open the mist. Christine clung to one of the pitons, with her left foot balanced on another. The mist was still too thick for me to see beyond her. 'You're nearly there,' I encouraged. 'Only a few more steps and we'll be at the top.'

'I can't!' Christine was frozen in fear. When she looked down, I saw her eyes were wide and her mouth gaping in terror. 'I want to let go!'

'I can see the summit!' Kate's voice boomed down to us. 'Not far now, girls!'

'There, you see?' I tried to urge Christine on. 'You've not far to go.'

'What's happening down there?' Charlie shouted. 'The rope's taut. I can't get any further up.'

'Christine's got the jitters,' I called up.

'Come on Christine,' Charlie encouraged. 'We're nearly there.'

'I can't!' Christine wailed.

'Let go then,' Kate shouted. 'Let go and we'll haul you up. You're just a lightweight anyway.' That was true. As well as the youngest, Christine was the lightest of us, a little nymph of a thing, barely five feet tall and slender as a teenager.

'No! I'll fall.'

'Come on,' I said. 'I'll help.' I did not know if the pitons could sustain our combined weights but reasoned that if it could support a full grown man, it could hold one woman and an elfin girl. I raised my voice. 'Take our weight,' I shouted and pulled myself up beside Christine.

I imagined the pitons bending under our feet. I imagined us tumbling down, pulling Kate and Lorna and the others behind us as we hurtled down, down, down to smash into a hundred pieces of splintered bone and mashed brains on the rocks so far beneath.

'You'll be all right.' The voice murmured in my ear. 'You won't come to any harm on this mountain.' There was nobody there of course. It was only my imagination that brought that reassuring voice and the soft music of bells and harps.

Balancing on the tip of the boots, I put my hand over Christine's and with difficulty, prised her grip free. 'Stretch up,' I kept my voice calm and low, trying not to think of the immense drop into the sucking void below. 'I've got you.'

Christine was trembling, her breathing harsh. 'I can't' she said.

'Come on.' I pushed her hand up the cold face of the rock, feeling as if I was the bully now. 'We're nearly there.'

'We've got your weight,' Kate, bless her, called from above.

'We're with you Christine,' Charlie shouted. 'All girls together.'

'Now!' I said, and reached up, dragging Christine with me.

Her scream nearly deafened me. 'It's all right,' I whispered, taking hold of the next piton. As I said, she was lightweight, and with the women above helping, we scrambled to the next hold, and the one after that. I held on, feeling my muscles strain and crack, feeling Christine's arms and legs wrap around me like a baby octopus, feeling her breath hot in my ear and wincing at her high-pitched screams. After a few moments, Christine's screaming faded to a constant whimper and her struggles diminished. Her grip on me remained constant.

'Here we are,' I nearly threw her over the lip of the cliff and onto the rocky shelf where Kate and Charlie waited.

'What are you making all the fuss about?' Kate welcomed her. 'You haven't grown up at all, have you?'

'She's terrified,' I said. 'Leave her alone, Kate.'

'I knew we should have left her behind, snivelling little witch.'

'Nobody can help being afraid,' Lorna had followed us up and hauled herself over the final lip. 'She needs help, not condemnation.'

'I'll help her,' Kate said, 'here, Chrissy, here's something to help you grow up.' Her slap rocked Christine back on her heels.

'That's enough.' I stepped between them. I could feel Christine's fear. It was tangible, like a force that drove away all reason. I could also feel Kate's anger and contempt. There was something else, something that I had not expected. I felt an undercurrent of rage from Christine, more intense than any I had experienced before. I had thought she was a terrified little mouse, content to obey her dominant friend. Now I felt something different, a deep vein of frustration. Christine was not happy with her position.

'You're nothing but a bully!' Mary pushed Kate back. 'You're no better than your ancestors!'

'She needed that!' Kate pushed back. 'I know her better than you do! She needed something to bring her back to herself!'

I put an arm around Christine. Mary could fend for herself, and I hoped she would put Kate in her place. 'It's all right, Christine. You're safe now.'

'She's not safe,' Christine muttered. 'I'm going to kill her.'

'No, you're not.' I said. 'She over-reacted, that's all. She should not have slapped you.' I raised my voice. 'I'm sure she'll apologise.'

Lorna was holding Mary, with Charlie speaking to Kate.

'I'll never apologise to a little snivelling weasel,' Kate said.

'Let's move on,' Charlie said. 'You should not have hit Christine.'

'She'll live,' Kate said.

I have always been aware of the feelings of others. Even as a child in the orphanage I could read the motives behind people's smiles and smooth words. At that moment I felt buffeted by the various feelings of the five women around me. Anger, hatred, disgust, fear, ambition, confusion, all erupted and fought for supremacy or survival in our tight little group. Although we were all together, we were also individuals, each with our own reasons for being here. It was up to the leader to bring us together, and in that Kate was failing.

'Let's see your face,' I brought Christine closer and examined her cheek. 'It's all right,' I said. 'There's barely a mark.'

'Thank you.' Christine said. 'Thank you, Brenda.'

And then the mist cleared with the startling suddenness that can be so unnerving to people unused to the Scottish west coast. One minute we stood within a wet grey blanket and the next we were on that bare hillside with the sun warming us and a panorama that God would have envied from his seat in heaven.

We stood on a false summit that sloped south and west, with views over the sea toward the dark smear of the Outer Hebrides. Above us was the vast void of the sky, now deep blue, with only shredded traces of cloud or mist. To the south stretched the coast of Sutherland and Ross, fringed by silver-white surf, with the high mountains blue-grey beacons. To the east, separated by sea-lochs and bog was the mainland with its rank after rank of peaks. Behind us, rising steeply was a mass of broken rocks that ended in a definite, well-defined pinnacle. An Cailleach waited.

'There's the summit,' Charlie said. 'Now, kiss and make up you two and let's get up there.'

'I'm sorry Kate,' Christine said. 'It was my fault.' I felt mixed emotions from her, from fear to self-loathing.

'Good.' Kate said. 'Now let's get on with this.' Turning her back, she headed for the summit.

As always, we followed, taking care not to slip on the shattered rock with its sharp-edges as we scrambled on hands and knees. Christine lagged behind to touch my hand. 'Thank you,' she whispered with a small smile. Her eyes were hazel, I noted, and very clear.

'Keep going, ladies!' Charlie raised her voice to a stentorian roar. 'We're nearly there!'

The last hundred feet or so was a hand-and-foot scramble, slipping on loose rocks, avoiding ankle-trapping holes and feeling the heart-pounding excitement that only climbers approaching a new summit can understand.

'Here we are.' Kate had to be first to the summit pinnacle. She clambered up the sharp granite, stood on top and lifted her stick high in the air. 'This is the highest spot. We've conquered An Cailleach!'

I could see the Mahoney party again. Mike Mahoney stood precisely where Kate was, looking behind him as Bill and Adam stumbled over the last of the broken rocks. He was smiling, his blue Irish eyes bright with pleasure and his tweed jacket torn across the sleeve. Adam joined him, with his freckles merging as he spoke. Bill was singing some music-hall song. I could feel their presence as if they were still here, I could almost reach out to touch them they were so real to me. I could smell the pipe-tobacco and hear the grate of their boots on the granite.

'They are still here.' That now-familiar voice intruded in my thoughts.

'I would see them if they were,' I replied automatically, without fear, for I knew that woman intended me no harm.

'You will meet them by-and-by' she said.

Four people were standing on the small mound that was the summit of An Cailleach; three men and one woman.

'Kate!' I called as the shapes metamorphosed into Kate, Charlie, Lorna and Mary. I noted that Christine remained below the mound and nobody asked her to join them.

'We've done it!' Charlie said. 'We're at the summit of An Cailleach. We beat the men!'

I knew that was not true, but I could not destroy Charlie's moment of triumph.

I have stood on the summit of scores of hills. Some were significant triumphs, others an anti-climax. It did not depend on the height or the amount of effort it took to climb them, for even small hills could create great emotion while some of the loftiest left me without any feeling whatsoever. Schiehallion gave me a surge of spirituality, as did small Arthur's Seat in Edinburgh. Ben Nevis was disturbing; I did not like that hill. Now as I joined the rest on the crowded summit of An Cailleach, I experienced something I had never felt before.

I felt as if I had come home.

That made no sense. I had never been on An Cailleach before in my life.

'You have never left,' that little voice in my head told me.

'Wait!' Charlie said. 'Let's celebrate this like no man ever can.'

'I'm not giving birth up here,' Lorna said.

'No, follow me!' Quickly unfastening her top, Charlie pulled it off and lifted her tweed sweater and the woollen shirt beneath. 'Give a hand here,' she said and turned her back to allow Christine to unfasten her brassiere. She turned around with a grin on her face and juggled her neat little breasts. 'There we are. No man can do that!'

Laughing, Kate followed, and within minutes we all stood on that summit pinnacle, exposing our breasts to the wind and showing our triumph in what I thought was a truly unique style. I would doubt that any first ascent has been celebrated quite as liberally as that one, and when I think back to that day, that picture springs to mind. We grinned at each other, enjoying the conviviality and then Kate reached inside her rucksack and produced a small silver hip flask.

'This was Adam's' she said. 'I'd prefer champagne, but this is whisky from our own distillery.' She took the first sip and passed it around. 'If it's good enough for the men, then we can do it too.'

'Quite right,' Charlie was next to drink.

I had had quite enough chilly exposure for one day so quickly got back inside my clothes. The top of a Scottish hill is not the best place to stand without one's upper clothing.

'We're not alone up here,' Lorna paused with the silver flask nearly touching her lips. 'Look over there.'

We all followed her pointing finger.

Chapter Nine

'What's that?' Charlie asked. 'Who's up here?'

Rather than reply, Lorna replaced her clothes, slipped off the rocky pinnacle and strode toward the western rim of the summit. One by one, we followed, with Charlie striving to overtake Lorna and Christine at the back.

'What is it? Who is it?' Charlie asked.

'I think it is the Mahoney party,' Lorna said. 'I'm truly sorry, Kate.'

White-faced under her weather-tan, Kate nodded and pushed forward. 'I came here to find them, Lorna.'

They lay together in a hollow in the ground, still wearing the clothes in which they had ascended An Cailleach. Three skeletons that no longer had tongues to tell their stories, three dead bodies that could not claim the first ascent, three corpses from years past. We were not first to conquer An Cailleach, but we should be the first to ascend her and return.

'Adam!' Kate said, and I did not deny her the truth. I had seen the Mahoney party in their hour of triumph, and now I saw them in their eternity of death, the three proud men who conquered An Cailleach and whose spirits remained on the dark mountain of the old woman.

'They rest in peace,' I said. I felt Mary look at me, her eyes narrowed. 'They achieved their objective and died doing what they loved to do.' I felt no sorrow, no sympathy for these men. They were climbers who died climbing, hill-men who remained on the hills, outdoorsmen who spent their last hours in God's free air, friends who would always be together. I hoped for such success in my life.

'Why?' Kate knelt beside the three skeletons. 'Why did they stay up here and die? Why did they not return? What happened?'

I did not know the answer. I still do not know the answer. I did not try to guess although the others advanced a dozen theories from the three men having a major argument and killing each other, to death by starvation or getting lost in the mist.

'Now we know what happened.' Kate looked at the three corpses. 'We will probably never know why.' She pointed to the man on the left. 'This is Adam.'

I agreed. I could see Adam standing proudly on the summit with his freckles merging with his grin.

'We should bury them here,' Lorna said. 'Maybe later somebody can take them back to the low country.'

'They belong here,' I said.

'It's not up to you to decide that,' Kate said. 'That's a family matter.'

'You are right,' I conceded. 'I apologise, Kate. It must be hard to see your brother like this.'

'At least I know where he is.' Kate said. 'It was worse not knowing.'

'There are tens of thousands of men still missing in France.' Lorna said. 'Blown to pieces, drowned in mud, lost forever,' she put an arm around Kate's shoulder. 'It's a comfort knowing where Adam is.'

'Maybe it's a comfort to you,' Kate retaliated. 'This is my brother lying here.'

'We might not have been the first up,' Charlie said once again, 'but we will be the first up and then back again. Where the men failed, we will succeed.' Taking out her notebook, she began to sketch the three skeletons.

'You heartless bitch,' Kate said, and I agreed with her. Charlie may have been a tireless campaigner for women's rights and a suffragette *par excellence*. She may have been an excellent journalist, forging a career in a world dominated by men, but when it came to compassion and sympathy, she had been well down the queue.

I half expected Kate to slap Charlie, but perhaps she reserved her violence for people she knew would not retaliate. Instead, she turned away and walked to the edge of the summit, where the tremendous western cliffs plummeted in unequal steps nearly three thousand feet to the churning sea. I watched her for a long two minutes before joining her.

Kate was weeping. Our determined, confident, vibrant leader's shoulders were shaking with her grief, her face was twisted and tears coursed down her face.

I stood at her side in silent sympathy. This secret display of emotion was a new side to Kate. To be honest, I rather appreciated it. I prefer people to have some sort of vulnerability; it makes them more human, more like me, and therefore makes relating to them much more comfortable. I touched her arm and felt her agony of mind.

'He's at peace now,' I whispered against the wind. 'And you can tell your parents that their son died in triumph.'

Kate shook me away. 'I always looked up to him,' she said. 'I always had hope that he might turn up at the door one day with that great big impish grin on his face, saying he had an impulse to travel the world on a tramp steamer or he had joined a Dundee sealing ship and got lost in the Arctic, or he joined the French Foreign Legion or *something*.'

I withdrew my hand. I did not even know if I had a brother, somewhere, searching for me. I did not even know my real name. 'He sounds like an adventurous man,' was all that I could say.

'None better.' Kate took a deep breath. 'We'll leave him up here until mother decides what's best to do with him, or with his body.' When she turned around the wind had already dried her tears, and her face was composed. The stiff upper lip had returned to the mask of the Scottish aristocrat, and nothing would now upset her equanimity.

We built a cairn for the Mahoney party, using some of the thousands of shattered and wind-and-rain smoothed stones that lay on the summit of An Cailleach. We placed the three men side by side on a level slab, protected their fragile bones with large boulders and roofed it as best we could before piling smaller stones on top. The clunk of stone on stone seemed very final, yet timeless, for, in Scotland, people had been burying their dead beneath cairns for countless centuries.

'There,' Kate said. 'A cairn fit for heroes. I wish I had a flag to place on top.'

'I have one,' Lorna surprised us by producing a small Union Flag. 'This flag graced the bonnet of my ambulance in Belgium back in '14 before the British Army permitted women drivers. It was with me right until the Armistice.' She placed it at the apex of the cairn, with larger stones to hold it in place. 'This is a suitable resting place for climbers, and an honourable last post for any flag.'

I saw Charlie sketching in her notebook. 'A double reason for the flag,' she said. 'It marks the graves of the three men and flies to show our achievements as women.'

'It will be a fine picture in your article,' I did not hide my sarcasm. 'What a pity you don't carry a camera as well.'

'I find them too bulky,' Charlie said. 'And sketches are so much more evocative, don't you think?'

'I'm sorry about your brother, Kate' Christine said.

Kate snorted. 'You did not know him. Why should you be sorry?'

I sensed Christine's hurt and gave her a wink. 'She doesn't mean it, Christine,' I said. 'She's upset.'

'I know,' Christine said. 'I'm trying to help her.'

'I know you are,' Kate touched Christine's arm. 'I'm sorry Christine.'

Ninety minutes before, we had flaunted ourselves on top of the summit pinnacle, as proud and carefree as any women in the world. Now we were sobered and chastened with all elation behind us.

'We'd better be heading back,' Lorna said. 'With luck, we'll make it in one long tramp although it will be well after dark before we're at the ford.'

'It'll be easier going downward,' Mary said. 'We know the route and what to watch out for.'

'Give me just five more minutes,' Charlie pleaded. 'Could you all gather on the summit so I can draw you?'

'Oh, we don't have time for that,' Kate said.

'I'll make you famous, Kate,' Charlie appealed to her vanity. 'The Honourable Kathleen Gordon, leader of the all-woman expedition that not only conquered An Cailleach but also solved the mystery of the missing Mahoney mission.' She grinned. 'Talk about alliteration!'

Kate glanced at her brother's cairn as if to apologise. 'Oh, go on then, if you must.'

We waited a further seven minutes by my watch as heavy clouds gathered above us and Lorna's Union flag crackled and rippled in the strengthening wind. Only when Charlie snapped shut her notebook did we stamp our feet, rap our sticks on the shattered granite of the summit and turn our attention to the return.

'If you're nervous on the hill,' I whispered to Christine, 'stay close to me and don't tell anybody. If you don't let on, Kate can't bully you.'

Reaching across, Christine squeezed my hand. 'Thank you, Brenda. I don't mind Kate, really I don't.'

The initial part was easy, sliding and slithering down to the series of pitons on the first cliff face. I stayed close to Christine to afford moral support, knowing she was near to panicking at the thought of descending that pegged wall of rock.

'I think we should use a rope,' I said.

'Oh, yes,' Christine agreed.

'That's the coward's way,' Kate said.

I felt Christine stiffen. 'Then I'm a coward,' I said. 'Come on, Kate, it will be much easier and just as fast. We've nothing to prove now that we've conquered An Cailleach.'

'Please, Katie,' Christine begged.

'Coward!' Kate jeered. 'I'm not taking up the hills again, Chrissie. You're a coward and a disgrace, what are you?'

I cringed at this ritual humiliation. 'Leave Christine alone, Kate.'

'She deserves it,' Kate said. 'More, she needs it if she is ever to grow up.'

'I've dropped and secured the rope,' Mary had ignored Kate's disapproval. 'I'll go down first and leave Kate to torment poor Christine.' Mary's look would have frozen an active volcano. 'Come on, the rest of you.' She swarmed down the rope, hand over hand and with hardly a pause. Snorting, Kate was next, and then Charlie while Lorna and I waited for Christine.

'Are you all right, Christine?' Her confidence was shattered. I could see her shaking and feel waves of her pain. 'I'll go next, and you follow me closely. I'll go slowly.'

'I'm all right.' Christine looked close to tears.

'I'll be at the coo's tail,' Lorna tried to sound cheerful.

'Off we go then,' I swung over the lip, felt my rucksack pull me backwards and held tight to the rope. Honestly, there must be a better way to climb down a cliff than in heavy boots and with a mighty pack. I clambered a few feet and waited with the wind tugging at me and the drop inviting me to fall. 'Right, Christine, on you come.'

'I'm coming.' Christine poised her tiny figure at the lip of the wall, her boots seemingly too large for her and her rucksack nearly as big as she was herself.

'I'm here if you need me,' Lorna said quietly.

The wind was increasing again, rocking me back and forth with that immense gulf beneath me and the odd spatter of rain washing my face. Christine whimpered as she took hold of the rope and backed over the edge of the rock face. I saw her boots scrabble for the first piton and then she started down, breathing hard as she fought to control her fear.

'That's the way, Christine,' I encouraged and reached for the next piton. 'Keep going.'

Glancing down, I saw Charlie scribbling in her notebook. Kate had already begun the next stage of the descent, heading over the broken boulders like a woman demented. Mary waited at the foot of the cliff, singing *Kisimuil's Galley* as she watched our descent.

'I'm falling!' Christine yelled. 'I can't hold on.'

'You can't fall, far,' Lorna said. 'We're tied together.

'Well done, Lorna,' I praised her quietly as I eased down another few feet. 'Come on Christine. You're doing well.'

Christine's right foot slipped off the piton three feet above my head. She squealed and gripped the rope while the nails on her left boot scraped sparks from the granite. Balancing with my foot on a piton and my left hand on the line, I reached up and took hold of her ankle.

'I'll guide you,' I gently placed her foot on the closest piton. 'Now rest a second, and we'll go for the next one.'

Although there were four other women on that hill, I felt as if I were alone with Christine. Nobody else mattered at that minute. I talked her down that cliff face, step by step, piton by piton while Kate vanished into the increasing rain and Mary watched us, her face white with anxiety and her *Kisimuil's Galley* becoming faster and more garbled by the minute.

'There we are!' I could not restrain myself from embracing Christine when we reached the foot of the cliff face. She was trembling, with tears be-slobbering her face.

'Oh, God I was so frightened,' Christine said. 'Where's Kate?'

'She's gone ahead,' Charlie said. 'She could not wait.'

'Oh,' I felt Christine's disappointment. 'Did she not try to help?'

'No,' Charlie held up her latest drawing. It showed Christine and me toiling down the rope with Christine looking suitably terrified. 'There you are, Chrissie, recorded for posterity as the weakest link in the chain.'

'That's not fair,' I said as Charlie snapped shut her notebook.

'Maybe it doesn't sound fair, but it's true.' Charlie said. 'We're here to prove that women are at least equal to men, not to show our weaknesses.'

'If somebody is afraid,' I pointed out, 'it takes more courage for them to do something that it would for somebody who does not know fear.'

'Don't show that picture, Charlie,' Lorna said. 'Then nobody will know.'

'I'm a reporter,' Charlie said. 'I report things as they are; the bad as well as the good.' Her smile was unpleasant. 'Women can report as accurately as men can.'

We moved on then, down the broken slope with the wind picking up and the rain growing heavier by the minute. I did not know how I felt. I should have been elated at our success. I was not. My mind was more set on the strange happenings, the ghosts of the Clearance village and that woman who did not exist, the washerwoman and the *caoineag*. I also felt sorry for Kate, despite her continual cruelty to Christine. It must have been terrible for her to discover the skeleton of her brother on the summit of An Cailleach. No wonder she acted up, her emotions must have been in turmoil.

My thoughts had distracted me, so I did not realise where we were. I had moved instinctively, following the others as we made good time down the slope. Now I looked up to recognise that we were slogging through a torrential downpour.

'The Witch's Step will be a nightmare in this,' Lorna said.

'I can't crawl over that again,' Christine nearly whispered. 'I just can't.'

'We'll leave you behind, then,' Kate showed no sympathy. 'You can remain here with the skeletons and the wild beasts.'

'I'll look after you, Christine,' I said. 'Don't worry.'

'We'll both look after you, Christine.' Lorna corrected me.

The wind increased, blasting from the west, carrying salt spray from the Atlantic and so powerful that we had to lean into it to continue. 'Use the wind,' Lorna advised. 'Let it take your weight.' Twice Christine stumbled, and the second time she fell flat on her face. I helped her up, and we linked arms, fighting to remain upright as the blast threatened to pluck us off the side of An Cailleach and throw us headlong into the mist-smothered abyss below.

'The weather's getting worse,' Lorna had to shout to be heard. 'We'd be foolish to continue in this.'

'I'm not staying another night on this hill,' Kate said. 'We press on.'

As soon as Kate spoke, the thunder sounded, followed immediately by lightning that split the heavens in a flash that had us all blinking.

'That was right above us,' Charlie sounded worried.

'The mountain gods are angry,' Lorna murmured.

'We're pressing on.' Kate said. 'Charlie, you and I and maybe Lorna could get back to the inn tonight. We could leave the others here to come at their own pace.'

'No, Kate.' Lorna shouted. 'We stay together. It's the only proper thing to do. We'll rest at the Shelter Stone until the worst passes. It would be foolish to split into small parties in this.'

'You're soft, the lot of you,' Kate nearly screamed the words. 'You're all weak, especially you, Christine.'

I felt Kate's anger and frustration, together with Christine's humiliation.

'Come on then, to the Shelter Stone,' Kate said, 'if you're too scared to carry on.'

We stumbled down the hill, sliding on the wet rock, splashing into newly formed peat-holes, cringing before the bitter onslaught of the wind and rain. Thunder grumbled and growled above our heads, with the occasional mighty crack that made us jump. One bolt of lightning slashed to earth a hundred yards from where we stood, leaving a stink of burning heather and the static of electricity.

I grabbed Christine's hand as she gave a little scream. 'It's all right, Christine!'

'Isn't this marvellous?' As Kate stood still the next flash illuminated her, and for an instant, I saw her like an old Celtic goddess, bareheaded on a slight ridge with her hair flying free and a panorama of sea and mountains at her back. I swear that she loved the drama of the weather, enjoying pitting herself against the worst that nature could do. Kate had one problem; she was born a century too late. What an explorer she would have made, or a pioneer woman.

'Here is it!' Everybody except Kate was pleased to get under shelter as we crowded under the flat stone slab we had left only that morning.

Kate counted us all in before pushing past to the same position she had occupied the previous night. I ensured that Christine was under cover, as far away from Kate as possible. We did not say much, sitting in tense silence as we munched stale sandwiches and listened to the storm lashing the hillside outside. The occasional lightning flash showed a line of tired faces and dripping jackets.

'We could do with a fire,' Lorna said. 'Has anybody got any matches? My box is wet.'

'Good idea but so are mine,' I said. 'Mary? Kate?'

They shook their heads.

'How about you, Charlie, you're the next thing to a man we have here, don't you smoke a pipe?' I tried to lighten the mood.

'I've never tried a pipe,' Charlie said. 'I've smoked cigarettes, cheroots and cigars though.' She glowered across to me. 'And I'm nothing like a man.'

'That's interesting,' Lorna said. 'Do you have any matches?'

'Yes,' Charlie produced a box of Scottish Bluebell matches and threw them across.

Without wood, we had to burn the moss that lined the inside of the shelter, together with anything combustible that we could find.

'Look!' Mary pointed to the rock face that removing the moss had unveiled. 'There's something carved into the stone here.'

'Probably Adam Gordon's life story,' Charlie said.

Kate shuffled across. 'It's only a mark in the stone.'

'No, it's more than that. Give me a hand here.' Mary began scraping off more moss, with Lorna and me helping. 'It's a picture.'

'Let me see,' Charlie grabbed back her matches and squeezed through the press. Striking a match, she held it up with the small flame augmenting the fading light. 'You're right, Mary, it's undoubtedly a picture.' She ran her fingers over the carving. 'I can't quite make it out, though. I think that's a man holding somebody head down.'

'It's a woman,' Mary said. 'Look at her shape; she has breasts. It's obviously a woman holding somebody head down in some sort of cauldron.'

'A witch's cauldron,' Lorna said. 'Or the Holy Grail. Maybe the Holy Grail is hidden here? Nobody would ever find it if it were!'

'No,' Mary shook her head. 'I think it's some sort of ritual. The woman is cleansing that other person.'

I knew they were not right. The image came to me of a ring of women watching while another gripped another and plunged her upside down and naked into a pond. 'It's a ritual drowning,' I said quietly. 'It's a human sacrifice in a drowning pond or cauldron.'

'An execution?' Kate asked.

'A human sacrifice.' I repeated. 'So it is a sort of execution, Kate.'

'Now that's just horrible,' Lorna said. 'Would that be your ancestors, Mary? The poor people from Penrioch? Would they be sacrificing people because of the Clearances?'

'No.' Although I spoke quietly, I was quite definite 'This evil far predated the Clearances.'

I felt Lorna looking at me. If anybody had asked me how I knew, I could not have told them. The knowledge was within me.

'Mary will still blame my family,' Kate said.

I did not join in the general laughter. By touching the carving, I could bring the scene to life in my head, with the gathering watching as the victim was plunged into the bitter-cold water. They were solemn rather than jubilant, gravely observing a religious ritual that had a purpose. They were not lip-licking sadists enjoying the death struggles of some terrified victim.

'Your family was not to blame, Kate,' I said. Once again, nobody commented. It was as if I had never spoken, or they wished I had not.

'Well this is cheerful,' Lorna said. 'Let's get the fire lit and spread some warmth around.'

Within a few moments, we were all coughing in the smoke and cursing Lorna for what we had agreed to be a good idea.

'This storm does not seem to be lifting,' Lorna looked beyond the Shelter Stone to where thunder still rumbled. We could hear the rain hammering on the ground outside and rivulets of water rushing down the slope. 'If anything, it's getting worse. I can hardly see my hand in front of my face.'

'We should have pushed on,' Kate said. 'That's what Adam would have done.'

'Adam's dead,' Charlie was abrupt. 'That's what his masculine pride got him, an early death on a bare hillside. Adam and all his friends.'

The silence was so brittle I could feel it crackling. 'That's enough, ladies,' I tried to calm things down. 'We're all tired and tense and a bit fed up just now. Let's all keep quiet and stay friendly.'

There was silence as Charlie and Kate glared at each other, but precious little friendship in our tight little group. All the bonhomie of the successful ascent had vanished, with resentment and suspicion taking its place. We sat together as six individuals, each with our own thoughts and fears, trapped by the weather and the situation we had brought on ourselves.

As the storm swept away the last of the daylight, it became apparent that we were stuck under the Shelter stone for the night. We huddled together without saying much, listening to the shriek of the wind, the constant batter of the rain and the slowly retreating crack of thunder. The occasional flicker of lightning revealed our strained, tired faces.

'The worst of the storm has passed,' Lorna peered outside. 'It's getting on for midnight now, though. We can't try the Witch's Step in the dark.' She returned to the rest of us and sat close to me. 'This time tomorrow we will laugh at this adventure.'

I glanced outside. That woman was there, silhouetted against the now-starlit sky. I could not see her face, only the gleam of her eyes as she watched me. I held her gaze and knew that something was going to happen. I moved slightly so that Christine had more room in which to lie and when I looked again the woman was gone. The feeling of dread remained as I fought my desire to sleep.

Chapter Ten

'Where's Kate?'

As so often happens in Scotland, a night of heavy rain was followed by a bright, sharp morning where the air was so brisk that one's skin tingled.

'Where's Kate?' Lorna woke us up, one by one. Christine had moved during the night and was nearest to the entrance, lying in a foetal ball. I shook her.

'Christine, have you seen Kate?'

'No.' Christine yawned and scratched her head, looking like a disgruntled spaniel puppy. 'She might be answering a call of nature.'

We allowed Kate ten minutes before we began to search, shouting her name as we scoured the hillside. Sunlight sparkled on a score of new rivulets that gushed toward Poll nan Ban while whaups bubbled in the distance.

'Kate!'

'She might have slipped and fallen,' I said.

Lorna organised the search, so we moved in ever larger circles from the Shelter Stone, following every possibility, looking in every nook and cranny, poking our sticks into the peat holes and checking behind the scattered rocks. Remembering my visitor of the previous night, I worked with a heavy heart, dreading what I might find.

'Over here! Over here!' When Mary shouted the words, we hurried to her side. 'Down there!' She pointed down the slope to the sparkling waters of Poll nan ban. 'What's that in the water?'

I knew without looking.

Face down and entirely naked, Kathleen Gordon floated in Poll nan Ban. Her black hair spread like a fan, her arms were extended and her legs apart.

'Oh, dear God in heaven,' Lorna muttered. 'Please no.'

We scrambled down the shallow slope to the lochan, each of us hoping that she might still be alive.

'Kate!' I shouted as my feet dislodged a mini avalanche of stones that rippled down the hill to splash into the clear water. Kate floated about twenty feet offshore, bobbing gently. A pair of black-headed gulls swam nearby.

We stood at the water's edge for only a moment before Mary threw off her clothes and plunged in. I followed a few seconds' later. The pool was far deeper than it appeared from above and so cold that I gasped with shock.

Mary reached Kate first and dragged her to me. Between the two of us, we pulled her ashore where Lorna was waiting.

'Give her here,' Lorna felt for a pulse and a heartbeat. 'She's dead. I'll try anyway. Help me turn her over.' We pushed Kate onto her front and Lorna tried to pump the water out of her lungs and revive her.

We watched in hope as the Great War ambulance driver tried to bring life back into the landowner's daughter. Lorna gasped and strove, trying all the skill she had learned in the war with her wounded soldiers. Nothing worked. Kate, our flawed, magnificent leader, lay still beside the clear waters of the lochan. I heard the call of an eagle and saw the massive birds circling above.

Eventually, Lorna looked up. 'It's no good,' she said. 'Kate's dead.'

I felt sick. 'Can you tell how she died?'

'I think she drowned,' Lorna said. 'She must have fallen down the hill into the lochan.'

'There's not a mark on her,' I pointed out. 'Surely if she had fallen from the Shelter Stone, there would be bumps and scrapes. And where are her clothes? Why is she naked?'

We looked at each other. 'What's happening here?' Charlie asked. 'Kate's dead on the same hill as her brother died.'

Christine was white-faced but more composed than I would have expected. She spoke in a tiny voice. 'I think we should get back to the Inn.'

'Kate would not have fallen,' Charlie said. 'She was the best climber of us all, as sure-footed as a goat. She had no reason to go to the edge of the ridge anyway.'

'She might have lost her way in the dark,' I pointed out.

'Oh, yes. Kate took off all her clothes and went for a walk in the middle of a storm,' Charlie said. 'I don't think that is very likely.'

I knew Charlie was correct. 'What else could have happened?'

'Somebody pushed her.' Charlie said what I had been thinking.

We were shocked into silence. 'Oh, dear God,' Lorna said. 'Do you mean one of us?'

'There's nobody else here,' Charlie pointed out.

'There might have been other climbers,' Lorna clutched at any straw.

'We haven't seen anybody for days,' Charlie said. 'And how would they manage to sneak in, grab Kate, take off her clothes and throw her into the lochan without any of us hearing anything? Why would they do that?'

'Maybe they raped her,' I could be as brutal as Charlie.

'I'll check.' Lorna the practical nurse said.

'Oh, God Lorna, do you have to?' Christine asked.

'It's the proper thing to do. Don't watch if it upsets you,' Lorna and I turned Kate onto her back. 'If she's been raped we'll know that it was a man.'

'Oh, no!' Christine covered her face and turned away. 'Oh, don't, Lorna! Poor Kate.'

I watched Lorna's rapid yet thorough examination. 'No,' Lorna shook her head. 'As far as I can see, there is no forced entry. No entry at all in fact.' She looked up. 'Kate was spared that, at least.'

'Poor Kate,' I said. 'She died without ever knowing that side of life.'

'She was my friend,' Christine turned around. 'I know most of you did not like her but she was my friend, and now she's dead.'

'You said you wanted to kill her,' Charlie reminded.

We all looked at Christine. I felt the suspicion grow among us. The peninsula's attack on us, Tigh-na-Beiste's attack on us, had changed shape. I did not know what had happened. I did know that the Rough Quarter had killed Kate, somehow. Now we were going to blame each other.

'It wasn't Christine,' I said. 'I don't know who or what killed Kate but it was not Christine.'

'What do you mean who or what?' Mary stepped towards me. 'If it were a wild beast, there would be tooth or claw marks, and I can't see any.'

'There is not a mark on her body,' Lorna confirmed. 'There is nothing to suggest any violence. I would say that she drowned.'

'She was a top-class swimmer,' Christine said. 'She was captain of the school swimming team.'

'Mary didn't like her either,' Charlie altered the angle of her accusation.

'I didn't like her, and I didn't kill her,' Mary said, 'you're very quick to accuse, Charlie. Maybe you're trying to divert suspicion from yourself.'

'I don't think any of us killed her,' I poured oil on troubled minds. 'We don't know what happened. I think we'd be better deciding what we'll do next.'

'Get back to the Inn as quickly as possible,' Lorna said. 'That's the only thing we can do. There are the two dead male climbers to report, the Mahoney party and now poor Kate. That's enough death for anybody.' She glanced at Charlie, 'and I don't want to hear you say that it'll make good copy.'

Charlie remained sensibly silent.

'Do we all agree on that?' Lorna asked. 'We get back to the Inn and report Kate's death to the police.'

There was a collective nod. Nobody wanted to remain on the peninsula.

'How about Kate?' I asked.

'We can't take her with us,' Lorna said. 'We can't carry her all that way across the saddle and over the Witch's Step. We'll have to leave her here, and somebody can take her home later.'

'We can't leave her here,' Charlie looked around at the lonely lochan with the pair of black-headed gulls and desolate slopes.

'Vote on it,' I said. 'Let the majority decide.'

Only Charlie voted to take Kate home.

'We can't leave her like this,' I pointed to Kate's naked body and then to the eagles circling above. 'We can't leave her for the eagles.'

'We'll do for Kate what we did for the Mahoney party,' Lorna agreed.

We carried Kate away from the water's edge and built a cairn around her as we had done with her brother only the previous day. This time we had no flag to mark her grave. This time we were entombing one of our own.

'Here lies the last of the Carnbrora Gordons,' Mary said. 'In a way, it's fitting that she should die on the same ground her ancestors cleared a hundred years ago.

'Carnbrora?' Charlie asked. 'What's that?'

'That's the name of Kate's estate,' Mary said. 'She would have been Lady Kathleen Gordon of Carnbrora.'

Charlie nodded. 'I didn't know that.' Stepping aside, she sketched the scene in her notebook. With terrible cynicism, I wondered if Charlie was secretly rejoicing in the death of one of our number. Death would certainly add drama to her article and boost her sales.

'The people of Penrioch are watching,' Mary said, with a far-away look in her eyes. I said nothing, thinking of that carving in the Shelter Stone and the ritual drowning of a woman. History had repeated itself.

'Why is this called the Women's Pool?' I asked.

Mary shook her head. 'I don't know.' She gave a sudden high-pitched laugh. 'Maybe somebody knew that Kate would die here.'

I knew she was wrong. I could see the gathering around the lochan, the earnest, solemn faces and the reflection of the moon on the water. I saw them bring forward the woman, whose look was worried rather than scared. She knew she was to be sacrificed and accepted her fate. Had Kate known it was her time? I saw the people take hold of their sacrifice and walk into the cold waters, then lift her, turn her upside down and plunge her head first into the lochan. I saw her legs kicking, churning the water into a furious froth as she struggled with the burning agony of drowning, and then her limbs gradually stilled. She was limp. She was dead.

The crowd sang and lifted their hands to the moon. The ripples of the lochan quietened. The executioner, solemn-faced, raised the body of the sacrifice and returned to the shore, at which point the whole procession carried her to a cave to be placed with those who had gone before.

'Is there a cave near here?'

Mary frowned. 'My grandmother used to speak of a cave somewhere on the peninsula, *An uaimh mor* she called it – The great cave. She said that people were banned from entering it. Even the kirk minister didn't go in.'

'Is it nearby?'

'I don't know, why?'

Why? I did not know why. 'It would be a good place to leave Kate, safe from prowling beasts and seagulls.'

'Too late now,' Lorna said. 'Anyway, Kate's fine as she is.' Of us all, Lorna seemed least affected by Kate's death. She had seen too many bodies to worry over one more.

'We should pray,' Mary said suddenly.

'Kate was never religious,' Christine shook her head. 'She used to make us go to church assembly at school though.'

'We should still pray,' Mary said. To my surprise, she bowed her head and began praying. 'Our father, who art in heaven…'

I listened for a few moments and joined in, as did Lorna and Christine. Charlie watched with a cynical little smile on her face.

'Won't you join us?' Mary invited.

'The Church is a patriarchal institution,' Charlie said. 'It is intended to keep women in their place. When the Moderator of the General Assembly of the Kirk and the Pope of Rome are both females, then I may believe in the equality of the Church and in God.'

'The Church and the Lord are two different things,' Mary said. 'And there is no single Church anyway. Ministers of the Kirk supported the Clearances while the Free Kirk helped the people during the Great Famine of the 1840s.'

I said nothing. The drowning scene in my head was old centuries before Christianity reached the shores of Scotland. My own beliefs... I did not have many views to call my own.

A pair of oystercatchers flew overhead, their piping calls echoing from the gaunt slopes of An Cailleach. Almost immediately Mary began another prayer, with the Gaelic words natural in this environment. Lorna raised her eyebrows and looked at me. I motioned her to be silent and listened. Although I could not speak a single word of the language, I understood what Mary said as she called down God's blessing and protection for the soul of Kate.

'Now,' Mary reverted to English and looked around us. 'Kate should be safe now.'

'Safe from what?' Charlie asked.

'Any spiritual attack,' Mary explained.

Charlie snorted in disdain. 'Maybe you'd better place your wee rowan cross on her grave.'

I saw Mary finger the cross. 'Keep that,' I advised. 'It means more to you than it would to Kate.'

The gratitude in Mary's glance told me all I needed to know. She knew there was something uncanny about this place. She knew that Kate's death had not been an accident and she was probably as scared and unsettled as I was.

'I thought not,' Charlie said. 'Like all you Christian people, you say the words and mean nothing.'

Mary stiffened. Giving Charlie a single frozen glance, she unfastened her cross and placed it on Kate's grave, then impulsively added the blue crystal she had worn ever since I met her. 'That is a *clach gorm*,' she said. 'It's a stone to protect from evil and belonged to my grandmother's great-grandmother.'

'How touching,' Charlie said. 'I'll add that to my story.'

'We can do no more for Kate,' I said. 'Let's get to the Inn and contact the police.'

'It's strange,' Christine spoke so quietly that I had to strain to hear her, 'it's strange that Kate should drown.'

'Why is that?'

Christine looked at the burial cairn as if afraid Kate would burst free of the stones and start to torment her again. 'When we were at school, Kate used to supervise swimming lessons. One of her tricks was to throw the non-swimmers into the deep end and hold them under.'

'I see. Kate held you under at the beach with the palm tree, too.'

'She did that to me more than once,' Christine said.

'I would keep that to yourself,' I said. 'You don't want to create any more suspicion.'

'No,' Christine looked away. When she spoke, her voice was so quiet I barely heard her. 'If I tell you something, will you promise not to tell anybody?'

'If you wish me to,' I said.

'My friends and I used to pray that Kate drowned. We made an image of her out of candle wax, stole hair from her brush and nail clippings and held it underwater in a puddle to try to drown her.'

I felt deep pain from Christine and imagined what depths of misery bullying had driven her to. 'She can't hurt you now,' I said. 'You're free.'

'Yes,' Christine said. 'I'm free.'

The others might think that Christine's tears were sorrow for her friend. I knew they were tears of gratitude and relief.

The entire peninsula seemed lighter after the death of Kate. I could feel a sense of vindication from the spectres of Penrioch. I could not see these long-dead people, yet I knew they had watched. I could also sense the presence of the women in the long robes, whoever they had been. Now they were watching me.

Chapter Eleven

We were a subdued bunch of women as we left the Shelter Stone and headed to the knife-edged saddle and the ferocious Witch's Step. With Kate gone, Lorna assumed the lead as the most experienced climber, although Charlie questioned her decisions more often that I liked.

We stood at the edge of the saddle, contemplating our route. It seemed even more difficult from here, slicing upward in a sickle-curve with the mist already formed below and the sister mountain of Bein a Ghlo also shrouded in cloud.

'There's only one way,' Lorna said. 'I'll lead, Charlie, you're next most experienced, you go last to help the others. Mary, you're after me, and Brenda will be with Christine.'

Nobody argued. I think we all just wished to be across the saddle and off this peninsula.

'We'll rope ourselves together,' Lorna said.

'Not me,' Charlie said. 'I don't want Christine slipping and dragging me down there,' she gestured to the abyss beside the saddle, where ribbed granite plunged down into shifting mist.

'It's safer for everybody,' Lorna said, 'and besides, Christine is a lightweight. I could pick her up and put her in my pocket.'

'I'll do things my way,' Charlie said. 'You rope up if you wish.'

'I'll be all right,' Christine said. 'Please don't argue about me.'

The wind picked up as we stepped onto the narrow ridge. Despite her brave words, I saw Christine hesitate immediately in front of me.

'It's all right, Christine,' I said. 'Take it one step at a time. You got over once; it will be easier going back.'

With slippery rock beneath her feet and that immense drop into nothingness on either side, I could understand Christine's fear. Lorna proved a more careful leader than Kate, turning to check on her charges every few steps. 'You'll be fine, Christine' she encouraged. 'I'll stop when we reach the Witch's Step so we can take it together.'

'I don't think I can do this,' Christine said. 'I don't think I can do the Witch's Step again.'

'I'll be there to help you,' I said. 'And so will Lorna and Mary.' I did not mention Charlie, who stalked in our rear, saying little but watching everything. Once Charlie stopped to throw a stone into the abyss at our side, and we all listened to see how long it took to land. After what seemed an interminable time we heard the tiniest chink.

'It's a long way down,' Charlie chirped staring into the mist that writhed and seethed below us. 'I would not like to fall down there.'

'Stay on the saddle then,' I said and moved on, tapping my stick against the smooth granite. I heard Mary singing ahead, with the sea-song *Kisimuil's Galley* incongruous up here on the heights.

As she had promised, Lorna waited at the Witch's Step. She greeted us with a smile that seemed out of place so soon after the death of Kate. 'Here we are then,' she said. 'Once we're over this we're as good as home and dry.'

'Not very dry,' Mary looked upward where a drizzle descended from the now-grey sky, gradually soaking through every layer of our clothes.

'There's still that cliff to get down after this,' Christine said.

'One thing at a time,' I studied the great cleft in the ridge. 'Remember, it will be even easier this time.'

'Why will it be easier?' Christine asked.

'We're all more experienced,' I said.

The twin ropes stretched across, swaying slightly in the wind and making me feel dizzy. I could not imagine how Christine felt. Or rather, I could. I felt panic bubbling inside her.

'Watch how Lorna crosses,' I said quietly, 'and we'll copy her technique. As Lorna said, once we were across the rest of the journey would be easy in comparison.

'This way, ladies.' Going down on her hands and knees, Lorna balanced on the twin ropes and began to crawl across. We watched the lines bend under her weight and halfway across with the chasm beneath her at its deepest, she stopped.

'What's she doing?' Mary asked, and raised her voice. 'Lorna, what are you doing?'

'I'm showing you how easy it is!' Lorna shouted. 'See?' She raised one foot from the rope, replaced it, and then lifted a hand. 'If I can do this, then anybody can cross with all hands and feet.' She resumed her passage, reaching the far side within five minutes. Turning, she waved to us.

'Well now,' Mary said. 'That was easy enough. Who's next?'

'You go next, Mary,' I said.

'Right-o.' Mary was deliberately cheerful. She dropped to all fours and began the crawl. Only then did I notice the pair of eagles that circled above. Once again I wondered about Duncan Og's tale of witches and watched Mary's cautious progress. Without any daring heroics, Mary reached the far side, stood up and waved. I could see the strain in her face.

'You next, Christine,' I said. I felt her sudden overwhelming panic. 'Just take it slow.'

'I can't,' Christine shook her head, stepping backwards. 'I'll fall.'

'You must,' I said. 'There's no other way off this hill. The other faces are sheer cliffs dropping to the sea. We have to go this way.'

'Please, Brenda, don't make me.' There were tears in Christine's eyes.

I hardened my heart. 'You must, Christine. We're roped together, remember, so there is no danger. Take a deep breath and take it one step at a time.'

'Can't you come with me?'

'The ropes won't hold both our weight,' I said. 'Go on. Take it slowly, and you'll be fine.'

It felt cruel to push Christine out like that. I could see her fear and I wondered why on earth she had come on this expedition in the first place. Was it to please Kate? Had Christine been seeking acceptance from the woman who had tormented her for years? I have heard of dogs fawning to the hand that beats them, and wives returning again and again to an abusive husband. Perhaps Christine was of the same bent, a tormented soul who needed her tormentor. I did not know. I hoped not. I was beginning to foster a liking for the elfin little woman.

'I'll take your pack,' I helped unfasten the straps. 'Now remember that you and I are roped together, so you are in no danger.'

'Yes, Brenda.' Slowly lowering herself to her hands and knees, Christine inched onto the ropes, her knuckles white with the strength of her grip. She was sobbing as she crept forward with the lines bending under her weight and that great sucking drop below.

'Oh, oh, I can't do this.'

'Yes, you can. You're doing well,' I encouraged. 'Keep moving.' The worst thing Christine could do was stop and look down. If she did, she was almost certain to freeze. 'Keep your eyes on Lorna,' I said. 'Lorna is waiting for you.'

Christine did as I advised. I could hear her nervous panting as she crawled along the rope bridge, one slow step at a time with the mist coiling and shifting beneath her and a constant drizzle of rain from a low dull sky.

'Hold my eyes,' Lorna said. 'Look at me.' Lorna had taken over the mantle of leadership since Kate had gone. Crouching at the end of the rope bridge, she extended her hands for Christine. 'Nearly there, Christine.'

And then Christine slipped. I don't know how it happened, but one moment she was nearing the end of the bridge, and the next her left hand and left foot were off the rope bridge, and she swung sideways, screaming. I felt the snap and tension of the rope around my waist and leaned back to take her weight. The sudden shock unbalanced me, so I staggered forward. For a terrifying moment I teetered on the brink of the abyss, facing that thousand-foot fall into cloud-shrouded nothingness, and then I took hold of the rock with both hands and steadied myself.

'Brenda!' I heard Christine's desperate scream. 'Brenda!'

The rope tightened around my waist. I grabbed it with both hands and waited for the terrifying jerk that would mean Christine had fallen. It did not come. I looked up. Christine was balanced on the one hand and one foot, facing sideways into the abyss. Her screams echoed below.

'I'm coming!' Fully aware that the ropes might not bear my weight, I dumped both my rucksack and Christine's before I slid onto the fragile bridge and pulled myself onward toward Christine. The void pulled at me, encouraging me to release my grip and plummet down forever. I fought back, concentrating on Christine as she screamed in terror.

'Hold on, Christine!'

I did not notice the eagle until it passed a few feet in front of me, so close that I could see every detail of every feather and the cold glint of its eyes. The beak looked viciously sharp and then it was gone. I ducked involuntarily and slid further forward with the rope slippery with rain and the wind pushing me this way and that.

'Brenda! Help me!' Christine was clinging with one hand, twisting so one minute she was on her side and the next she was nearly upside down with her screams echoing in the vastness beneath.

'I'm coming!' I shouted. 'Only a few minutes more, Christine!'

'I've got you.' Lorna's calm voice ended the screaming. 'I've got you, Christine, you're safe.'

Looking up, I saw Lorna ease Christine onto the far side of the Step. She was holding Christine like an older sister, comforting her as she brought her to safety. I wondered how many wounded soldiers had seen Lorna like that, a ministering angel who saved their life or gave them companionship as they took the final step from life to death.

Already two-thirds of the way across, I crawled the final few yards and dragged myself to safety. 'There we are, Christine,' I forced a death's head grin. 'I told you it would be easy.'

Christine lay on the narrow ridge, panting in gradually reducing fear. 'Thank you for coming for me.'

'It was Lorna who saved you,' I said.

Christine pushed herself to her knees. 'Thank you, Lorna.'

Lorna smiled. 'I couldn't let you fall. Think of the mess.'

'My rucksack,' Christine's voice rose. 'I've left my rucksack.'

'Me too,' I said. 'I'm sure we can do without. After losing Kate, I won't be worried about the contents of a bag.'

'You don't understand,' Christine said. 'My mother gave me that bag. I need it.'

'Charlie!' I shouted across the Step, 'could you bring Christine's bag over with you, please?'

'Tell her to come and get it herself,' Charlie said. 'I've got enough to carry with my own bag and my journalistic tools.'

By the time I could think of a response Charlie was already on the ropes, pulling herself over with more skill than I could ever manage. She arrived on our side of the Step within a few minutes, not even out of breath.

'You can go over for your rucksack now, Christine' she said cruelly. 'We'll wait for you.'

'No,' Christine shook her head, staring at the twin ropes. 'No, I can't.'

'I'll go for them,' I said. 'My bag's there too.'

I eased myself back across that fragile bridge with the drop inviting me to let go and the eagles circling, calling harshly. I was shaking when I reached the far side and picked up Christine's bag. It was heavier than I had expected as I buckled it on my back, took a deep breath and crouched down for the return.

The eagles watched me, and I thought of the two witches. *What if..? No, that was arrant nonsense.* I pulled myself over the Step, feeling the cold sweat of fear forming on my forehead and dampening my back. After this trip, I told myself, I would limit my adventures to the Pentland Hills, the low range just outside Edinburgh, or even the Botanical Garden inside the city. Breathing harshly, I arrived safely, with Christine's outstretched arms waiting for me, and Charlie busy with her notebook.

'There you go,' I passed the bag over to Christine. 'No wonder you're tired lugging that around. What's in it? Lead weights?'

'Books and papers,' Christine said. 'It's something I've been working on. I'll tell you later.'

'Aye, not just now,' I said. 'I'll fetch my bag across.'

'I'm faster than you,' Lorna put her hand on my shoulder, 'and we have a bit to go yet. Wait here.'

I did not argue. Lorna was far more skilled than I was in the hills and I had no desire for another trip across the ropes. I hardly watched as Lorna swarmed across, her hands and feet moving in unison and the lines swinging gently beneath her.

'I wish I could do that,' Christine said.

'She's good, isn't she?' Mary agreed.

I do not know from where the eagles came. They soared above Lorna as she lifted my rucksack and began the return journey. As she reached the halfway point of the rope bridge, they plunged down on her. I gasped and shouted out a warning:

'Lorna!'

The first bird raked its talons across Lorna's hands. She pulled one hand back, trying to fend the eagle off.

'Lorna!' I searched desperately for a weapon, lifted a chunk of rock and threw it. It missed by yards and plummeted uselessly into the mist far below. Mary and Christine joined me in lifting loose pieces of rock and hurling them at the birds.

'Be careful you don't hit Lorna,' Charlie put away her notebook and came to help.

The second bird came from Lorna's other side, diving to peck with its enormous curved beak. I saw Lorna writhe at the sudden pain as the eagle's beak tore into the back of her leg.

'Get away!' We were screaming at the eagles, throwing stones and rocks without any effect, watching as they circled Lorna, dived and clawed at her. Lorna struggled on, desperate to reach the end of that fragile rope bridge. Keeping her head down, she tried to fend off the birds with one hand.

'Keep coming!' I lifted a large, jagged rock. 'Come on Lorna!'

I threw the rock, saw it miss by at least a foot and then the birds soared upwards, so high that they were almost out of sight in the rain-sodden sky.

'Come on Lorna.' I took hold of her arm and helped her back onto the ridge. Bleeding from deep cuts to her hands and leg, Lorna handed over my rucksack and stood there, shaking.

'What was that for? What was that for? I've never known eagles to act like that before.'

'We must be near their nest,' Mary said. 'I can't think of any other reason. Thank goodness they've gone. Let's get off this saddle and out of this place.'

We moved off, quicker than before and with Mary frantically humming *Kisimuil's Galley*. I heard the whirr of wings and looked up to see the eagles attack again. Lorna ducked, but this time the eagles struck Mary. She turned to face them, threw a round-house punch, overbalanced and staggered on the edge of the ridge.

Dumping my rucksack, I rushed forward, slipping on the loose stones. 'Mary!' I came close, saw the panic in her eyes and stretched out my hand to help. 'Take my hand, Mary!'

Mary grasped at me, missed and stumbled backwards. For one everlasting second, she stared straight into my eyes, mouthed my name once and then she fell, agonisingly slowly, back from the ridge.

'Mary!'

What had the tinker woman at the castle said? 'Be careful when you are safe from the big step.' Mary had survived the Witch's Step only to fall when she thought herself safe.

Her scream lasted far longer than I expected, a long drawn out howl as she spiralled through the air and vanished into the mist. It seemed an age before we heard the terrible crunch as she hit the rocks far beneath and then, horribly, her screaming redoubled.

'Oh, dear God in heaven,' Lorna said. 'What do we do now?'

'We can't just leave her there,' I stared uselessly into the mist. 'She must be in terrible agony.'

'We have to go down to her,' Lorna said. 'It's the only proper thing to do.'

'And then what?' Charlie answered her own question. 'You were a nurse, Lorna, you can help her.'

'I was an ambulance driver,' Lorna said. 'I know some basic nursing. No more.'

I continued to look down into the mist. We had never seen the bottom of the chasm. This hill was well named as the mountain of the mist, for the covering seemed permanent. 'Is there a way down there?'

'Nobody has ever tried, as far as I am aware,' Lorna said.

'We can't climb down from here, these sides are like glass,' I pointed to the vertical slopes in case Lorna could not see them. 'It might be easier from Bein a Ghlo.'

Mary's screams increased, distorted by the mist, unearthly, tearing at my heart, and ripping into my soul. I cringed.

'We must help her,' Christine grabbed my arm. 'Please Brenda. We can't leave her in pain.'

'Come on.' Lorna increased her speed until she was nearly trotting along that knife-edged ridge with the mist boiling beneath us and the eagles still circling high above. We followed, with even Christine keeping up, glancing down into the abyss.

'Hold on, Mary, we're coming as fast as we can,' Lorna shouted. 'Please hold on.'

Beinn a' Ghlo was no friendlier than the saddle had been. The hill flanks were granite, weeping with moisture and seared with foaming burns.

'How do we get down there?' I looked to Lorna as the most experienced of us.

'We can't,' Charlie said. 'It's impossible.'

'We have to,' Christine said to me. 'We can't leave her.'

'Rope together,' Lorna made a quick decision. 'We're going to get wet.'

'What?' Charlie stared at her.

'We're going down one of the burn channels.' Lorna said. 'You can stay here if you like, Charlie but I'm going down.'

'I'm coming too,' Christine said. She was white-faced and shaking, yet her jaw was set.

'So am I,' I said, although I was terrified by even the sound of the burn as it roared down in a series of cascades, leaping from dark pool to dark pool into the unseen depths.

'You're a fool!' Charlie said. 'You can't help her even if you do get down.'

'I'd rather be a fool than a woman without a heart,' I said.

'Stay then, Charlie,' Lorna said. 'Run ahead to the inn and get help.' Without another word, Lorna looped the rope around her waist and passed it to me. I followed suit with my heart hammering and Mary's mixed screams and whimpers in my ears.

'Are you sure you want to come?' Lorna asked Christine, who nodded.

'Yes.' Christine's voice was small.

'Good girl.' Lorna nodded. 'On we go then.'

Lorna began the descent, slithering on loose rocks as she clambered to the edge of the burn with us only yards behind. Down in the gulley, the thunder of the burn dominated so we had to shout to be heard. The water was milk-white as it cascaded down, with the occasional peaty brown pool of unknown depth in which strangely-shaped rocks lingered amidst trailing green weed. I remembered stories of water-bulls and other aquatic horrors, pushed them from my mind and concentrated on the matter at hand. The only consolation was that the bellow of the burn drowned the sounds of Mary's agony.

After only a hundred yards or so, the burn cascaded into a waterfall, hurtling down in a silver-white thread to a pool fifty feet below. Without hesitation, Lorna hammered a piton into a crack between two water-rounded boulders, tied her rope and climbed down, facing the fall and with her back to the drop.

'Are you all right, Christine?' I yelled into her ear.

Christine nodded, courageous girl that she was, and I waited until Lorna was safe beside the pool before I trusted myself to the rope.

'Follow me down!' I shouted.

The rock was slippery wet and the waterfall deafening as I descended. Ignoring the chill of the water, I felt my way, step by step, biting my lip to conceal my fear. I had never done anything like this before and wondered if Lorna had.

'Got you,' Lorna's hands were firm on my waist. 'Is Christine coming?'

'She is.'

'We'll wait then. It might have been better if she had gone with Charlie!'

'No!' I shook my head. 'Charlie would not look after her.'

We watched Christine negotiate the waterfall, moving slowly and clumsily. My heart leapt when she slipped, recovered and splashed at our side, breathing heavily.

'Well done!' Lorna shouted.

We looked downward at the mist. If anything it seemed even thicker from here, grey-white and clammy, an opaque mattress of unknown depth between us and the ground.

'Come on,' Lorna said. 'We'll leave the rope for our return.'

I did not ask how we were going to carry Mary back up. My only thought was to get down to the valley floor and ease her pain, somehow.

For the next hundred feet or so we only had to scramble down the narrow bed of the burn. Over uncountable aeons the burn had carved its passage through the gulley, grinding down the granite with a constant torrent that left rounded, green-slimed boulders along the base and sides as smooth as glass. We moved as quickly as the conditions permitted, sliding from rock to water-slimed rock, now ankle deep in bitter water, now plunging up to our waists but always moving downward.

In one place the burn split into two, divided by an outcrop of rock on which grew a pair of birch trees. Below, the water foamed in twin falls, each a maelstrom of fury. Lorna led us to the right side, gripping on tiny ledges and half-seen handholds as we plunged onward.

'We're entering the mist!' Lorna shouted.

I gripped Christine's arm. 'Are you all right?'

Christine nodded quickly, forcing a brave smile. Her breathing came in short, ragged gasps.

So dense it muffled sounds, the mist engulfed us. We held hands where we could and tugged on the rope when we separated.

'This is a nightmare,' I shouted.

'We'll get there,' Lorna assured me. 'How are you holding out, Christine?'

'I'm fine,' Christine mouthed.

A hundred feet into the mist, the burn vanished. We stood on a shelf of rock, watching the water thunder into a black hole and disappear.

'What now?' I yelled.

'Now we climb,' Lorna pointed to the slope beside the shelf. 'We have to get out of the gulley and then head down to the bottom of the valley or whatever is in this muck.' She indicated the mist, which seemed thick enough to cut into chunks and use to build houses.

The first fifty feet were vertical but blessed with a plethora of handholds. After that, it was only a steep slope, and we were out of the gulley and above the valley floor. 'Do you want to stay here, Christine? We'll pick you up on our return.'

Christine shook her head. 'I'm coming with you.'

I agreed with her. I would not wish to remain on that desolate spot, a bare, rain swept shelf on a misty hillside in the middle of nowhere. If there is a Hell, then I could not think of a better place for it.

'Come on then.' Lorna accepted Christine's decision. She moved on, expecting us to follow. We did.

Our next obstacle was a sheer drop of some thirty feet down to a scree slope. I looked and shrugged. After what we had been through, it was simplicity itself. Securing her penultimate rope around a prominent knob of rock, Lorna dropped it down the vertical incline. It hung there, moving slightly in the wind.

'I'll go first,' Lorna backed over the edge of the ledge and walked herself downwards. 'It's easy' she said. 'You next, Christine. Take it easy now.'

Christine took a deep breath and followed. Her eyes held mine for the first few feet and then she concentrated on the descent. Lorna caught her as she reached the bottom. I was last and sighed with relief when I hit the ground.

I stopped smiling when Mary screamed again, long and low.

'Come on ladies,' Lorna said.

The slope was bare in front of us, speckled with erratic rocks and unutterably bleak, with the mist swirling around, creating strange shapes and unusual patterns. We scrambled down, gasping, scraping knees and shins off rocks, twisting ankles as our feet gave way beneath us and occasionally swearing.

'Look up,' Lorna said.

The mist spread horizontally above us, a lowering grey sky that shifted and altered shape, sending down serpentine tendrils to sweep across the rough ground.

'We are separated from the world,' I said.

'Where's Mary?' Lorna scanned the ground. The screaming had stopped. Now there was only a long bleating whine that set my hair on end.

'That way,' I had never known Christine as decisive as she set off at a fast walking pace.

I had thought we would find ourselves in a narrow glen. I was wrong. We were in a corrie, a tremendous spoon-shaped ice-gouged hollow between the two mountains, with a succession of lochans and ragged boulder-strewn depressions. Above us, the grey-white blanket of mist created a sense of confining unreality, as if we were walking through a constricting outdoors room. I felt as if we were the first women on the moon, the first humans to enter this mysterious place.

'There she is,' Lorna hurried forward, sliding on the greasy surface. We followed, our boots splashing on the sodden ground and our packs thumping against our backs.

Grey-pink brains seeped through the shards of Mary's skull as she lay on her face with her head pulped against a rock. Blood had formed a pool around her, her legs were splayed at a horrible angle, and one arm was bent beneath her body.

'She's dead,' Lorna said at once. 'The fall would have killed her.'

'No,' Christine shook her head. 'That can't be right. She's still alive. We heard her screaming. I know we did.'

'I can still hear her,' I said as the long, eerie bleating wail sounded again. I thought of the *caoineag. Was it that I could hear?*

Christine saw the snipe rise from its rocky bed, its eerie call echoing around us.

'The *gabhar adhaire*,' I do not know from where my words came. 'That's the Gaelic name for the snipe. It means air goat because of the noise it makes. The mist must have distorted the snipe's call into the screams we heard.' I looked around at the desolation. 'We have wasted hours for nothing.'

Lorna was kneeling beside Mary, checking without hope for any signs of life. 'It was not for nothing, Brenda. We found Mary. At least she's not in pain.'

'No,' I said. 'Mary's not in pain.' I saw them come for her, the long column of men, women and children drifting over the bleak landscape, old men and young women, young men and old women, all silent. They formed around Mary, lifted her body and eased away toward Penrioch. Mary Ablach's kin had come to take her home. The circle was complete, and she was where she belonged.

'We can't carry her,' Lorna rose from Mary's body. 'And we can't bury her in this thin soil. We'll build a cairn around her as we did with Kate.'

'Yes,' I shook away my vision. Something on this peninsula was affecting my mind. I had not seen these people carry Mary away. I had imagined it.

'I liked Mary,' Christine said. 'Is there nothing you can do, Lorna?'

'No,' Lorna closed Mary's eyes. 'We can only bury her; it's the proper thing to do.' She looked around. 'I would prefer we left her elsewhere, though. This is a bad place.'

'Have you ever read Conan Doyle's *Lost World*, Brenda?' Christine asked.

I shook my head. This was not the time to discuss literature.

'It's about a plateau in South America cut off from the world. This place is like that. Cut off by the hills and the mist. There are no dinosaurs here though.'

I could not respond to that. I knew there were other things here, things I could not explain.

'No,' Lorna spoke quietly. 'There are no dinosaurs here.'

'I hope Charlie's all right.' Christine said.

We laid Mary in a slight hollow and built a cairn around her from the plentiful supply of rocks. That was the third burial cairn we had raised in three days, which was three cairns too many. I cannot say how I felt. Numb, if anything, as if I were watching somebody else's life. There were some scrubby trees nearby, wind-tortured and stunted. Lorna fashioned a cross, and we placed it at her head.

'If she had held on to her rowan cross and her blue crystal she might still be alive,' I said. Nobody contradicted me. In this strange place, we all jumped at shadows.

'I don't want to leave her alone,' Christine said.

I thought of the image I had seen. 'Mary's not alone,' I said. 'She is with her ancestors.' I could only shrug when Lorna threw me an odd look.

'Now we have to get out of here,' Lorna said, 'without losing anybody else. I wish we had all stayed together. I wish Charlie had remained with us.'

'So do I.' Although I did not like Charlie, I did not wish any harm to befall her. The thought of her wandering around this peninsula alone was quite alarming.

'It will be dark soon,' Christine said.

'It's quite a climb to get back to Bein a Ghlo.' Lorna looked upward. 'Do we chance it in the dark?'

'Yes,' I said. 'We're running out of food, we've had two deaths, and we've had enough of this place. It's time to get back to civilisation.'

'Yes,' I was surprised that Christine agreed. 'I can't stay here,' she said. 'It's too horrible.'

'Very well then,' Lorna said. 'Keep together.' Although she was calm and had seen death a thousand times at the Front, I could see that she was shaken.

'Are you all right?' I asked.

Lorna nodded. 'It's different,' she guessed my thoughts. 'One expects death in war. One is prepared for it, even though it can be utterly hideous. One has a framework in which to work and a team to help and support. I did not expect anything like that here.'

Of us all, it was now Christine who seemed the most composed. 'That's seven deaths in this peninsula' she said. 'There were the two men on the beach, the Mahoney expedition, Kate and now Mary.'

I nodded. 'We'd better take great care that there are no more.' How many shrouds had the washerwoman worked on at the ford? Five. Would the shrouds only refer to members of our expedition or everybody who was out here? I did not know. Mary would have known.

If I discounted the Mahoney expedition, there had been four deaths so far, the two men and two of us. One shroud remained. Would there be another death?

'I hated her, you know,' Christine said.

I had guessed that.

'Who did you hate?' Lorna asked.

'Kate.' Christine said. 'I used to dream about killing her in all sorts of different ways.'

Lorna hesitated before asking the inevitable question. 'Did you kill her, Christine?'

'No.' Christine replied at once. 'I'm glad she's dead, though.'

I did not have to speak, knowing that Christine wished to unburden herself.

'When we are a school, Kate used to bully me all the time. She made me into her slave.' Christine said. 'When other people were around she was as nice as could be, pretending to help me with my homework and that sort of thing.'

Lorna was also quiet as Christine recounted old memories. We stumbled through the gathering dark with the spirit of Mary accompanying us. I heard that weird call again. Was that the snipe, or was it Mary's soul departing from her body, hoping to rise to heaven but trapped by the malignancy of this hidden corrie in the Rough Bounds. Faint in the mist I heard music, a familiar voice singing *Mairi's Wedding,* then *Kisimuil's Galley.*

'When we left school Kate found me a job as her secretary. I desperately wanted away but it was a position, and there was no alternative. One must eat.' Christine looked at me as if pleading for understanding. I understood. Some people have that sort of power over others; a dominant personality will control the lives of those around her.

'There are few jobs at present,' I encouraged. I could not blame Christine for her predicament. She could not help her personality any more than I could help mine. We are as Mother Nature made us.

'Everybody needs somebody,' Christine seemed to tap into the core of my loneliness. 'And everybody needs to eat.'

I understood Christine. While the others had a need to push forward on some personal crusade, Christine possessed a much quieter character. I smiled at her. 'You're all right, Chrissie,' I said.

'Please don't call me that.' Christine's voice was urgent. 'Kate called me that. I hated it.'

'I won't use that name again,' I promised.

We splashed across the floor of that corrie to the foot of the slope and looked up for the burn, hidden in the evening dim. It sounded sinister with its constant roar, like some beast hunting for prey.

'Look,' Christine's night vision was superior to mine as she pointed to a gleam of white thirty yards away. 'The burn is coming out of a cave up there. It may be easier to get up that way than that bare slope with the cliff wall.'

'Good thinking, Christine.' Like me, Lorna was surprised that Christine ventured an opinion.

We stared up at the hillside. In the gathering gloom, it looked more ominous than ever, with each rock a potential hazard and each dark shape transmogrified into a threat, real or imagined. The burn rushed from the cave entrance, boiling and eddying around countless water-slicked boulders on its mad rush into the corrie.

'I don't think we should try the climb in the night,' Lorna made the decision that we were all thinking.

'We might be able to shelter in the cave.' I said. 'As long as it's relatively dry.' I did not fancy sitting in a slimy wet hole in the ground.

'My candles are in the rucksack if anybody can be bothered finding them.' Lorna said.

None of us could. We were too tired so groped our way from the gloom of the corrie into the darkness of the cave and hoped for relief. The entrance closed around us.

'It's dry in here,' Christine's voice echoed from the rock. 'And the ground is fairly level.'

'There is shelter from the wind and rain as well.' Lorna said. 'I am surprised. Maybe things are going to turn our way for a change. We'll stay here overnight and be off at the first crack of dawn.'

Once again we were destined for another night on this peninsula, and this time with two of our party to mourn. We ventured sufficiently far into the cave to escape the weather and huddled down in a corner, with the sound of the burn our constant companion.

'Did Mary have any relations? A husband? Parents?' Lorna was first to mention Mary's loss.

'She had a mother,' I said. 'Somewhere in Edinburgh, I believe.'

'I'll find out,' Lorna said. 'I'll break the news to them; it's the proper thing to do.' She lowered her voice. 'I've done that sort of thing often enough in the past.'

'Kate had parents,' Christine said. 'Lord and Lady Gordon of Carnbrora. Since Adam died, she was the heir to everything.'

'That will be a loss,' Lorna said.

'Only to the Gordons,' Christine said.

'It's strange that both Mary and Kate had an ancestral history here.' I shook my head. 'What a terrible trip this has been. I'll be glad to get away from here.'

'We all will,' Lorna said.

'How are your cuts, Lorna?' I asked. 'I've never seen an eagle act like that before.'

Lorna rubbed at her leg. 'I'll live,' she said. 'It'll be stiff in the morning, but I'll live.' She shook her head. 'It's been a terrible day. Let's hope that tomorrow is better. If you have any food left, eat a little and save a bit for breakfast. Good night now.' She lay down and was sleeping within a minute.

'Brenda,' Christine whispered. 'I must talk to you.'

'I'm listening,' I cleared a space on the ground to lie down. Suddenly I felt exhausted as the endeavours and tragedies of the day hit home. 'Best let it keep until tomorrow, Christine. I must sleep now.'

'There's something I must tell you,' Christine said. 'It's important.'

I heard her voice as if from a long distance away as sleep crept over me. 'It'll have to wait, Christine.'

Chapter Twelve

I did not know where I was when I awoke from a troubled sleep. Grey light filtered through the entrance of the cave, creeping over the sleeping bodies of Lorna and Christine. I lay still, watching the light play on Christine's face, highlighting her cheekbones and her snub nose. I loved the way her hair masked her eyes. I smiled until I remembered the deaths of Kate and Mary.

The snipe was active again, its call eerily echoing around the cave. I sat up and felt for what was left of the food I had brought, thanking Kate for forcing the inn to provide a decent packed lunch. Stale marmalade sandwiches were a lot better than nothing, while there was plenty of fresh water in the burn. I knelt and cupped the flowing water in both hands. It was cold and clear and tasted of sand.

'Are you awake?' Christine had followed me to the burn. She crouched at my side.

'Just about. How are you feeling?'

Christine knelt on all fours to lap at the water like a dog. 'I'm fine,' she looked up. 'How are you?'

'I mean how do you feel about Kate and Mary?' I said.

'I'll miss Mary,' Christine said.

'You knew Kate a lot longer than you knew Mary,' I tried to find out more about their symbiotic relationship.

'I was scared of Kate,' Christine said. 'I told you that I wanted to kill her. When I was at school, planning her death was the only thing that kept me from running away or killing myself.' Her smile was so innocent that it did not belong to the words.

'I see.' I drank more water. 'Did you feel the same way after you left school?'

'Not much different,' Christine said. 'I needed her for the employment, and she needed me as somebody to bully and prove how powerful she was.' Christine smiled. 'Not any more.'

Something was chilling about the way Christine accepted Kate's death with such equanimity. 'I see.'

'Anyway,' Christine glanced over to ensure that Lorna was still asleep. 'I want to talk to you about something completely different.'

'What is it?' I asked.

'It's about you,' Christine said, 'and who you are.'

'I am Brenda Smith,' I gave my automatic response.

'No,' Christine shook her head. 'Not that name. I mean who you really are.'

I stood up. I knew nothing about my early life. I grew up in an orphanage in Perth, and then with a family who told me all they knew. The orphanage gave me the name of Smith and had used it ever since. 'Nobody knows who I really am.'

'I do.' Christine said.

Suspicion quickly replaced my initial interest. 'How can you know?'

'You know that I worked for Kate,' Christine said. 'And Kate helped her parents run her estates.'

'I only know what you have told me,' I said.

'Kate's parents don't just own an estate up here in Sutherland; they also own land in Perthshire.' Christine told me. 'They finance and run orphanages in Aberfoyle and Perth.' She gave a quick, nervous smile. 'Despite what Mary thinks- sorry, thought – the Gordons are not the devils incarnate. They give a lot back to the local communities.'

I gave an impatient nod. 'Yes, good, please carry on.'

'I had access to all the records,' Christine said. 'I knew you were an orphan from Perthshire, so I looked you up.' She smiled across to me. 'I always liked you, Brenda, ever since you joined the climbing club.'

'Thank you.' I was not sure what else I should say.

'At first, I could not find you,' Christine said. 'I was looking for Brenda Smith, you see.'

I stepped back, suddenly interested. All my life I had wondered who I was, now this strange young woman seemed to know more about me than I did myself. 'Carry on.'

The sound of the burn seemed to diminish as if it also wished to hear my life history. Sufficient light filtered through the cave entrance to illuminate Christine's face, with her delicate features and eager hazel eyes.

'There was a new-born baby left at the door of the orphanage at Aberfoyle on the morning of 1st November 1895.' Christine put a hand on my arm. 'There was no name or anything with the child, so they named it Brenda, after the woman who found her and Smith because that was a common name.'

I nodded. 'That much I knew.'

Christine smiled. 'Did you know that there was a woman taken into the infirmary in Dundee the same day who had recently given birth? She denied it, and the police charged her with concealment of pregnancy. That was in the *Dundee Courier*.'

'I did not know that,' I said. 'Is that related?'

'Yes.' Christine said. 'She came from Achnashee farm, a mile or two from Aberfoyle.'

'Oh?' My heart gave a little leap. *Was that my mother?*

'Yes. Achnashee is Gaelic for the sacred field or something like that. Fairy field perhaps.' Christine smiled coyly. 'Do you want to know the woman's name?'

'I would like that,' I tried to control my nervousness. *Would I find out the name of my mother?*

'Roberta Kirk,' Christine said.

'Roberta Kirk.' I ran the name through my head. 'Roberta is an unusual name. I suspect her parents wished for a boy and had already picked out the name Robert.' I could suddenly hear everything very clearly, from the rush of the burn to an unknown bird whistling outside. 'Do you think Roberta Kirk was my mother?'

'Yes,' Christine said. 'I am almost certain. She was from the same place and had given birth to a baby at the same time.'

'But why abandon me?' I asked.

'The shame of being an unmarried mother in a rural community,' Christine said simply. 'How could she live with that?' Suddenly she was not the innocent young girl but a very perceptive and understanding young woman with bright, intelligent eyes and a gentle smile on her lips.

I had to sit down. 'Thank you, Christine. I'll have to think about all that.' A shaft of dawn sun eased into the cave and glossed the surface of the burn. I lowered my voice to little more than a whisper. 'I want to meet my mother, wherever she is. I have to tell her that… ' I did not know what I had to tell her. I only wanted to see her, to look into her eyes. I wanted to *matter* to somebody.

'She died in the infirmary,' Christine said. 'I'm sorry Brenda.' Reaching over, she touched my arm. 'I'm sorry to raise your hopes like that.'

'I might have relatives elsewhere,' I said. I was used to masking my disappointments and rejections. My hurt would return later when I was alone.

'Does the name not mean anything to you?' Christine asked.

'Roberta Kirk? No,' I shook my head. 'I've never heard it before.'

'Well,' Christine leaned closer to me. 'You must hear this…'

'What are you two talking about?' Lorna's voice boomed through the cave. 'Come on, let's get some breakfast and get on our way. I want to get back to the inn today and away from this terrible place.'

Lorna's words brought back to me the reality of our situation with two members of our party dead and the male climbers' deaths to report as well. My past would have to wait for the future. The present took precedence. 'Thank you, Christine,' I wanted to hug her. 'We'll have to talk about this later.'

Lorna hurriedly finished off the last of her sandwiches, and we got ourselves ready to journey on, although my mind was buzzing with speculation about who I might be. Brenda *Kirk*? I quite liked that name.

'This cave slopes upward,' Christine's confidence seemed to be growing by the minute. All she had needed was somebody to take her seriously. I listened to her with some pride, like an elder sister. 'I'm sure this is the same burn that we followed coming down so hopefully we can follow it and save ourselves that first climb.'

Lorna looked at me with her eyebrows raised. She had also noted the change in Christine. 'I think this woman is talking sense, Brenda. It seems the only proper thing to do. Do you agree?'

'With all my heart,' I said and saw Christine flush with pleasure.

The first part of the slope was gentle but we had to duck our heads as the cave narrowed in size.

'It's lucky you're only a little 'un,' Lorna said, and Christine laughed. We had not forgotten the deaths of Kate and Mary, but there was no point in dwelling on such things. We had to keep our spirits up.

As the roof lowered, so the space between the cave wall and the burn diminished, forcing us to walk in single file and then to creep upwards along a narrow ledge, nearly scraping our heads on the roof and with the burn foaming on our left.

'If it gets any more constricting,' Lorna shouted against the roaring water, 'we'll either have to walk up the burn or return to the corrie outside. We'll have to decide soon.'

I nodded, and at that moment the cave levelled out into what appeared to be a large cavern. The noise immediately decreased, and we fumbled in the sudden space.

'Wait,' Lorna said. 'Now we need a light. Look in my rucksack, Christine.'

It only took Christine a minute to unearth a box of matches and the stub of a candle. She scraped a flame, applied it to the wick of the candle and when the flame increased we almost immediately we wished she had left us in the dark.

The skull sat on top of a pillar or rock, its mouth gaping open and its eyes staring at us. While I recoiled in horror, Christine gasped and dropped the candle. It rolled around the ground, casting alternate light and shadow before the flame died entirely and left us in the dark.

'What was that?' I asked foolishly.

'It was a skull,' Lorna said. 'Find the candle, and get it back on.'

We scrabbled on the dusty floor of the cave until Christine lifted the candle and scraped a match. Wavering light pooled around the cavern, as we clustered together for comfort.

The skull seemed to stare at us, its mouth wide in a soundless scream.

'I wonder what happened here.' Lorna was first to recover her nerve.

'I've read about massacres in caves,' Christine approached the skull and held her candle beside it. 'Some clan would raid another, who would hide in a cave and the first lot would smoke them to death.'

'Oh, how romantic,' Lorna said. 'Walter Scott never mentioned anything like that in his books.'

The light reflected from the white bone, posing a mystery to which we would never know the full answer. 'I don't think this was a clan massacre,' I said as the image appeared before me.

A group of men and women in simple clothing carried a dead body into the cave. Singing a low song, they laid the body on the ground and slowly, reverently, cut off the head and the limbs. Blood seeped onto the ground and dripped into the burn as a woman lifted the disembodied head and placed it on the pillar of rock. The others gathered around, still singing.

'I think this was a much older evil.' I said.

I remembered the drowning at the pool. Now there was a skull preserved in this cave. What was the connection? Water. There was water at the pool, and there was water in the burn. Had this been a sacrifice to a water god?

Water was the source of life. Water flowed through and over the flanks of An Cailleach. Water was her blood. Water formed the basis of the veil of mist she wore to hide her face from the presumptuous scrutiny of men.

'There are others,' Christine held her candle high, revealing more skulls set in niches on the face of the cave and on columns of rock. They returned our stares through empty eye sockets, skull after skull that decorated the walls of the entire cavern.

'How many are there?' Christine stepped closer to me. I could feel the warmth of her body.

'Hundreds,' I said. I do not know where I got that information. 'A skull for each sacrifice and a sacrifice to the water each year.'

'What is this place?' Lorna chose to ignore my speculations.

'It is a temple, a holy place to store the venerated dead.' I could feel the sanctity, like the holy island of Iona or the ruins of the Border Abbeys. 'You'll have seen much worse in the war.'

'Much,' Lorna said. 'These poor people are beyond suffering now.'

'Unless their souls are still in torment,' I said. 'I wonder who they were, and why they were selected to be sacrificed.'

'These are the unwanted.' The woman stood in the darkest recess of the cavern, beyond the yellow glow of the candle. Her voice was low and clear, and I knew that nobody saw her except for me. 'These were the orphans and the unclaimed, the children of broken marriages, the scions of dead mothers, the prisoners of war and the unknown. They were honoured to be chosen for it gave purpose to their existence.'

'I was unwanted,' I said. 'I am not known,' I said. 'Nobody knows who I am. I don't know who I am.' I saw myself in the position of these sacrificed women. I saw myself becoming central to the existence of these people who lived on the flanks of An Cailleach. Was that why I had come? Had the hill called me across the breadth of Scotland to sacrifice me?

The woman stepped closer to me with darkness shielding her face and only her eyes clear and bright and intense.

'Find out, Brenda. Find out who you are. Will you find yourself upside down in the drowning pool and your head thrust on a spike to watch the water for all eternity? Or is there some other reason for your birth?'

'How do I find out?' I asked.

'Ask the right people the right questions,' the woman said.

I stretched my hand out to her. 'Help me,' I said.

I spoke to nobody but shadows. The woman was gone as quickly as silently as she had appeared, leaving me in that cave of the dead with the burn rumbling and gushing on one side and the grinning skulls on the other. I could feel the souls of the dead pleading for a release I could not grant them. Suddenly I saw another head in that cavern. Kate's face sat there, accusing me with forceful eyes. Beside her lay an empty niche, awaiting a tenant. A man stepped forward, benign-eyed as he strove to save me from that fate. I had seen him before at the inn. I knew that man without having ever spoken to him.

Other forces rose, whispering voices in my mind and fat fingers clutching at me. I knew they were the priests of that long-dormant order. They wanted me in the drowning pool. They wanted to sacrifice me to the blood-water of An Cailleach, so my skull would be here forever. A tall female threw back her hood and reached for me, with cold water dripping from her fingers.

'No!' I denied out loud and cracked my stick on the hard ground.

'No what?' Lorna was looking at me in surprise. 'What's the matter, Brenda? These skulls don't bite. They're long past hurting anybody.'

'Oh,' I looked at Christine's suddenly knowing eyes. 'Oh, no, I'm not scared of the skulls,' I said. 'I just wish we would get out of here. I'm not looking forward to telling people about Kate and Mary.'

'Nor am I,' Lorna said 'Come on then.'

That strange woman was still watching me. I tried to shake off her image. I knew that this peninsula affected us all in different ways, enhancing some aspect of our personality. Lorna was more prone to bad memories of her wartime experiences, Mary had become bitterer about her ancestor's fate, Kate's bullying predominated, and Christine was more hesitant while Charlie delved more into her role as a suffragette and journalist. I had wondered how the peninsula or the spirits in it, would affect me.

Now I knew. The peninsula attacked my insecurities of self. An Cailleach sensed that ignorance of my birth weakened me. It attacked that vulnerability through impossible fears. I straightened my shoulders. Well, I was a full-grown woman now, not some little child clinging to her doll in the darkness of the orphanage, crying for the mother she had never known.

'I am no child to be scared of shadows,' I said out loud. 'Let the past remain in the past.'

'Over here,' Christine's voice was low and clear as she tapped her stick on the ground.

More bones, femurs and scapulas, clavicles and sternums, ribs, radius and humerus, an eclectic collection of the discarded. Lorna picked her way through them, identifying each one. 'These must belong to the skulls,' she said. 'Oh, dear God, what's this?'

It was a tiny skeleton, complete in every detail except the head.

'A child,' Lorna said. 'They've killed a child.'

'More than one,' Christine said. 'Look over here.'

In an offshoot of the cavern, a score of niches lines the wall. A tiny skeleton sat in each niche, headless and forlorn. I could feel the pain of these children, unwanted by the world, abandoned to the cruel religion that demanded a sacrifice so that An Cailleach could live. What kind of people were we, to hold human life so cheap?

Charlie would say that it was all the fault of men, while women would be gentler, more sensible and kinder. Thinking back to what I knew of history, I doubted that. Neither Catherine the Great of Russia nor Queen Elizabeth of England had been renowned for their gentleness, while Bloody Mary had been as big a monster as ever lived. I thought of the women who marched on Paris and who watched the heads roll during the French Revolution. No, I thought, we are no more the gentler sex than we are an inferior gender to the male. If women were in charge, the world would roll on much as before.

In the last century, hundreds if not thousands of women had murdered their unwanted children. I had been fortunate to avoid that fate; my mother had compassion for her bastard if that was what I was, and the landowner, Kate's parents, had funded an orphanage. We were all bound together, each entity a single strand in a complex rope woven with history, family, tradition and money. I was part of a story whose final chapter was yet to be written.

Turn the page, Brenda, uncoil the rope and see what An Cailleach wants with you.

'What now?' I had been walking instinctively as my mind wandered. I came back to reality with a start. We were at the foot of an underground waterfall, with Christine's candle casting flickering light over the milky-white water that thundered past us. I could not see the top of the fall.

'Do we go up there?' Lorna pointed to the near vertical incline beside the fall, 'or do we go back?'

'What would Kate do?' Christine asked.

'She would go on,' I said, 'up the *Easan gruamach* – the gloomy waterfalls.'

'From where did you get that name?' Lorna asked.

I shrugged. 'I must have read it somewhere.' I knew that was not true. I had never read that name. Even if I had, I doubted if I would have remembered the pronunciation and the translation.

'The climb does not look too bad,' Lorna accepted my explanation. 'Shall we rope ourselves together?'

'Yes, please,' Christine said. 'We're safer united.'

We tied ourselves with our penultimate length of rope and began the climb. As Lorna had said, it did not look too bad, a dark wall streaming with water but provided with a myriad hand and footholds.

Climbing in a cave is like no other kind of climbing. One moves in the dark, with rock all around rather than clear air. There may be insects but no birds, often one is damp and cold, and always one is uncomfortable. That climb was no different as we ascended the wall beside the artery of An Cailleach, with my thoughts racing and little Christina clambering like a champion a few feet above my head.

We felt the cold first and then realised the dark was fading around us. The passageway around the burn narrowed, and then we emerged onto the same slope we had descended the previous evening, with the mist beneath us and ominous black clouds gathering above Bein a Ghlo. I took a deep breath of the chill air, glad to be free of the confines of the cave.

'Well, Christine,' Lorna said. 'You were correct, that cave was an easier route. I didn't like the old skulls though.'

Christine shook her head. 'They were scary,' she said.

'Now let's push on and get home,' I stamped my feet. 'I don't want any more tragedy.'

'Look over there,' Christine pointed with her stick. 'Somebody is running on the hillside.'

'That's Charlie,' Lorna said at once. 'Why is she running in this direction?'

I felt an immediate slide of disappointment. I had hoped that Charlie was safe back at the inn and had sent a party over to collect the bodies of Kate and Mary.

'Charlie! Charlie!' Lorna waved her stick with her voice carrying over the hillside to where Charlie ran.

Charlie started and turned toward us. She was bare-headed and without rucksack or stick. She lifted a hand, staggering.

'Something's wrong,' Christine said.

We hurried on, chancing a twisted ankle or worse on the treacherous ground where rocks could slip underfoot, and heather frequently hid deep holes.

'Charlie!' Lorna caught her as she stumbled. 'Where are you going?'

'Is it really you?' Charlie's face was smeared with mud, tear-stained and swollen with insect bites. 'Oh, please God tell me that it's you.'

'It's us,' Lorna held Charlie by the shoulders. 'It's all right; it's us.'

'Did you see them?' Charlie spoke rapidly. 'Did you see them? They're coming after me.'

'We didn't see anybody,' I looked around the bleak hillside, wondering what further horrors An Cailleach could throw at us.

Charlie, tough, aggressive Charlie, began to sob. 'Oh, don't let them get me, please don't let them get me.'

'Nobody will get you,' Lorna promised. 'You're safe with us. We won't let any harm befall you.'

'Who was it?' Christine asked. 'Who is trying to get you?'

'The men,' Charlie said. 'The men are chasing me.' She clung to Lorna as if to a saviour.

I gripped my staff and searched the hillside. A fluctuating wind stirred the heather, making bushes move to look like people. A trio of deer trotted past, unheeding. I did not see any men.

'Tell us what happened,' Lorna said. 'Take a deep breath and take your time.'

Charlie nodded. 'When I left you I hurried on. I wanted to get to the inn and send out a rescue party. But when I got to the Shelter Stone the men were waiting for me.'

'We haven't seen any men,' Lorna gripped her stick tightly. Remembering what she had been and what she had experienced, I doubted that any man or group of men would overawe Lorna. I felt Christine move closer to me.

'How many men?' I asked. 'What were they like?'

Charlie swallowed hard and ran a hand through her hair. 'There were three men, one a fellow with a moustache, another with freckles and the third was younger with a long face and hands covered in black hair.'

I could not have described the Mahoney expedition better myself. Or at least, I could not have defined my image of the Mahoney expedition better.

Lorna glanced at me as if warning me to keep my mouth shut. 'What happened?' She asked Charlie.

'When I got to the Shelter Stone they lunged at me,' Charlie said. 'All three of them tried to grab me. I dropped my pack and ran away with them chasing me.'

'Why did they do that?' Lorna asked. 'Did they say anything?'

'No,' Charlie shook her head. 'They didn't say anything, but I saw the naked lust in their eyes. I knew what they wanted all right and they were not going to get it from me.'

I stepped back. An Cailleach had her way of attacking us at a spot where we were most vulnerable. She had enhanced Kate's domineering streak, increased Christine's vulnerability, given Lorna nightmares about her wartime experiences and now introduced Charlie to her worst nightmare. A trio of men had attacked Charlie, the supreme suffragette.

'Did you escape?' I asked.

'I ran into the hills, and I've been hiding ever since.' Charlie looked around her, wide-eyed. 'They're still watching me. I know that they are.'

'You're safe with us,' Lorna tried to soothe away her fears. 'Nobody will bother you while we're here. We'll stay together now and head for the inn.'

'I'm not going back to the Shelter Stone,' Charlie shook her head.

Lorna glanced at me. I nodded agreement. 'We'll avoid it,' Lorna said, 'if that's all right with you, Christine?'

Unused to being consulted, Christine gabbled out. 'Yes, if you think so.'

'Let's keep moving then.'

'What about Mary?' Charlie asked. 'How is she?'

'Mary died in the fall,' Lorna said. 'It was not her we heard, it was only a bird calling.'

It was a distraction, I realised. An Cailleach had distracted us with the snipe, so our party divided, and she could attack Charlie. She was aware of our weaknesses and exploited them. An Cailleach was a devious mountain, but I was up to her tricks. I would not be fooled again.

I tapped my staff on a rock. Every day here brought its dramas; thank goodness we were heading away. Allowing Lorna to set the pace, I walked in the rear, continually turning around to see if anybody was following us. I was not sure that I believed in Charlie's three men, but on the other hand, I did not believe in the washerwoman at the ford either, or the caoineag, and I had seen them plainly enough. I thought of the eagles attacking Lorna and Mary, gripped my stick and watched for the three men.

'Come on, An Cailleach,' I murmured, 'I'm ready for you.'

The wind rustling through the heather sounded like distant laughter.

Chapter Thirteen

We stood halfway down the slope that led to Penrioch and Tigh-na-Beiste, with the bogland glittering in the weak sunshine and the bubbling call of a curlew melancholic above the constant hum of insects.

The long trek across Bein a Ghlo had calmed Charlie a little although she was still not herself. 'You won't leave me?'

'No, we won't' Lorna said. 'We'll stick together all the way home.' She nodded to the west where purple clouds bruised the sky. 'There's heavy weather coming, so we had better keep moving.'

'It's all right, Charlie.' I said. 'I'm keeping watch for any men. We'll be back at the inn around dusk.'

Charlie nodded. 'Christine,' she said. 'I'm sorry for how I acted yesterday.'

'That's all right, Charlie,' Christine accepted the apology with the magnanimity I would have expected from her. 'We're all under nervous strain here. Nobody is acting as they normally do.'

'Shake and make up,' Lorna said. 'It's the only proper thing to do.'

'You always like to do the proper thing,' Christine's hand was out in an instant, and I felt a subtle twinge of jealousy when she also gave Charlie a quick kiss on the cheek.

'That's the way,' Lorna approved. 'Now let's get going.'

We began the walk downhill with Lorna's arm around Charlie's shoulder and Christine close to me. I felt as if I had been adopted, or had replaced Kate in Charlie's affections. That kiss had rankled though, and I wondered how I could inveigle Christine into kissing me as well.

The rain began with an isolated spatter that increased to a steady downpour and then the heavens opened and a deluge hammered us, forcing us to walk with our heads down and our boots sloshing in puddles. What had been small trickles quickly turned into brown-and-white burns that foamed and roared down the hill flanks, some in deep gulleys and others over-topping the beds they had carved into the granite.

'We can't go on in this,' Charlie said.

'We must,' Lorna said, 'if we're to get over the ford before dark.'

Keeping my head down, I plodded on. I agreed with Charlie but did not wish to appear weak.

'Where's the nearest shelter?' Charlie shouted.

'Tigh na Beiste' Lorna replied. 'We'll pass over the bogland, and then we'll pass Tigh-na-Beiste.' She hardened her voice. 'We won't stop.'

Even the name made me wince. Which was worse, spending hours out here in the driving rain or sheltering in a building that had turned this expedition into a nightmare? 'I agree,' I said. 'We don't have the time to shelter. We should press on and get to the inn. I for one have had enough of this peninsula and its disasters.'

'I agree,' Christine said. 'Sorry, Charlie but I want to get out of here.'

Charlie nodded, and we pressed on, slipping and sliding down the slope toward the bog.

By now the rain had subsided into a miserable, misty drizzle that obscured our vision and seeped through every layer of clothing, so walking was uncomfortable and damp trousers chafed the inside of our thighs and other more intimate places.

'Tonight we'll sleep in warm, soft beds,' Lorna tried to cheer us all up.

'I want a bath first,' I said. 'I want to luxuriate in a long hot bath, wash my hair and smell clean again, rather than stinking of peat and dirt and sweat and other things that I refuse to mention.'

'Food,' Charlie said. 'I want real food rather than mouldy sandwiches. I want a pot of hot tea and fresh salmon or a chunk of beef and vegetables.'

'How about you, Christine? What do you want most?' Lorna asked.

'I don't know,' Christine said. 'I always let Kate decide. Without her, I don't know what I want.'

'You're your own woman,' I chided her gently. 'You choose now.'

'Oh,' Christine took off her hat and ran forked fingers through her hair. 'I want a bath and food and a soft bed.'

'When we get back home, I'll sleep for two days, Lorna said.

'I want to check on my real family,' I altered the course of the conversation. 'Christine has discovered what my real name might be. I want to see if I have any living relatives.'

I had hoped for a reaction. All I got was silence. We plodded on with our boots squelching on the ground and our feet encased in sodden stockings. I could feel blisters forming on my left heel and between the toes of my right foot. This is my last expedition, I thought. I am not putting myself through this torture again. From now on it's a sedentary life for me, sitting by my own fireside in the evening and maybe indulging in some gentle gardening at the weekend. The furthest I will venture is to the coffee shop at Jenners department store in Princes Street, and if I want the countryside, I will take a gentle walk around the Botanical Garden, or up Arthur's Seat if I wish to be daring.

I heard the mocking laughter.

'Who was that?' I asked.

'Who was what?' Lorna looked sideways at me.

'I thought I heard somebody laughing.'

'Nobody's laughing,' Lorna said. 'Maybe you heard one of these snipes or a whaup. There are plenty of them around.'

'That must be it,' I said, knowing full well that it was no bird I had heard. Somebody was mocking my plans for the future. Who? It might have been that strange woman or the man with the gentle eyes. It may have been An Cailleach herself, the evil witch that had turned herself into an eagle to kill Mary.

Now it was my turn to be stupid. How could a hill turn itself into an eagle? That was just superstitious nonsense gleaned from old wife's tales. I forced the thoughts away. I was over-tired and under nervous strain from the deaths of Mary and Kate. That's all that was wrong with me; nothing else.

The laughter came again, a wild cackle that emanated from the hill-side.

'Go away,' I mumbled. 'I can't hear you.'

The laughter came a third time, more raucous than ever. 'Can you hear yourself?' The voice asked. 'Can you hear your own voice talk-ing?'

'You can't hurt me,' I said. 'I won't fall for any more of your de-ceptions.'

'Your deceptions,' the voice echoed. 'Your deceptions.'

'Brenda?' Christine was shaking my arm. 'Are you all right? You're talking to yourself.'

'Am I?' I attempted to look surprised.

I had never adequately looked at Christine before. Now I saw that she was a beautiful young woman with a snub nose and a lovely heart-shaped face. When she smiled, as she did now, her eyes crinkled at the corners, and her teeth were even and white.

'You are,' Christine was smiling. 'You were arguing with yourself.'

'Well, I said. 'If I were doing that, at least I would win the debate.'

Christine's laugh held the tinkling of silver bells. 'That's true,' she said. 'Will you ever come back here?'

'No,' I ignored the mocking laughter and shook my head. 'I have no intention of returning here.'

'Oh,' Christine shook the moisture from her hair with a gesture rather like a springer spaniel drying itself. Her eyes were equally soft and puppy-like. 'I have.'

'You would return here even after all that has happened? The loss of Kate and Mary and finding these two dead men, and now,' I gestured to Charlie, 'whatever happened to Charlie.'

'Oh, yes,' Christine said. 'That's why I want to come back. There are so many mysteries here. I want to unravel them and find out what makes this place so terrible.' She smiled again. 'I like to unpick mysteries,' she said. 'That's why I tried to find out about you, Brenda. You were a mystery. You still are.'

'I'm no mystery.' I said. 'I'm just an unwanted orphan of the storm.'

Christine laughed again. 'You're even a mystery to yourself,' she said. 'Brenda Kirk suits you.'

'If that's my name,' I said.

'It is,' Christine was suddenly serious. Her smile dissipated, so her face altered from a mischievous elf into a studious academic. I had never seen such a fascinating transformation. 'And you should know more about your family Brenda. Or about one of your ancestors in particular.'

'Do you know more than you are saying?'

'I know more than I have said so far,' Christine said. 'I need time and space to tell you. We need somewhere private without anybody else present.'

'Why is that?'

'Because you won't believe what I have to tell you.'

I looked at her solemn face. 'Why would I not believe you?' I asked.

'Because what I have to say is unbelievable.'

I was not sure how to reply to that, so said nothing as we trudged on into the recurring mist. At least we were heading home, downcast at the loss of two of our women, tired, hungry and aching, but moving in the right direction. Every step saw us leaving An Cailleach's malevolent influence further behind. Yet every step also brought us close to Tigh-na-Beiste with its memories of evil men and terrible events.

'They're back,' Charlie's voice broke into the slide of mist and hiss of the rain. 'Over there. The men are back.'

We all turned to peer where Charlie had pointed. The mist had thickened again, slithering down the hillside, gathering in grey-white patches in pockets of low ground, clinging to isolated rocks to alter their shapes and deceive our eyes.

'I can't see anything,' Lorna said. 'Mist can play tricks with our eyes, Charlie. Anyway, they won't try anything with the four of us here.' She gripped her stick hard and lifted it like a club. 'Just let them try, that's all, just let them try!'

I hefted my own staff. 'We're with you, Charlie. Nobody will hurt you while I'm around.' Brought up in an orphanage, and then as an adopted child, I was well used to taking care of myself. The boys in my orphanage had been a tough crowd, while adopted children had a rough time at school. Teachers and pupils often picked on us as motherless, unwanted and therefore, in their eyes, blameworthy children guilty of the terrible sin of being unsupported. I was used to receiving and giving hard knocks and pity help any man who tried to assault me. As An Cailleach had challenged me: *gin ye daur.*

'Hurry, please hurry!' Glancing over her shoulder, Charlie increased her pace, so she nearly ran down that slithering slope. An Cailleach had found the weakness in the confident, brash, nearly aggressive suffragette of only a few days ago and had broken her.

'Stay with us,' I shouted. 'We're stronger together.'

'They're chasing me, not you,' Charlie said.

'Nobody will hurt you when I'm here,' I promised. 'I'll kill them.' *They are already dead,* I said to myself. *If Charlie's attackers are the Mahoney group, then I can no more kill them than … Than I can work out who my own mysterious apparition is?*

Oh dear God what is happening here?

Lorna gripped Charlie's arm. 'Brenda's right,' she said. 'Stay with us, and nothing will happen to you.'

Perhaps An Cailleach heightened our ability to feel each other's emotions, for Christine was next to be affected. 'I can see them,' she said. 'I saw movement back there.'

'There's nobody here except us,' level-headed Lorna was the voice of common sense. 'Keep calm.'

I took a deep breath to calm my now racing heart. 'Let's stop for a moment,' I said. 'Gather our thoughts and see what we can see.'

'If we stop they'll catch us.' Charlie was badly scared. A night alone on An Cailleach had shattered her nerves.

'Let them,' I hefted my stick, fully ready for a fight with any number of men. I had been petrified, soaked, dangled over cliffs and forced to watch the death of two of my companions. If any flesh-and-blood man tried to attack us, I would crack his skull and joy in his yells for mercy.

'Everybody halt.' There was something nearly military in Lorna's order. We stopped and listened. I heard the patter of the rain on our clothes, the low gurgle of the burns and the melancholic, bubbling cry of a curlew somewhere on the hillside. I also heard, on the fringes of reason, the echo of voices, slow whispering through the mist. I could not make out the words or even the form of words, but the voices were real, muttering among the heather and rocks.

'Can you hear them?' Charlie was near hysteria. 'They're watching us. They're talking about us.'

'I can't hear anything,' Lorna said. 'Keep calm, Charlotte.' She sharpened her voice. 'Charlotte Gunn! Listen to me! There's nobody here except us!'

We were silent again except for our laboured breathing. I heard the burn talking, its voice low and sinister. 'Be careful' it said as it surged over the rocks. I heard the heather whisper as it blew this way and that. 'They're coming, they're coming for you, they're coming,' it said. I heard the wind calling my name. 'Brenda Kirk, Brenda Kirk.' Behind everything, I heard the deep grumble of An Cailleach as she extended her hands to enclose me and pull me in. 'You're mine,' she said. 'You're mine Brenda Kirk.'

'No!' I shouted out loud. 'You're not real! I can't hear anything! You're all in my imagination!'

Christine's little hand slid inside mine. 'It's all right, Brenda. I'm here. It's all right.'

It was not all right. It was anything but all right. I squeezed poor Christine's hand as if my life depended on it, which it did not, or my soul, which might have been in danger. 'Thank you, Christine.'

'Can anybody see anything?' Lorna's voice was like steel. 'Stop imagining things ladies and concentrate on what is real, not what the mist makes you think.'

Feeling my heart hammering like a wild thing, I did as Lorna said and stared into the clinging white mist.

'Take one-quarter of the hill and concentrate on that,' Lorna said. 'Then move to the next section. Move in a slow circle.'

'*Deisil*, sunwise, right handed and lucky,' Mary's voice whispered inside my head.

'You're dead,' I told her, yet I obeyed her command, moving in the same direction as the circuit of the sun, the same way the Celts had moved for luck and our fishermen still did in some Scottish ports. Only Christine moved *tuaithiuil*, widdershins, left to right.

We stared upward, hoping not to see what we feared most. I saw a figure looming up, tall and supple and dangerous, and readied my staff to fend off an attacker. It was an elder tree, twisted by the wind, mist-shrouded and harmless. A crouching creature turned out to be a rock, a gleam of metal the run of a burn. One by one, I eliminated every possible source of danger in that part of the hill before I moved on to the next.

'Can anybody see anything?' Lorna's voice held us together. Her personality dominated our little group, binding us together with bonds forged in friendship and fear.

'No,' I answered first. 'Only rocks and trees.'

'Nothing,' Christine took hold of my hand, her fingers intertwined with mine. 'All serene, Lorna!'

'I can't see anything either,' Lorna said. 'How about you, Charlie?'

Charlie hesitated before she spoke as if she was scared to confess. 'No,' she said at last. 'I can't. They must be hiding.'

'Very well then,' Lorna said. 'We'll continue. We'll walk slowly and keep close together. If anybody sees or hears anything, or thinks they see or hear anything, speak out at once so we can all check it. I don't want anybody to be alone in this.'

'It's An Cailleach,' I said quietly. 'It's the hill herself.'

'I don't know or care what it is,' Lorna replied. 'I only know there's something wrong here and I've not gone through four years of man-made hell, dealing with broken bodies and broken minds, to be defeated by some imaginary fears on a bloody Scottish hill!'

It was the first time I had heard Lorna swear. The fact that she did proved that An Cailleach had also strained her nerves. That knowledge did nothing to settle my mind.

I had anticipated trouble at the cliff-face, but we scrambled down the rope like champions, with Christine biting her lip to control her fear.

'Good girl,' I approved, to be rewarded with a smile.

'Well done,' Lorna said, patting Christine's shoulder. Swarming back up, she unfastened the rope and threw it far away. 'If we are being followed, the men can find their own rope.'

Charlie's laugh was as near to hysteria as anything I have ever heard.

'Come on, ladies,' Lorna said. 'Nearly there.'

We scrambled down the slope, chancing twisted ankles and scraped skin in our haste to escape. After a remarkably short time, the bog-land stretched before us, as eerie and desolate as before, with swathes of mist spreading from the lowest levels and clinging to the black peat holes, while patches of bright green tempted the unwary onto the deep peaty mud. Two curlews whirred overhead, and a snipe gave its bleating call.

'The causeway is about here,' Lorna said. 'I wish we had thought to mark it with a stick or something.'

'There was a group of rowan trees,' I remembered. 'Three of them, I think, all wind-bent and battered.' I scanned what I thought was the edge of the bog, seeing stunted trees appearing and disappearing in the fluky mist.

'We'll be lucky to find anything in this muck,' Christine said. 'Maybe we should split up and spread out.'

'No,' I said. 'We stick together.'

'Sorry, Brenda,' Christine at once reverted to the meek little girl she had been with Kate.

I controlled my sudden panic. 'It's all right Christine. I wasn't rebuking you. It was a perfectly sensible suggestion. I just don't want to lose you, that's all.'

Christine smiled at once. 'Oh, thank you, Brenda. I don't want to lose you, either.'

'Over there!' Charlie pointed. 'Is that not our copse of rowans?'

We trudged to the spot with our boots splashing up mud with every step. Mist trailed in great tendrils from the weeping branches of the trees, half concealing what few leaves remained, like the grey hairs on an elderly man's balding head.

'It's a copse of rowan,' I said doubtfully. 'I hope that it's the right copse.' There were other groups of trees in the vicinity, straggled clumps in twos and threes on this side of the bog.

Lorna thrust her stick into the mud around the trees. 'It is the right copse,' she said. 'The ground is quite firm under the first inch of peat. Shall I go first?'

Kate would never have asked.

'We can take it in turns,' I said. 'It's not fair that you should be in the most danger all the time.'

Charlie glanced over her shoulder. 'Brenda's right. We should take it in turns.'

'All right. Five minutes each,' Lorna stepped onto the causeway, testing each step with her stick. We followed, with Charlie close behind Lorna and Christine and I making up the rear. As before, I felt tense as soon as we stepped onto the causeway. The knowledge that we were all walking on bundles of old heather stalks was not a comfort.

'We're moving at a fair pace,' I said.

'And there's nobody behind us,' Christine added. 'Not long now and we'll all be safe at the inn.'

The mist drifted in front, concealing the causeway and slowing us down. 'My turn to lead,' Charlie pushed past Lorna. 'Come on, Lorna, you can't have all the fun.'

'That's more like our Charlie,' Lorna passed over her stick. 'Don't forget to test the ground.'

'I won't' Charlie gave a quick grin. 'What a marvellous article this will make. My editor will be tickled pink.' She forged ahead, prodding the stick into the ground. 'Wait!' She held up her hand. 'There's nothing here.'

'There was a dog-leg twist remember,' Christine called from behind me. 'We put a table across the gap.'

'It must have floated away with all the rain.' Charlie's confidence of only a minute ago had already vanished.

'It can't have gone far,' I pushed forward. 'Poke with your stick.'

'I am poking,' Charlie leaned forward and thrust in her stick. 'There's no bottom here.'

We heard the voices drifting across the bogland, vague and faint. Charlie looked up. 'What was that?'

'I don't know.' I said. 'I heard them too.'

'What's wrong?' Lorna asked.

'We heard voices.' I said.

'There's nobody here except us,' Lorna said. 'And nobody is on the causeway either. It's only the mist playing tricks with your imagination.'

'I'm telling you,' Charlie said. 'I heard somebody. These men are back.'

'They're not on the causeway, and they can't walk on water, so they're not on the bog. Concentrate on finding the table top and forget anything else.' Lorna shook her head. 'I've seen this sort of thing before, you know. Lots of men that came out of the trenches thought they saw and heard things that were not there. It's all to do with a strain on the nerves.'

I gripped my staff tightly, scanning the mist. Although I knew that nobody could walk across the surface of the peat bog, and nobody could pass us on the causeway, I remained nervous. Far too many strange things had happened on this peninsula.

'Over there,' I could see something solid beneath the dark surface of the bog. 'That's our route.' Stretching over, I tapped with my stick. 'Found it, folks! Panic over! Come on.' I took the first step and breathed a sigh of relief when my boot landed on wood, part-hidden by half-an-inch of dark water. 'Come on, Charlie.'

A bank of mist rolled over us then, clinging close and rendering everything outside our little world invisible. I could not even see Lorna, a mere three yards away.

'Hurry, Brenda!' Nearly pushing me over in her haste, Charlie strode in front.

'The causeway is over to the right,' I remembered. 'Be careful Charlie.'

'We're fine now,' Charlie turned toward me. She smiled, and an expression of utter panic crossed her face. I have never seen anybody look so scared. 'Brenda!'

'What is it?' For one second I was paralysed. 'What's wrong?'

The figures loomed up through the mist, tall and broad and muscular. There were three of them, striding over the bogland with their hands outstretched. Knowing they could not be real, I swung my stick. 'Get out of here! Get out of my mind! Get out of my life!'

My staff hissed through empty air, with the force of the blow nearly unbalancing me. I recovered, ready to do battle with man, woman, monster or witch. The figures vanished as suddenly and completely as they had appeared, yet in that short space of time, Charlie had gone.

'Charlie?' Flapping my hand before me in a vain attempt to clear away the mist, I peered along the causeway. 'Charlie? Where are you? Charlie!'

She was fifteen yards away, a nebulous shadow in the mist, fast diminishing. 'Charlie! You're off the causeway! Charlotte Gunn! Charleeee!'

'What's happening?' Lorna called from further back. 'Brenda! What's happening?' I heard her sharp footsteps on the causeway as she marched towards me. I had no time to wait; I had to help Charlie before she lost herself in the bog.

'Charlie!' I stepped into the mud, finding it less deep than I had feared. 'I'm coming for you, Charlie!'

I heard the splash of heavy footsteps and a gurgling cry. 'Charlie?'

For an instant, a gap appeared in the mist, and I saw Charlie, blundering into the bog at right angles from the causeway, sinking deeper and deeper with every clumsy footstep. I raised my voice in a shriek that Christine and Lorna joined in. 'Charlie, you're going the wrong direction. Come back!'

When Charlie looked back over her shoulder, I saw the panic in her eyes. It is something I will never forget if I live another week or another thousand years. If all the terror and horror of humanity could be collected together and distilled into a single look, then Charlie's expression would surpass it. I looked into the madness of the damned.

'Charlie!' Without thinking, I leapt further into the bog and splashed toward her, lifting my legs high to escape the suction of the mud. I was aware of the mud engulfing my feet and legs, aware that beneath me was an unknown depth of peat, yet I had to try. I could not watch Charlie splashing to her death without doing something to help.

Charlie stopped moving. She was thigh deep in mud and still striving to run. 'Charlie!' I was five yards behind her with the bog dragging at my legs. I felt myself sinking deeper. 'Charlie, keep still, it's worse if you struggle.' I stretched forward as far as I could, without hope. We were too far apart. I could only watch in agony.

'Don't let them get me!' Charlie forced herself around, so she was facing me. Trapped in the mud, I could not help as Charlie slowly sunk, inch by terrible inch. The dark peat sucked at her hips and then around her waist. For a moment I thought that her jacket would save her as it ballooned up, trapping air like a lifebelt. I was wrong. It only slowed the inevitable, prolonging her suffering.

'Don't let me die here, oh, God Brenda please don't let me die here.'

'We're coming!' I heard the welcome voices of Lorna and Christine. They were laboriously and oh-so-slowly pushing the table top across the surface of the mud, using their bare hands to paddle it as if it were a raft.

'Hold on, Charlie,' I said. 'Help is coming.'

Mary's death had been terrible, but at least it was quick. Watching Charlie slowly sink was infinitely worse. I watched the mud slither up to her chest and further until it was lapping at her throat and then her chin.

'Brenda,' she stared at me, her eyes wide. If I had been slowly drowning in a peat bog, I might have hoped for the insensibility of insanity. An Cailleach afforded Charlie no such mercy. She pulled Charlie down inch by terrible inch, allowing her the full horror of knowing what was happening. I shared in Charlie's fear, empathetic to her pain, watching her suffer without the ability to help.

'We're coming!' Lorna threw her last climbing rope forward. It landed three feet from Charlie, who stared at it. With her hands trapped under the mud, she could not reach out. I tried to inch forward, only for the mud to suck me further down. I had been so preoccupied with Charlie's fate that I had nearly forgotten that I was also trapped. I could feel myself sliding slowly into the bog. I did not want to die here in this cursed peninsula.

'Brenda!' Christine was only six feet away, crouched on the table top. 'We'll rescue you, Brenda.'

'Get Charlie first,' I said. 'I'm all right.'

The mud had reached Charlie's lower lip now. She leaned her head back to get some more air, hoping for another few moments in which Lorna and Christine could rescue her. Lorna inched to the front of their makeshift raft and leaned forward, stretching out her arm as far as she could. There was still two feet of black peat-mud between her fingertips and Charlie.

'I can't reach!' Lorna said.

The mud was over Charlie's lip now, seeping into her mouth. She spat some out, the effort forcing her further down. 'Oh please,' the mud muffled her voice. 'Don't let me drown like this.'

I could not help. I saw the despair in Charlie's eyes as she slid another half-inch. The mud covered her mouth and bubbled at her nose. Panic filled her eyes. Tears filled mine as Charlie slipped under with only her eyes showing. I saw the commotion around her nose as she desperately tried to breath and then her eyes glazed and she slid fully under. Her hair floated for a few seconds, and she was gone. An Cailleach had taken her as thoroughly as a woman eats a slice of chocolate cake.

'Oh, dear God in heaven.' I hardly felt Christine loop the rope under my arms and gradually, slowly, they began the process of hauling me from the mud. I was sure that another pair of hands helped. I could not say who or how. I only knew that I was not destined to drown in the peat bog that day.

No. Oh, no. An Cailleach had quite another fate reserved for me. I was crying when Lorna dragged me onto the causeway. As I looked over at the bog, the sun emerged to burn away the mist. The dog-leg of the causeway was clearly marked, and there was nobody in sight except us.

Chapter Fourteen

'Poor Charlie,' Christine said.

I lay on the ground at the eastern side of the peat bog with mud caking me from my waist to the soles of my feet, still shocked by Charlie's death and my own escape.

'Poor Charlie,' Christine repeated. 'I remember her saying how much she hated that bog.'

'An Cailleach has taken three of us,' I said. 'Please God she is satisfied now, and the rest of us can escape.'

Lorna sat on the ground with her head in her hands. 'Oh my God, what a horrible way to go. Three good women, all killed on a Scottish hill. What next? What will I tell their relatives?'

'The truth,' I said. 'You can only tell them the literal truth. Kate fell into the lochan in the dark, Mary fell off the saddle and Charlie wandered into the bog.'

Christine lay on her side, staring at me as if she had never seen me before. 'You could have died too, Brenda.'

I nodded. 'I know.' I looked back over the peat bog, wondering if anybody could ever retrieve Charlie's body or if she was destined to remain there forever, preserved as part of An Cailleach.

'I'm glad you didn't.' Christine said.

'So am I. Thank you.' I felt physically and emotionally drained. I wanted only to lie here and allow the rain to wash over me. The prospect of getting up and walking further on seemed beyond my strength.

'How are you, Brenda?' Lorna asked.

'I'm all right,' I lied.

'What happened to make Charlie take fright like that? We had calmed her down after her earlier scares.'

'I wish I knew,' I said. 'We both saw what we thought were people coming behind us. I shouted at them to get away and the next thing I knew, Charlie was charging into the bog.'

'That would be us that she saw,' Lorna said. 'It's the mist. It distorts shapes and sizes.'

I knew that Lorna was wrong. It was not only the mist. It was An Cailleach herself, killing us all one by one. She had killed our leader first, and then Mary with her local knowledge. Then An Cailleach murdered Charlie, with her determination to succeed. Who was next? Would it be Christine, the youngest of us all? Or Lorna, who had stepped up to become our leader? Or would it be me, the orphan? Perhaps I would be last because I had worked out who was killing us. Maybe An Cailleach would toy with me, killing the others one by one and letting me suffer all the more. I knew that evil witch with her cunning, devious ways.

Or had An Cailleach already tried? I had survived one attempt when Lorna and Christine dragged me out of the mire. Would I be so fortunate a second time?

Duncan Og's story returned to me. Two witches had killed Lord Walter Comyn. One had turned herself into An Cailleach, the old hag. I knew it was superstitious nonsense and a fairy tale to frighten children to bed but who was that woman who stalked me and who nobody else had seen? Was she the witch, or the spirit of An Cailleach herself? All these ideas were utter nonsense of course. Yet who could explain the two eagles that attacked Mary, or Kate's naked body floating in the lochan, or Charlie's sudden terror when she blundered into the bog. And who was the kindly-eyed old man whom I had seen twice?

And then I remembered the Washerwoman of the Ford. She had five shrouds, and we had experienced five deaths. There had been the two male climbers, Kate, Mary and now Charlie. Did that mean that there were no more to come? Were the rest of us safe? Or had the five shrouds only related to our particular party? I did not know.

I only knew then that, however repugnant the thought of moving, I could not lie beside the bog, forever. I must rise, force myself to move and escape from this place.

'We'll have to leave here,' I said. 'The old hag is killing us one by one.'

'We are leaving,' Lorna was calm as ever. 'As soon as you recover your strength we'll be on our way.'

'You'd better get some of that mud off you,' Christine said. 'It will be most uncomfortable, and it will slow you down.'

'Yes, thank you.' Standing up, I began to brush the mud off me. Christine came over to help; sliding off my jacket and helping me remove my damp, peat-encrusted trousers. I had not realised how galling they had become until I stood in my underwear, not caring about the rain.

'That's better,' Christine said. 'We'll soon have the worst of this muck off. Now, what were you saying about an old hag?'

As we worked at shifting the peat, I told them what I thought. I spoke about the woman who appeared to me and about the visions of the past I had experienced. I told them about my belief that An Cailleach herself was hunting us. I reminded them of Duncan Og's story of the witches and how the witches had killed Mary.

They listened to me with Christine making all the right noises in all the right places while Lorna looked sympathetic.

'That's all very interesting,' Lorna, trust her to be efficient, had unearthed a brush from the recesses of her rucksack. 'Now use your reason, Brenda. You know that there is no such a thing as a witch, and nobody can change herself into an eagle. It just cannot happen. You know that witches are not mountains. That's also not possible. You're not thinking straight, Brenda after that fright you had.'

I shook my head, watching as Christine worked on my trousers, removing layers of peaty mud. She held them up to her cheek, shook her head and carried on. 'I know it sounds crazy,' I said.

'It is crazy,' Lorna said. 'We have been subjected to a series of unfortunate and tragic accidents, that's all.'

'How would you explain the behaviour of the eagles?' I asked.

'We must have disturbed their nest,' Lorna said.

'At this time of year?' I shook my head. 'I don't think so. Any young will be long gone. Now Kate, how was she found naked in the lochan?'

'She must have fallen in,' Lorna said. 'She must have gone outside the Shelter Stone for some reason, a call of nature perhaps, and fallen down the slope.'

'Stark naked?'

'You're nearly naked now,' Lorna pointed out. 'In speaking of that, get your clothes on and let's get away from this hellish place.'

I agreed with that and, thanking Christine with a smile, I pulled on my damp and unpleasant trousers. 'They feel a lot better, thank you.'

Christine's eyes brightened with even that little piece of praise. I understood her a lot better. Christine was one of these people who lived for approval. I presumed that Kate had controlled her by using the bullying to enhance the effect of the limited praise when it came. 'You're a good friend, Christine.' Well, I was no Kate. I would not resort to bullying on any level.

'Thank you,' Christine's smile would have charmed an angel.

We set off again, marching slowly and steadily with our heads down and An Cailleach spitting rain down on us. Wet and miserable, I wished I had kept my discoveries to myself. Now Lorna believed I was unbalanced, as crazy as Charlie had been. Thank goodness that Christine had not agreed with Lorna, although I wondered what she thought about me now.

'I don't think you're crazy,' Christine could have read my mind.

'Do you believe what I said?'

'I don't know,' Christine said. 'Your ideas are a little different, Brenda, as is this whole place. But I've still got things to tell you about yourself. When I do, you might have other perceptions.'

My interest returned. 'Tell me now.'

'I can't,' Christina said. 'You'll need peace to listen.' She patted my arm. 'You'll understand when I tell you, and then you and I can discuss things together.'

'I'd like that,' I said and enjoyed the pleasure my words gave her.

I tried not to look at the old Clearance village of Penrioch or at Tigh-na-Beiste as we hurried past. The memories were too vivid, and I could still hear Mary's singing coursing through my head. I knew I would never listen to *Mari's Wedding* or *Kisimuil's Galley* again without thinking of her. The evil of Tigh-na-Beiste seemed to reach out, chilling me even as I averted my eyes. If it was a hundred years before I saw that house again it would be too soon.

'Not far now.' Christine was trying to cheer me up. 'Just down to the ford, Brenda.'

'Thank goodness,' I said, 'oh thank goodness.'

The prospect of escaping from this place gave me energy. I hurried ahead of the others, nearly running in my eagerness to get away. 'Come on, Lorna. Come on, Christine.'

'You're feeling better, I see,' Lorna smiled at me.

'Much,' I blinked through the increasing rain. One thing about this part of Scotland, there would never be a drought.

'We'll speak in the Inn,' I said to Christine for I was genuinely interested in hearing what she had to say.

Christine's smile was so enigmatic that I wondered anew what secret knowledge she had. At that moment my feelings were very confused. A huge part of me wished to be away from this peninsula and safe in a civilised environment. Another part of me quailed from telling the world that we had lost half our group and I physically recoiled from relating the circumstances of their deaths. One small, rebellious part wished to spend more time here, to return to An Cailleach and dare her to do her worst, to call her bluff and prove I was good enough for her. And lastly, there was a strange, warm glow whenever I thought of Christine, which was an entirely novel experience for me. I was looking forward to being alone with her. I was looking forward to hearing my story from her lips. There was more. I could not articulate how I felt, even to myself.

I could hear the rush of Allt an loin, the sound as sweet as the most exquisite music. Beyond that, only a couple of stern hours walk, was the inn, a warm bath, food, hot tea, conversation and a soft bed. Beyond the ford was civilisation; beyond the crossing was safety. Beyond the ford was Christine.

'Nearly there,' I shouted the words. 'Come on ladies.'

We hurried the final couple of hundred yards to the ford. I could nearly taste the hot, sweet tea; I could feel the soft sheets easing over my bathed and clean body. I could almost feel the relief of being safe from the malevolence of Tigh-na-Beiste and the brooding presence of An Cailleach.

'Oh my God,' Lorna said. 'Oh no, oh, my God.'

Lorna had stopped fifty yards from the great Bore Stone that marked the peninsular edge of the ford with water lapping at her feet. 'The ford,' Lorna said. 'What's happened to the ford?'

'It's been raining,' Christine said. 'It's been raining a lot.'

I said nothing. If I had the strength, I would have burst into tears. Instead, I sunk to my knees and stared at the ford.

When we had tramped the opposite direction a few days previously, the ford had been little more than thigh deep and twenty yards in width. Now, after days of intermittent rain, it was five times that width and very much deeper. Water surged half way up the Bore Stone while the branches of the lone rowan tree at the mainland side dipped and swayed in the current.

'We can't cross that,' Lorna said. 'We'll have to wait until the water goes down.'

I looked at the sky, pregnant with rain. 'That could take days.'

'Or longer,' Christine felt for my hand. 'It's all right, Brenda. Everything will be all right.'

I squeezed her hand in desperation, unable to voice my fears.

'What should we do, ladies?' Lorna sounded as despondent as I felt.

The river level had increased even as we stood beside the ford. Now water surged around Lorna's boots.

'Look,' Lorna stepped back from the edge of the ford. 'Across there.'

The washerwoman was hard at work, kneeling at the side of the ford, kneading a long white garment. I knew, with sick certainty, that it would be a shroud.

'You!' I shouted, hoping to be heard above the roar of the ford. 'You! Washerwoman!'

She continued to work, kneading the garment in the water, taking it out, pounding it on a rounded boulder, inspecting it and replacing it in the water.

'Can we all see her?' I asked.

'The woman washing her clothes,' Lorna said at once. 'I see her as plainly as I see you.'

'I see her too,' Christine said.

Mary told me that she means death,' I said. 'She is washing the shroud that covers the body of her who is to die.'

'She only has one shroud,' Christine pointed out.

'So one more of us have to die.' I said. 'An Cailleach will take one more as payment for defiling her with our presence.'

'No.' Lorna said. 'That is only a woman washing clothes. Nothing more and nothing less. She's probably some old crofter woman.' She sighed. 'Well, we certainly can't cross here today. We'll stay on this side for another night and try again tomorrow.'

'Maybe there is another way across,' I said.

'There is the bog, and there is the burn.' Lorna said. 'I've had enough of bogs after Charlie and this burn is too deep to wade and too wide to jump. Sorry, Brenda but we are here until the ford is passable.' She looked upward. 'The heavens are about to open again. We'll spend the night in Tigh-na-Beiste.'

I shuddered at the prospect. 'Is there nowhere else?'

'There's the Shelter Stone,' Lorna said brutally, 'or the cave we were in last night.'

Was that only last night? The death of Charlie seemed to have elongated the day.

Christine gave hesitant voice. 'Both are a very long trek away.'

'I agree,' Lorna said. 'That's why we have to stay in Tigh-na-Beiste. Believe me, Brenda, it's not my first choice either, but there is fuel and shelter there, and I would like to be dry and at least a little warm again.'

Those two luxuries were very appealing. I remembered the images. I thought of the cold and damp, balanced the two discomforts of heavy rain or numbing depression with warmth and opted for the heat. 'What do you think, Christine?'

'I'm fine with whatever you say yourself,' Christine's eyes were as soft as a puppy as she looked at me.

'You must have an opinion,' Lorna said.

Christine shrugged and smiled.

'Tigh-nan-Beiste it is,' I realised that once again I had made the final decision. At that second I would have done anything to get out of my wet clothes and get some heat in my bones. Nothing else mattered. I tried to push the Washerwoman to the back of my mind.

We made the trek back in silence save for the grumbling of our stomachs. I wished I had saved some food. I shrugged. I used to hope that my mother would come into the orphanage and take me home, or that somebody would be my friend. Wishing for dreams does not make them happen.

'We could catch a fish.' Christine had the wonderful knack of reading my thoughts. 'How does anybody fancy a bit of trout?'

'That sounds marvellous,' I said. 'Are you an angler? Don't you need a line and bait and rod?'

'I need a length of string, a worm and a hook,' Christine said. 'Or I could sing them to the surface.'

'Sing them?' Lorna frowned.

'Oh, yes. I can charm the fish.'

Looking at Christine's face, I could nearly believe her. If I were a fish, I would have risen to the surface for her.

'Here,' Lorna perched on a rounded rock at the side of the path. 'Give me a minute.' Producing a knife from her rucksack, she teased out a long strand from what remained of her climbing rope. 'Here's a bit string.'

'That's a good start,' Christine said. 'Now I need a hook.'

I had a collection of pins and needles in my rucksack in case of emergency. I handed them over to Christine. 'Are these any good?'

'Could not be better,' Christine said. 'And bait is easy. In this weather, the worms will be teeming just under the ground. I'll go fishing while you two get the fire on.'

I had never seen Christine happier as she basked in our approval. As well as seeking praise, Christine evidently wished to be useful. Under Kate's strict control she had never been able to reveal that side of her personality. It is strange how the death of one person could bring out the best in another. An Cailleach was an unusual old witch, I thought, to rebuild young Christine by removing the person who had stunted her potential. I looked forward to watching Christine develop.

'Careful you don't fall in the river,' Lorna said.

'Yes,' I added. 'I'll be worried about you.'

Christine's smile was radiant. 'I'll be along before you know it,' she said. 'Thank you!'

Tigh-na-Beiste waited for us, cowering under the lash of the rain. Dampness had swollen the front door, so we struggled to push it open and enter the house of many memories. I looked around, remembering Kate's raucous laugh and Charlie's brusque confidence. I could nearly hear Mary's voice singing *Mairi's Wedding*. All gone now vanished with the women themselves.

'Right,' Lorna was all efficiency as she bustled around the room. 'We need firewood,' she said. 'Break up whatever furniture is left. Anything you can find. I want this room warm. Sitting around in soaking wet clothes will bring all sorts of problems.'

I needed the relief of doing something positive so enthusiastically broke up three of the six chairs and the remnants of the old chest-of-drawers that stood in the corner of the room. I left the frame of the freestanding mirror to its own devices and carried the splintered fragments of furniture to Lorna as she cleaned out the fire to enable a free current of air.

'Not enough.' Lorna only glanced at my offering. She was busy with old newspapers that had been used to line the drawers, crumpling them into balls and adding kindling. 'More. Bring me more.'

Leaving the living room, I tramped upstairs to the bedrooms. One was empty; the other had an antique double bed of solid oak. When I could not break it, I searched the house for a tool. Outside in the garden was an outhouse, heavy with cobwebs and riddled with damp, but containing sufficient tools to gladden the heart of a master carpenter. Unfortunately, years of disuse had also brought layers of red rust. There were three axes of various sizes, one that would be suitable for any Viking warrior, one that was about the same size and weight of a hatchet and a third somewhere in between. I selected the middle one and ran upstairs to hack away to my heart's content.

There is something fundamentally satisfying about destruction. It wakens a primaeval urge to reduce a creation to its basic components. I don't know why that should be; perhaps it is born of frustration against a world that does not immediately provide one with all one's desires. I only know that when I lifted that rusty old axe, I felt supreme joy in smashing the bed to fragments.

'Hurry up!' Lorna's voice floated from below. 'The fire's waiting.'

Grabbing a great armful of splintered timber, I thundered down the stairs. 'Here we are.'

'That's better,' Lorna approved.

With the fire smoking in the grate and Lorna sitting on one of the chairs we had decided to retain, that front room looked decidedly cheerful. There was no atmosphere of foreboding that I had experienced last time. Perhaps, I hoped, it had dissipated and would not return?

'That warmth is very welcome,' I said.

'I hope that Christine is successful,' Lorna said. 'My stomach thinks my throat has been cut.'

'I wish Mary were here, and Charlie and Kate,' I said.

'No.' Leaning forward, Lorna put a hand on my arm. 'Don't think of them. It's not healthy. You never think of the ones that have gone. That's how the boys coped in France. Live for the minute, not for the past.'

It was good advice, if hard to take when the deaths were so raw and vivid in my mind. My memories of Charlie's dying gurgles, of Mary's final scream and of Kate's naked body floating in the lochan would remain with me forever.

'It's hard,' I said. 'I've never known such loss before.'

'Have you never experienced the death of a relative or friend?' Lorna remembered my position. 'No, of course not. Sorry, Brenda, I was forgetting. Yes, it is hard. You will mourn later when you are alone.'

I nodded. 'I did not realise that friendship can come with such a high price.'

'All things worth having have a high price,' Lorna said. 'Now, we'll gather as much firewood as we can,' Lorna said, 'then we can dry off our clothes. We'll relax more when Christine returns.' She glanced out of the small, multi-paned window. 'I hope she's all right out there. I may go and look for her.'

'I'll do that,' I said in sudden dread of some accident befalling little Christine. 'I'll bring down more wood first.'

'So what will I do?' Lorna asked.

'Make sure the fire doesn't go out,' I said. 'I'm already looking forward to coming back to a warm house.' I hesitated for only a minute. 'There's an old outhouse round the back, I wonder if there's a tin bath in there.'

'Oh, the luxury of a bath!' Lorna looked up at me in sudden anticipation. 'What a marvellous conception!' She smiled. 'When we were in France that was the thing we missed most. A long soak in a bath was more important than a soft bed or decent food, or even being away from shell fire and broken bodies. A bath was the height of luxury.'

'Did you never miss men?'

'We were with men all day and every day.' Lorna's eyes shadowed with memory. 'Most were very young, just boys, poor, poor boys trying to be brave. They tried so hard and were always polite to the nurses however badly injured they were.'

'No, that's not what I meant,' I said. 'I mean the physical side of things.'

'Oh, that!' Lorna shook her head. 'No. We were too busy and when you see naked men every day and all day, some of the attraction palls. No. Any interest I had died at the front.'

I nodded. 'I'll go and look for Christine.'

The rain was as heavy as ever, pelting down as I left Tigh-na-Beiste and trudged, head down toward the ford. It was a good hour's walk, so I put my best foot forward.

'Christine!' I shouted. Evening was colouring the sky with a hazy sun setting in an orange-ochre blaze between two banks of dark grey cloud. For a moment I stopped to absorb the beauty, for the west coast can do that. One minute you are worrying about the death of your colleagues and the next the splendour and the scenery transports you to a different place, somewhere between heaven and earth where only beauty matters and the wonder is so all-encompassing that it is nearly painful.

'Oh my word, that is lovely.'

And then the two clouds merged, absorbing the sun and I was alone with the melancholic wonder that only the west of Scotland can provide.

'Christine!' I recollected my mission. 'Are you all right?'

My voice faced with the light. I thought with horror that Christine may have fallen into the rushing burn. I imagined the current powering her slight body downstream to the sea, or crashing her against the unforgiving rocks. I shook my head. No; no that had not happened. I would not find her floating face up in the morning. Even the thought made me physically sick.

'Christine! Please answer me!'

I hurried now, regretful of the slender moments I had spent watching the sun go down. 'Christine!'

'Brenda! Over here!' Christine's voice was so welcome that I laughed.

'Oh, thank God!' When I saw Christine walking toward me, holding something, I could not restrain my impulse to take her in a great bear-hug. 'I was so worried!'

'Thank you!' Christine allowed me to crush her for a long minute. 'I didn't think I mattered that much to you!'

'Of course, you matter!' I released her, gazing into her bright hazel eyes. 'You matter a great deal, you silly little nymph!'

Christine giggled. 'Look what I caught.' She held up three decent sized trout.

I hugged her again for I was ravenous. 'A veritable feast,' I said. 'Come on, Christine, the fire is on, and we've a bit of a walk before us.'

The room was warm when we stepped in, with Lorna greeting us with a smile. 'Well done, Christine,' she said. 'We'll eat well tonight. You were right about the bath, Brenda. It needed a bit of a scrub, but the pump in the garden still works and its clean now.'

The bath was of galvanised zinc and big enough to sit in. We stared at it in longing.

'We'll need hot water,' Christine said, 'and soap. I only brought sufficient soap for my hands and face.'

'Look in the cupboards,' Lorna said. 'If there was a woman in this house she will have a store of soap. I know I always have.'

'So have I,' I could have wept at the thought of my tidy little house in Stockbridge.

Christine said nothing but she was still young so one must forgive her.

Ignoring the scurrying spiders and great silver webs, we raked through the cupboards. We found a welcome box of candles, vast stores of blue and white china, a striped blue and white milk jug and sufficient cutlery to equip a hotel. Christine found the soap, a whole box full of solid green cakes, each one enough to wash an entire street.

'Now we're there,' Lorna said. 'Some hot water and we're off. We need a kettle or a pail, anything to heat water in.'

'The outhouse,' I dived for the door, nearly laughing in my excitement. I returned with a great iron pot, battered beyond description but almost entire. Lorna washed it at the pump to remove the worst of the rust as Christine held a candle high. Yellow light pooled across what had once been a very productive garden.

'Look,' Christine lifted the rank weeds with the toe of her boot. 'These are potato shaws mixed with the nettles. There might be some tatties still here.'

We dug with enthusiasm, lifting each battered shaw. We retrieved a decent haul of potatoes, mostly very small, discarded those with imperfections and carried the remainder inside the house, delighted with our good fortune.

'This house is a good provider,' Lorna said. 'We'll eat well tonight.'

Filling the pot at the pump, we placed it on the fire and added more wood.

We had not forgotten the loss of Kate, Mary and Charlie. Their memory was always at the back of our minds, sometimes at the forefront. We just chose not to dwell on things we could not alter. We needed a break from the horror of the expedition. For the sake of our sanity, we needed refreshment. Our laughter was slightly frantic, our movements hectic and we were all only a whisper from hysteria. We carried on, of course; what else could we do?

It took three full pots to even half fill the bath, and we all looked at the steaming water in some awe. 'Who's first?' Lorna asked.

'Christine,' I said. 'She's the youngest.'

'No,' Christine said. 'You need it most after falling in the bog. It should be you.'

'We'll toss for it.' Lorna produced three pennies from her purse. 'Odd woman out gets the bath.'

We looked at each other and at the hot water. We tossed, staring in hope as the three brown coins spun in the air. I had heads, as did Christine while Lorna's penny landed tails up.

'You first Lorna,' I said.

'Good!' Lorna was laughing, her eyes bright but tears not far away. 'You two can cook the dinner.' She stripped in seconds and squeezed into the bath with her knees up near her ears and the water lapping around her. We watched her, smiling, and handed her the soap.

Filling the pot once more, I tipped in the scrubbed and peeled potatoes while Christine prepared the trout. There was a grill near the fireplace, excellent for the fish and we waited in some anticipation for the first decent meal we had enjoyed in days.

'We'll run short of wood unless we use these chairs,' Christine said. 'Are there more upstairs?'

'No,' I shook my head. 'I've emptied the two bedrooms, and there's only the locked room left.'

'What's in the locked room?'

'I don't know. The door's locked.'

'I'll break it open,' Christine ran upstairs, and we heard half a dozen thumps, the crash of breaking wood and then the hollow thumping of her feet.

'Brenda!' Christine shrieked my name. When I left the room at a run, I nearly banged into Christine charging down the stairs. 'Charlie must have come here. Her rucksack was in that room.' She held it out as if in proof.

'I wonder why she went back up the hills,' I said. I knew that Charlie had not returned to Tigh-na-Beiste. Someone or something had placed Charlie's rucksack here for a reason. Despite the fire, I felt the familiar chill run through me.

'She must have gone to look for us,' Lorna spoke from behind a mask of soap-suds. 'Good for her. I thought her magazine article was more important to her than we were.'

I tried to smile. I knew better. An Cailleach had played its evil game with Charlie and dragged us back to this house. Maybe we were destined never to leave this peninsula. Once again I felt the chill hopelessness of Tigh-na-Beiste.

'What are you doing?' Lorna asked as Christine opened Charlie's rucksack.

'Seeing if Charlie had any food left,' Christine said. 'It's no good to her, now.'

I said nothing although to me it seemed like robbing the dead. I was slightly disappointed in Christine.

'Here's Charlie's notebook,' Christine produced the thick, leather-bound volume. 'She'll never get her article published now.'

'Pass it over,' I held out my hand imperiously. 'Let's see what Charlie's been writing.'

'That's not fair to Charlie,' Lorna said.

'If she complains, I'll stop,' I opened the book. Growing up in an orphanage makes one inquisitive about other people's affairs.

Charlie's writing was small and neat, with every letter immaculately formed. Naturally, I looked for my own name. She had been fair and accurate, calling me 'a quiet loner,' which was correct, and describing our journey without exaggeration. What did surprise me was her mention of seeing the 'others'. I had considered Charlie to be a hard-headed, practical journalist yet her notebook had a dozen mentions of what she called 'others'. I read the descriptions with some interest, as Charlie wrote about 'things that were not quite human' and 'strange creatures that should not be here.' As I read, I realised that there had been more to Charlie than merely a thrusting journalist and wished I could have known her better. There were occasional mentions of men in her notes. The two bodies on the beach, the three corpses on the summit on An Cailleach and the three men who she was convinced followed her whenever she was alone.

'Poor Charlie,' I whispered.

'Is it a good article?' Lorna asked.

'Charlie was a good writer,' I said. I had ignored the illustrations. Now I looked at them. Charlie had caught our features with some accuracy. Some pictures included an extra figure that I recognised as the mysterious woman. There was also a hurried sketch of three people that must have been her 'others' with only vague features on their faces and nothing distinguishable about them except that they were undeniably male.

I closed the book with a bang and hurriedly thrust it back inside the rucksack. I did not understand.

If Charlie had seen that woman, why had she not mentioned it? Or, had that woman added her own image in some unimaginable manner? I shook my head. *No. That's utter nonsense. Tigh-na-Beiste was inside my head again, playing subtle games with my thoughts.*

'Brenda?' Lorna was looking at me, her eyebrows raised. 'Are you all right?'

'I was thinking about Charlie.'

'Charlie's gone,' Lorna said. 'We'll mourn her when we get home. At present we use every device to get through this experience including hot baths and hot food. Put Charlie's rucksack away so we can't see it.'

I nodded. 'That's good advice.'

'Wait. Charlie had food too,' Christine remembered why she had opened the rucksack. She produced a flat tin box. 'The very last of the sandwiches. Charlie must have been hoarding them for a rainy day.'

'Stale bread and cheese,' I tried to force a smile although those images of the strange women unsettled me more than I wished to admit. 'Yum.'

'No, they're strawberry jam,' Christine said. 'Want one?' She offered them to me. I shook my head.

'Marmalade or nothing,' I said.

Christine laughed. 'You are loyal to your marmalade.' She lowered her voice. 'You're a loyal woman, Brenda.'

'I'll have a sandwich, then' Lorna raised her voice. 'Thank you, Charlie.' She shook her head. 'Imagine sitting in a tin bath in front of a smoky fire of old furniture and thinking you're in the lap of luxury.'

'You'll have seen worse,' I said.

'Yes,' Lorna bit into the first of the sandwiches. 'I've seen worse. There was a time after the Somme when we were ferrying wounded from the front in a constant stream. There were so many we had to pack the ambulance like sardines and the floor was awash with blood. We had 30,000 casualties in the first hour, over 17,000 dead the first day of a battle that lasted five months.'

'All passed now,' I did not wish Lorna to return to these dark memories. 'The war is over, we won, and there will be no more wars.'

'Please God you are right,' Lorna said. 'Please God. Anyway, this water is getting cold, so I'll get out and let one of you ladies have her turn.'

'Christine next,' I offered. 'I'll go last.'

'No, you should be next.' Christine said.

'No, Christine. You're next.' Emptying out the potatoes, I left them for Christine to get ready and left the house to fill the pot at the pump.

The woman was waiting for me, unsmiling. Unprepared, I could only stare at her while my mind wrestled with her presence.

'Who are you?' As I stepped toward her, she backed away, always maintaining the same distance between us.

'Who are you?' she responded. 'Find that out first.'

'I am Brenda Smith,' I said, 'or maybe Brenda Kirk.'

'When you know yourself you will know me,' the woman said. As always she was maddeningly obscure as if hiding behind a gauze veil.

'Are you An Cailleach?' I asked. 'Are you the witch?'

'I am who I am,' the woman said.

'That tells me nothing.' I was growing tired of this game. 'Go away and leave me in peace.'

'If I go away, you will never be in peace,' the woman said. 'You will never cease wondering who I am, and why I came to speak to you. You have fretted all your life, worrying who you are, Brenda Smith or Kirk. This is your time to find out when the world has torn itself asunder in war and evil has wrenched apart the gateways between worlds. Things will never be the same again.'

I did not understand much of what the woman said and fastened only on one thing I knew to be correct. The question of my identity had haunted me since early childhood. 'Do you know who I am?'

The woman's laugh was long and low and mocking. I ran toward her in sudden anger, swinging the pot as if it were a weapon. I did not see her move yet she must have struck me for I fell to the ground, stunned. When I rose, she was gone, and the candlelight shone welcoming through the window of Tigh-na-Beiste.

Filling up the pot, I returned to the house. Christine had been busy, so we had trout and potatoes to eat, with smiling faces to greet me and the fire keeping the darkness outside. We ate quickly, as befitting hungry women and cared not a whit for greasy fingers and a lack of table manners that would have shocked our peers in the civilised world.

'What happened?' Christine asked.

'When?'

'What happened when you went outside? You were white-faced when you came back in.'

'You're a perceptive little woman, aren't you?' I was not sure how much to tell without exposing myself to ridicule.

Christine was persistent. 'Did you see that woman again?'

'Yes,' I told them what had happened and waited for the mockery.

Christine took hold of my hand. 'Poor you,' she said in sympathy while Lorna nodded acceptance. 'We'll speak later.'

I lifted a forkful of trout. 'You're a good little cook,' I knew that praise would distract Christine, who smiled and blushed simultaneously.

'I'm not.'

'You are.' While we had been eating, I had poured two pots full of hot water into the tub. I added a third and indicated that Christine should get in.

She stripped slowly, never taking her eyes from me. 'Are you sure I can go next?' She stood naked in front of me, slim and elegant and disturbingly appealing. I am sure she knew the effect she had on me.

'In you get,' I said.

Four inches shorter than Lorna, Christine sank into the water and smiled at me as I handed her the soap. 'Thank you, Brenda,' she said.

I had to jerk my eyes away as a host of unbidden sensations and thoughts rushed through me. I saw Lorna looking at me sideways and guessed what she was thinking. She was jealous.

'No,' I said roughly. Was this some new attack by An Cailleach? Was the old hag attacking my sexuality and friendships as well?

'Are you all right Brenda?' Christine turned within the tub, sending water cascading over the sides and onto the floor. 'Is that woman back?'

How did she read me so well? 'I'm all right,' I lied. 'You get washed now.' I spoke to her as I had spoken to the small children at the orphanage, or as I would have spoken to a younger sister or a daughter. The sense of relief was so intense that I could have laughed. That was what I felt. That was this new emotion that disturbed me. It was sisterly affection, nothing more sinister than that. On an impulse, I bent forward and kissed the top of Christine's head.

'What was that for?' Christine's smile was broad.

'Just because,' I felt Lorna's eyes on me. I could not explain what I did not fully understand. I only knew that I wanted Christine to myself without a third party present.

I fretted after that, surreptitiously watching Christine as she washed, exulting in every movement, savouring every smooth curve and hidden valley. I knew I was wrong, I knew it was terrible of me to exploit her in this manner, yet there was a dark excitement in allowing this new aspect of me to take temporary control. I hated me at the same time as my pleasure increased.

That woman was watching me. I could not see her, yet she was there, inside the room, inside me and looking out, encouraging me to observe, to taste the sweetness of something I had never before considered.

'Brenda?' Christine was watching me with the hint of a smile lifting the corner of her mouth. 'Are you all right?'

I recoiled from my deliciously scandalous day-dream to the sordid reality of a smoky room in a semi-derelict house. 'Just tired,' I said.

'You were asleep on your feet,' Christine said. 'I'm coming out of the tub now.'

I knew that Lorna was watching as avidly as I was. I could feel her gaze devouring my Christine, yet we remained perfectly civil to each other on the surface. There had been too much ill feeling in our little group to pander to more, at least openly.

I was next into the bath. I had deliberately chosen to be last so I could wallow in hot water without the guilty feeling that I was denying somebody else the pleasure. Now sorrowful thoughts tainted my enjoyment. I remembered Mary and heard her singing echoing around this room. I remembered Kate with her confidence. I remembered Charlie, driven by her desire to push the cause of women in this world. In such a confined tub I could not lie back, so I huddled forward and allowed the warm water to soak away some of the dirt and a small portion of my aches and pains.

I was aware of the warm water smoothing down my shoulders and over my back. I opened my eyes to see Christine smiling at me, gently pouring the contents of the pot over me.

'Would you like me to wash your back?'

I shook my head. 'No, thank you.'

'I used to wash Kate's. Ever since I was at school with her, I washed her back.'

I wondered anew at the nature of their symbiotic relationship. Looking into Christine's eyes, I saw that now familiar deep yearning, that desire for approval and acceptance. 'I've never had anybody wash my back since I was three years old.'

'Never?' Christine seemed appalled.

'Never.' *Should I explain further? Not yet.* But even as I made that decision, I released a little of myself. 'I avoid people.'

I saw Lorna slump into a chair beside the fire. Her eyes were closed, and she was asleep in seconds as the stresses of the day took their toll.

Christine's touch was gentle as she began to wash my back. I did not object.

'Why do you avoid people, Brenda?'

Why did I avoid people? 'I don't know.' I replied automatically, erecting the barrier I had hidden behind for so many years.

'Don't you trust people? Do you think they will hurt you in some way?' Christine worked on my shoulders, lathering the hard soap and easing away some of my aches. Her voice was as tender as her hands, honey-smooth inside my head. I closed my eyes again, savouring this new experience.

'Maybe it is a mixture of both.' *Why was I telling Christine these things? I never tell anybody about myself.* 'Maybe it was because I am an orphan.' I struggled with my defences.

'I see.' Christine's hands drifted down my arms to my hands, relaxing my biceps and triceps, massaging my wrists and fingers. 'Do you feel different from other people? Do you sometimes think that you are different even from other orphans?'

How does Christine know that? I allowed her to soap my flanks and onto my breasts. Nobody, man, woman or child, had ever touched me there since I was five years old. I raised my arm to allow her. *Dear God, what was this woman doing to me?*

'It's all right,' Christine said. 'Everything is all right. Everything is exactly as it should be, as it is meant to be and as it was always intended to be.' Her eyes were as soft as I presumed a lover's to be, or a mother's.

Her hands eased across my breasts to my stomach, soaping, washing, cleansing away my aches and my worries. I did not object.

'Would you like to stand, Brenda?' Christine did not command, she requested so that the decision was mine. I stood and allowed her to soap and smooth me below the waist, front and back, missing nothing yet not intruding. Everything seemed perfectly natural.

A piece of wood fell in the fire, sending a shower of bright sparks onto the hearth where they glowed for a minute and slowly died.

'Do you wish to sit back down?' Christine asked, 'or do you want to step out of the tub now. I've washed your clothes, and they are drying nicely by the fire.'

I stepped out of the bath and reached for my small towel.

'May I?' Christine's towel was larger and softer than mine. 'I've been warming it by the fire for you,' she began to dry me, starting with my hair and working her way down slowly. 'There now.' Before I realised it, she was kneeling at my feet, towelling my calves. 'Clean as a whistle and shining brightly.'

'Nobody's ever done that for me before,' I said. 'I don't know what to say.'

'You don't need to say anything.'

'Thank you.'

'Friends don't need to say thank you to each other.' For an instant, Christine looked sad. 'We are friends aren't we?'

'Yes,' I said. I knew that Christine would smile at that, just as I knew she would blush and look away.

'I'm glad,' Christine said. 'I think we should put Lorna to bed now.'

Lorna was dead to the world. We made a cosy little nest for her in front of the fire, covered her with our dry, long-discarded skirts to keep her warm and returned to the chairs. With most of our clothes still drying, we wore only our under things.

'Now,' Christine smiled across to me. 'I can tell you what I've been dying to tell you ever since we began this adventure. We never seemed to get time alone together, did we?'

'We're alone now,' I said. 'Lorna is sleeping like a baby.'

Christine nodded. 'Good. Now, Brenda, you may have to suspend your disbelief a little when I tell you this.'

'After being on this peninsula,' I said, 'nothing can surprise me.'

'I told you that I discovered your mother's name was Kirk.' Christine wriggled herself into a more comfortable position on the hard chair.

'Yes,' I said. 'When we get back I intend to search for any living relatives.'

Christine looked downcast. 'Sometimes a good friend is better than a relative.'

'I have kept people at arm's length,' I said. 'I don't have any good friends.' When I saw the hurt on her face, I quickly added. 'Except you, if you wish to be a good friend and not just a friend.'

'Would you like me to be your good friend?' Christine's answer was equally rapid. 'Your particular friend as Jane Austen would have put it?'

'I would like that,' I said, knowing that any other answer would hurt her. I did not wish to harm Christine with her elfin face and telltale eyes.

'I will be the best, most particular friend you could ever wish,' Christine promised.

'I believe you,' I wondered if she wished me to reply in kind. 'I will be the best friend I can for you,' I said. 'Although, Christine I haven't had much practice. Children from many families are discouraged from befriending orphans and by the time I became an adult I hadn't got the knack of making friends.'

Christine's smile wrapped around me like a cloak. 'Will I be your first ever best friend?'

'You will,' I said.

'That's good.' There was more than mere 'good' in her eyes. There was desperate yearning for acceptance and approval. I knew I would feel immensely guilty if I ever hurt this young woman. 'Have you ever heard about a minister named Robert Kirk?'

'I have not,' I said with my interest quickening. 'Robert Kirk? If my mother was named Roberta, could he be my grandfather?'

'He lived in the 17th century,' Christine's gaze did not stray from my face.

'He was not my grandfather then.' I killed off any slight hope.

'Probably not,' Christine bent over the side of her chair and opened her rucksack. 'You will recall that I carry books with me?'

'I remember you explaining how heavy your bag was!' I wondered at the sudden change of subject.

Christine passed over a small, cheaply-bound book. 'Here. Read this. Robert Kirk was the minister at Aberfoyle.'

'Where Roberta came from?' I was a bit disappointed when I looked at the book. Entitled *The Secret Commonwealth of Elves, Fauns and Fairies*, it seemed to be a children's fairy story.

'Yes,' Christine said. 'Where your mother came from.'

I flicked through the pages, not in the mood for reading. 'What is it about?'

'Robert Kirk believed in fairyland,' Christine began. 'He thought he could hear the fairies at a hill near Aberfoyle.'

'The Fairy Hill,' I suddenly remembered. 'I know of that place.'

'Read the book when you can,' Christine said. 'Please.'

I could not deny her, although I had no time for fairy stories and no belief in fairies. 'I will,' I promised. 'We'd better get to sleep now. I hope that tomorrow is better than today.' I held the book; the fact that Christina had given it to me was more important than the content.

I do not know what was on my mind as I tried to settle that night. Charlie's face was there, with her eyes pleading for help I could not give, and Mary's final scream. I saw Kate's floating body once more, and that mysterious woman with the enigmatic words. Overall, I saw Christine's eyes, watching me, searching for acceptance, and felt her light touch on my skin. And always, underlying everything there was the sense of foreboding, of being watched, of An Cailleach brooding over me.

The screaming woke me.

Chapter Fifteen

'It's Lorna.' Christine stood at my side, shaking, with her hands at her face. 'Do something, Brenda.'

I sat up. 'Lorna, I'm coming!

The fire was dead without even a single red ember. The room was in darkness, with a high wind clattering at the windows and roaring down the lum. I scratched a match and lit a candle. Wavering yellow light pooled over the room, highlighting Christine's cheekbones, making deep pits of her eyes.

'Lorna!'

Still stupid with sleep, I pulled myself to my feet. Lorna was asleep, twisting and turning in her nest, so the rug was a tangle around her legs. Sweat gleamed on her face, dampened her snarled hair and plastered her surprisingly fashionable chiffon slip to her body. Crouching at her side, I shook her shoulder. 'Lorna, wake up. It's all right.'

Lorna slept on, screaming through her nightmares, now with her arms thrashing to push me away.

'Lorna!' I shook harder. 'Oh dear God please awake!'

'Wake her,' Brenda. Please wake her.' Christine hopped from one foot to the other, flapping her hands.

I slapped Lorna's face, gently and then with more force. She continued to scream kicking and punching at imaginary foes. 'Lorna!' Lying beside her, I pulled her close to restrain her, whispering what I hoped were soothing words into her ear.

'Oh, dear God help me.'

Lorna awoke with a jerk and grabbed at me, tears in her eyes and nails like claws digging into my body. I did not heed the pain.

'It's all right, Lorna,' I said. 'You're safe here. It's me, Brenda. It's all right.'

Lorna was sodden with sweat, and her breath was foul. I did not care. I could feel the hammer of her heart through the thin material of her slip. 'It's all right,' I said. 'You're safe.'

'I had a nightmare,' Lorna said at last. Her grip relaxed, and she gabbled her words. 'I had a nightmare. I was back at the Front with the ambulances and Kate and Mary were on board, and we ran over Charlie as she drowned in the mud in front of us.'

'It's all right,' I said. 'It's only a dream.'

Lorna sat up, calming down. 'Sorry ladies. I hate these nightmares. I can't control them.'

'We know that,' I said. 'We're here.'

I knew that this house and this whole area were affecting Lorna as it affected all of us. Once we were away, we would all be calmer, Lorna's nightmares would ease, I would stop having crazy thoughts, and Christine would gain confidence.

'We'll try the ford again tomorrow,' I tried to reassure everybody. 'The rain is off so the water should recede.'

Lorna nodded. 'Yes, we'll do that.' She looked around the room. 'It's terribly dark. Light a lamp, please.'

We had no lamps, so Christine scrabbled for another two candles and held their wicks over the flame. I don't know if the increased light made the room look better or worse.

'The dark nights were the worst,' Lorna continued, 'when the guns lit up the whole horizon, and we lay awake watching the flashes and heard the sounds. Like thunder, on and on and on, a mechanical roar of men being killed and torn to pieces. When we heard the guns like that we knew that they would come soon, the wounded and the injured, the pieces of men that pleaded for death and the boys who hoped we could put them back together again, the blinded and the mutilated, the boys who sobbed for their mothers and the men who apologised for giving us trouble.' Lorna spoke in a long, disjointed mutter. She looked up. 'Could you light a candle, please? Just one? A candle to push back the dark?'

I glanced at Christina, and she lit another candle, holding it close to Lorna before placing it on the mantelpiece. The little yellow lights flickered in a draught, throwing wavering shadows over the three of us. I heard somebody singing *Kisimuil's Galley* and knew that Mary was also here, unseen. Mary did not scare me.

Lorna was sobbing on my shoulder. 'They were all so grateful to us, the married men with pictures of their wives and children and the boys, just little 16-year-old boys, with legs and arms blown off and faces disfigured. There are hundreds and thousands of them in a never-ending column of suffering and pain, always waiting for me, hoping for help I cannot give.'

Lorna looked up, and I knew she was seeing the faces and torn bodies of her boys. They had never left her. I imagined what she saw, the endless khaki columns of the suffering, the price of politician's promises, and the cost of meretricious glory.

I could not help. I could only hold Lorna close to me and wait until her sobbing stopped. I hated Tigh-na-Beiste then, hated it more than I had ever hated anything before in my life. This terrible house was magnifying Lorna's memories, combining them together; condensing them into an unendurable nightmare that I knew threatened her sanity.

'We'll leave here tomorrow,' I repeated. 'We'll get across the ford somehow, and we'll never come back.'

'Settle back to sleep now,' Christine said. 'We won't leave you.'

Now wide awake, I sat back on my bedside chair and watched the candle-light battle the lords of darkness that was more spiritual than physical. I was acutely aware of Christine sitting opposite. I smiled at her, and she smiled back.

'This time tomorrow,' I said, 'we will be back.'

'Yes,' Christine said. 'This time tomorrow we will be home.'

Home. That was such an evocative word that meant so much. Home to some people meant family and comfort. To others, home meant a tiny single room in a decrepit tenement. The fortunate thought of home as a detached bungalow with a pleasant garden while the very lucky called their mansion home and often despised those born to lesser fortune. People needed a sense of home, somewhere they felt valued, somewhere they belonged, and their own little bit of the world.

'What is your home like, Christine?' I asked.

Joy brightened her face. I had shown interest in her. It was so easy to bring pleasure to this young woman. 'I live a two-roomed flat in Edinburgh,' she said. 'A part of the city called Canonmills.'

'I know it,' I said. 'It's near the Water of Leith and the Botanical Garden.'

'That's right!' Christine said. 'Do you know the Botanics?'

'Very well indeed,' I said. 'I walk there of an evening.'

'It's a magical place,' Christine said. 'We can walk there together.'

For some reason, the prospect of walking through that peaceful oasis made me emotional. I felt suddenly homesick for the magnificent glasshouses and the sound of blackbirds through the trees. 'Yes,' I said. 'I will look forward to that.'

'You must live nearby,' Christine said.

'I live in Stockbridge, not far at all.' I thought of my one-roomed flat in Raeburn Place, with the blacksmith's forge at the back. I wished I was there now.

We were silent again as the candle flames gradually burned their way down the wicks. I lifted the book that Christine had given me and leafed through the pages.

'Have you ever heard of a co-walker?' Christine's voice was clear.

'I have not,' I said.

'Look,' Christine gently took the book from my fingers and found a page. 'It tells you about them here.' She traced the words with her finger. 'A twin brother and companion in every way like a man, haunting him as his shadow.'

That was chillingly familiar.

'And here again,' Christine read out the words ' "the shape of some man in two places; that is a superterranean and a subterranean inhabitant perfectly resembling one another in all points ... a reflex man." '

'I see,' I was not sure what point Christine was trying to make.

'Now tell me about this woman that visits you,' Christine said.

'I can never see her properly,' the small hairs on the back of my neck rose erect at the very thought of that strange woman. 'Only her eyes are clear.'

'What colour are they?' Christine asked.

'Brown,' I said.

'The same colour as yours,' Christine said. 'How tall is she?'

I struggled to remember. 'I don't know.'

'Is she taller than you, or shorter?'

'About the same.'

'This woman is the same height as you, with the same colour of eyes.' Christine said. 'And she echoes your words when you speak.'

'Yes,' I began to see where Christine was steering this conversation. 'I don't believe in co-walkers though.'

'Of course, you don't. You don't believe in fairyland either. What did this woman say to you? She said they you would know who she is when you know yourself.'

'Yes, something like that,' I agreed.

'Is that not a clue? She is your co-walker; she is your spiritual self.'

'I don't think so,' I said, although I did not wish to hurt Christine by negating her theory. 'I think she is somebody I am imagining. There is an evil in this house or a power that enhances some part of us. It made Kate more of a bully, it makes Lorna's nightmares worse, and it makes me imagine people. I was lonely for a long time; I used to create imaginary friends.'

'You will never be lonely as long as I am here,' Christine said.

I closed my eyes at those words. 'Thank you.' I wished I could believe her, but I had heard similar promises throughout my life. I remembered my hurt as children I had thought to be friends joined the majority in ridiculing and tormenting the lonely little girl that I had been. Christine knew all about me. I would like to know more about her.

I opened my eyes. 'You know the Latin names of trees and flowers, and about causeways. Do you consider yourself to be an intellectual?'

Christine shook her head. 'Not really.' She considered for a few moments. 'No, not at all.'

'You researched my name for me. That was very kind of you.' I was trying to work out this woman.

'You were lost,' Christine said simply.

Reaching across, I took hold of her hand. 'That was very kind of you,' I repeated. 'Thank you.'

Brenda Kirk. I ran the name through my mind. *Brenda Kirk. It is an excellent name, a strong name. Can I get used to it after being Brenda Smith for so long? Brenda Kirk. I would have to look up my mother's name and ancestry.*

'Roberta Kirk was the only daughter of Robert Kirk,' Christine answered my unspoken question.

'My grandfather? How far back did you research?'

'As far back as I could.' Christine said. 'Your grandfather was a ploughman.'

'Why did you do that?' I was genuinely bewildered. 'Why did you go to all that trouble for a relative stranger? We had only met three or four times before and then for a couple of days hill-walking.'

'You needed me to,' Christine said. 'As I said, you were lost.' She was silent for a long time as the failing candles cast dark shadows over her face. 'And I needed to because you were lost.'

I frowned. This house seemed to produce mystery after mystery. 'We hardly spoke, Christine. What made you think I was lost?'

'You looked lost.' Christine said. 'You know that you can sense atmosphere in places. For instance, when we arrived at Dunalt, you knew immediately that there were no spirits.'

'It was sterile,' I said.

'Exactly so,' Christine agreed. 'Yet you could not sense the presence of the family of tinkers.'

I nodded. 'Could you?'

'Yes,' Christine said simply. 'I know people. I could sense that you were searching for yourself.'

I wondered how somebody who knew people could be so needful of acceptance. I would find out later, for we had plenty of time. 'Do you know what my people did?' I asked.

'Your mother was a domestic servant in a big house,' Christine said. 'I could not find who your father was. It's possible that he was the master of the house.' She smiled. 'You might have blue blood in your veins if you want it.'

'Do you know his name?'

'It may have been Adam Gordon,' Christine's eyes twinkled. 'Kate's uncle.'

I started and thought of Penrioch and the attitude of the landowners to the people there. 'I don't wish blue blood,' I said.

'No. Your Kirk blood is good enough for anybody.' Christine seemed to have all the facts at her fingertips.

'Tell me all,' I savoured Christine's smile of pure pleasure.

'The Reverend Robert Kirk, your ancestor, was one of the most interesting men that 17th century Scotland produced,' Christine settled back in her chair, with the candlelight enhancing her delicate features and reflecting the gleam in her eyes. 'He was the seventh son, which, as you must know, made him susceptible to second sight and such-like powers.'

I nodded, although I had never heard such a thing before.

'He became the Minister of Aberfoyle, a place you know well.'

I nodded again as old memories resurfaced.

'Well,' Christine's face seemed to glow in the candlelight. 'Our Reverend Kirk was a highly intelligent fellow, bi-lingual in Gaelic and English, plus he spoke Latin and Greek. He was one of the first to publish the Bible in Gaelic. You have the book that he wrote, although you haven't had time to read it yet. When you do, you will find out that he could communicate with the People of Peace, the *Daoine Sidhe*.'

'The who?' I had never heard the term before.

'The People of Peace.' Christine repeated. 'That is the term Scots used to describe the beings that lived in the mounds and under the surface of the earth, the ones who were here before the Celts arrived, or possibly before humans arrived.'

Now I was intrigued. 'I've never heard of the People of Peace.'

'You have.' Christine said. 'They were also called fairies.'

'Oh,' I tried to digest that piece of news. 'So Robert Kirk's book is not a fairy story for children, then.'

Christine shook her head. 'It might be one of the most important books ever written on the subject.' She settled back in her chair. 'Robert Kirk used to listen to the People of Peace on the Fairy Hill at Aberfoyle. He travelled around the Highlands finding out what they knew about the spirit world and then wrote your book.'

I listened in silence.

'You have the gift of discerning atmosphere in a place,' Christine said. 'Perhaps you also have the power that the Reverend Robert Kirk had.'

'I have never spoken to a fairy, a person of peace,' I said. After a few days on this peninsula, I did not scoff. *I can believe nearly anything now.*

'Are you sure? How would you know?' Christine asked. 'Do you think they come complete with gossamer wings like Barrie's Tinker-bell? The old folk were afraid of them, in case they stole their children or hurt their cattle. The People of Peace are not delicate little creatures but, as Kirk said supernatural beings 'of a middle nature betwixt man and angel.''

I shifted slightly in my chair, thinking of that mystery woman who haunted me. She had been of middle size and seemed to be able to appear and disappear at will. Could she be one of these People of Peace, or perhaps a co-walker? I shook my head in complete confusion.

'One day,' Christine said, 'the Reverend Kirk was found dead, lying face down on the Fairy Hill. People thought that he had a heart attack and brought him home to lie for a few days before they buried him.'

I nodded. 'And the mystery died with the reverend.' I said.

'Not at all,' Christine said. 'The local people believed that the People of Peace were annoyed that he revealed their secrets and said that he was not dead at all. The locals said that his coffin was filled with rocks and the People of Peace had taken him inside the hill to be the chaplain of the Fairy Queen. Others said that his spirit is still trapped in a pine tree on top of Doon Hill, the other name for the Fairy Hill.'

'I see.' Vague tales of the fairy realm had circulated around the orphanage and my primary school. In such a God-fearing place as Aberfoyle was then, the minister ensured that such stories were squashed at once, with the teacher's tawse supporting him as a fearful implement of persuasion.

'There are other tales,' Christine leaned forward in her chair, so she was close to me. I have never seen such an intense expression on anybody's face as she had that evening. 'The Reverend Kirk appeared, or rather his spirit appeared, to his cousin, Graham of Duchray and told him that the Reverend was still alive and in fairyland. He pleaded for Duchray to release him. The Reverend said that he would appear at the baptism of his child, for he had left his wife pregnant.'

'How like a man,' I tried to inject some humour. 'Getting his wife pregnant and then running away to Fairyland.'

'We're better without them,' Christine agreed with a smile. 'The Reverend claimed that when his spirit materialised at the baptism, Duchray should throw a knife over his head to release him from his captivity. The People of Peace are said to be scared of iron, you see. Well, as you can imagine, Duchray was a bit sceptical. However, the Reverend, or something that looked like him, appeared at the Christening but Duchray was too astonished to do anything about it. Robert Kirk walked right past him, throwing him a look of reproachful despair. He has never been seen since.'

'So he is still with the People of Peace?' I found it hard to use the word 'fairyland'.

'He is still with the People of Peace,' Christine confirmed.

Unsure what to say, I said nothing as the final candle guttered and died.

'Now here is a twist,' Christine's voice carried through the dark room. 'There is an ancient fort on Doon Hill, maybe one that the People of Peace used before humans came. And Jules Verne used the setting for one of his books.'

'Do you think it is true?' I asked.

'I think there is truth in the story,' Christine said.

'Do you believe in the People of Peace?' I did not. Even after all the strange events on that peninsula, I could not convince myself to believe in fairies and a fairy queen. On the other hand, I did not want to scoff and ruin a budding friendship.

'I believe.'

'Then so might I.' I still could not commit myself. I was willing to suspend my disbelief up to a point, but the rational part of my mind still worked.

'Belief is in your blood, Brenda Kirk.' Christine said. 'Especially if you are a descendant of the Reverend Robert Kirk.'

'How much do you know about the People of Peace?' I was enjoying Christine's company in a manner that only lonely people will understand.

'A lot,' Christine said, and then Lorna began to dream again. She was silent at first, and then muttered a little, moving her hands as if to fend off some invisible attacker.

'There goes Lorna,' I sighed. 'We'd best light another candle.' I brushed against Christine as I moved to Lorna. That slight touch tingled like the sting of a bee.

'It's all right, Lorna, I'm here. You're safe.'

I crouched beside Lorna when she began to moan and held her hand when the moans intensified into low groans.

'It's all right,' Lorna,' I said.

Lorna stared directly at me. 'It is not all right,' she spoke as clearly as if she was sitting at home and fully awake. 'They're all dead, you know.'

Her words startled me. 'It's all right,' I repeated. 'We're here with you.'

'They're all dead.' Lorna said.

'She's still sleeping,' Christine said. 'She's talking in her sleep.'

'We'll calm Lorna down, and then we'd better get some sleep too,' I said, knowing that Christine would accept whatever I said. I was not sure if I liked having this power over somebody else, even if I would never abuse it.

Lorna sat up. 'We had to leave them,' she said. 'We had no choice. We had to leave them behind.'

'Of course, you did,' I said. 'You could do nothing else.' I settled her back down in her rug. 'It's all in the past now, Lorna.'

I waited beside her until she closed her eyes again and her breathing became regular.

'Time for us to sleep, Christine,' I said. 'You can tell me about the People of Peace tomorrow when we are back at the Inn.'

It was well before dawn when I awoke, but still too late to do anything to help Lorna.

She was hanging by her neck in the stairwell, and she was stone dead.

Chapter Sixteen

'Oh, dear God.' I stared at Lorna for a full three minutes before I could summon the strength to move. 'Oh, Lorna, Lorna. Why?'

Lorna had fastened her final climbing rope around one of the beams of the ceiling and looped the other end around her neck. Her death had not been quick and to judge from the expression on her face, it had not been easy. I could not look at her bulging eyes or her tongue that protruded from the side of her mouth. Her bladder had also relaxed, for there is no dignity in death.

'The nightmares killed her,' Christine was at my side, holding my arm. 'She did not survive the war. It got her in the end.'

'It wasn't the war,' I said. 'It was this house or this peninsula.' *It was An Cailleach,* I thought. *It was the mountain herself, striking us down one by one. An Cailleach had probed us all for our weaknesses and exploited them to her advantage. Even Lorna, the strongest of us all, had proved vulnerable. Lorna the compassionate, Lorna the nurse who had survived the worst that war had thrown at her, was dead. An Cailleach had taken Lorna's greatest gift, her caring for others, into a weapon and twisted her memories of helping into a lance that damaged her brain, so she killed herself.*

'Should we get her down?' Christine asked.

I nodded, once again making the decision. 'Yes. We cannot leave Lorna like that.' I took a deep breath, trying to gather my strength for the next ordeal. 'That's four of us gone,' I said. *The washerwoman had washed Lorna's shroud.*

'I know,' Christine said. 'Only we two are left.'

We unfastened the rope from the beam above and gently lowered Lorna to the floor before removing the noose from her neck. Unable to cope with the horror in her eyes, I closed them with a muttered prayer. We carried Lorna into the living room and laid her body on top of her nest, beside the fire.

'She's with her boys now,' Christine said. 'All the boys and all the men that she helped cross over to the other side.'

I nodded. 'Lorna's boys will be making her welcome.' I would have liked to give her a full military funeral, or have her interred in St Giles Cathedral in Edinburgh or make some other mark of distinction for Lorna Menzies, ambulance driver, climber and a woman I had hoped would sometime be my friend. As Lorna would have said, it would be the only proper thing to do. As it was, she would be scorned for her suicide and buried in disgrace.

'We must leave here,' I said. 'What a horrible thing to happen.' I tried to push my emotions away. I had both liked and respected Lorna. She was the strongest of us all, the best and most reliable person I had ever met, but if I dwelt on her death Tigh-na- Beiste or An Cailleach would take advantage.

'We will leave when you say, Brenda,' Christine said.

I sighed. 'It's your decision as well, Christine. You have as much a say as I do.' I decided to make our situation plain. 'If we are to be friends, Christine, then we must be equal friends.'

'Oh,' Christine stared at me with her mouth open. 'Yes, Brenda.'

That was not quite the response I had expected. 'When do you think we should leave, Christine?'

Christine's gaze fixed on me. 'We will leave when you know the truth, Brenda.' There was no hesitation in her answer.

'I don't understand,' I said.

'I know.' Christine spoke softly. 'I know you don't understand.' She stepped closer to me. 'Thank you for accepting me as an equal, Brenda.

That means more to me than anything.' Reaching out, she touched my arm. 'I think we should leave Lorna in this room and go upstairs until it's dawn.'

I had forgotten the time. A glance out the window showed the waiting darkness. 'We'll do that,' I agreed. I had no fear of remaining in the same room as Lorna's body; she would never harm me, alive or dead. I only thought it would be disrespectful for Christine and me to stay beside her.

We trooped upstairs, passing the beam from which Lorna had hung and entered one of the bedrooms.

'I can't sleep,' Christine said.

'Nor can I.' I said. 'What did you mean about leaving when I know the truth?'

'Ask yourself that same question,' Christine slid down the wall beneath the window and sat, legs apart, facing me. 'Tell me when you know the answer.' She winked, as she had done once before, flicked out her tongue and closed her eyes.

I sat opposite her on the stained wooden floorboards, listened to the wind grumbling down the chimney and allowed the tears to flow for Lorna.

'Brenda Kirk,' the strange woman stood inside the doorway, looking at me. 'Come with me, Brenda Kirk.'

'Who are you?' I asked. 'Where is Christine?'

'Christine is here,' the strange woman said.

I looked around the room. I could not see Christine. 'Who are you?' I asked again.

'You know the answer to that,' the woman said.

Remembering what Christine had said, I peered closer, trying to see clearly, but the air seemed to be clouded. Nothing was clear. 'Are you my co-walker?'

'Are you my co-walker?' As so often before, the woman echoed my question. 'Come with me, Brenda Kirk.'

'Where are you taking me?'

'Home,' the woman said. 'I'm taking you to the place you belong, the place you have wanted to be all your life.'

Christine had vanished. I was alone with this strange woman. My curiosity battled with fear and curiosity walked away victorious. 'Take me,' I said. 'Show me what you wish to show me and then,' I tried to recall what Mary had said to the tinkers a week and a lifetime ago, 'God between you and me.'

I don't know what I expected the words to do. I did not expect the woman to shake her head. 'God cannot be between you and me, Brenda, and well you know it.' She extended her arm as if to take my hand. I declined, keeping outside her reach.

'Allow yourself to trust, Brenda Kirk.'

'I do not trust,' I said.

'Then watch and listen and learn.' The woman spoke quietly. 'You must learn to trust those who need you.'

We were walking side by side through a dark landscape, yet I did not have to feel my way. The route seemed as familiar as my own street, with every rock and every overflowing water-course an old friend. The wind soothed my face as the wild mountain goats watched passively. Even the deer accepted our presence as normal, grazing without interruption.

We strode up Bein a Ghlo and over the saddle to An Cailleach without a pause. The slopes levelled before us, the causeway over the bog was as visible as the King's Highway, and two eagles guided us over the double rope bridge across the Witch's Step as smoothly as if it were on the North Bridge in Edinburgh.

'Where are you taking me?' I already knew the answer.

An Cailleach waited for us, bare, cold and windswept, her honest granite slopes austere against the western sky. The woman took my hand and led me to the pinnacle on the summit where the six of us had celebrated only a few bitter days before. I stood there, barefooted and part of the mountain.

'Who are you?' I asked again.

'I am you,' the woman told me. 'And you are me.'

'I don't understand,' I said.

'I am the person you see in the mirror, where your left is my right, and my left is your right. I am the voice that wants to say no when you wish to say yes. I am the one who pushes you on when you wish to stop, and who holds you back when the road is too busy or the snow too deep.'

I shook my head. I was not afraid. 'I still don't understand.'

'Yes you do,' the woman said. 'You just don't realise that you do.'

The wind was cool, refreshing around my flanks. I turned in a circle, sun-wise and saw the world in all its stark glory. I belonged here, grim and solid on this peninsula where I had stood for uncounted centuries. I was An Cailleach, the old woman, the hag, the witch, and the eagles, myself forever.

'We are in duplicate,' the woman turned widdershins, the opposite direction and we stopped facing each other. She held out her hands, and I grasped them, left hand to right, and right hand to left as we locked gazes.

'I am only one,' I said.

'Two eyes, two ears, two lungs, two hands and two feet.' The woman said.

'One mouth, one nose, one heart,' I stopped there.

'You will meet a mouth with lips to merge with yours and a tongue to add to your words. You will meet a face with a nose to point your mutual direction and a heart to mend your constant pain of loneliness.'

'I am alone,' I said.

'We are in pairs,' the woman contradicted me. 'You came here in three sets of two. Kate and Lorna. Charlie and Mary. Christine and you. The dominant, the seekers and the lonely, each pair with a mission and each individual needing something different yet similar.'

'You're talking in riddles,' I said as my feet seemed to merge with the granite of An Cailleach.

'Unravel the riddles, Brenda Kirk.' The woman was closer, so close that her face was nearly touching mine.

'Are you half of me?' I saw my reflection in the woman's eyes, I saw a lost little girl searching for love, a child seeking acceptance, a lonely youth hiding in the wild places, a young woman yearning for hope. I saw maturity with lines of growing despair. I saw the bright hopelessness of old age and the gradual acceptance of a solitary death. Life and death merged, and only the spirit remained to soar in final triumph or remain solid between the water that gave birth to all life and the land that provided nourishment. Above were the sun and the moon that regulated the days and the seasons.

'I am you,' the strange woman replied, 'and you are me.'

I was sinking into An Cailleach. The two eagles circled above, watching, gradually coming closer until they landed at my side, huge, feathered creatures with hooked beaks and talons sharp enough to rend a grown man. I was not scared for they were part of me, as I was part of them.

'Why did you kill Mary?' I asked the eagles.

'We did not kill Mary.' They did not speak yet I heard their answer. They preened themselves, acting in unison.

'I saw you kill Mary,' I said. 'She was no threat to you.'

'You killed Mary,' they told me. 'She was a threat to you.'

'In what way was Mary a threat to me?' I remembered watching Mary fall, toppling head over heels into the mist as her scream echoed around the lost corrie.

'She threatened your friendship,' the eagles responded. 'You were jealous of her.'

'That's a lie,' I heard the heat in my voice. 'I was not jealous, and I did not kill Mary.'

I relived the scene, with Mary safe on the saddle beside the Witch's Step. *I was beside her as she hummed Kisimuil's Galley and we stepped out again. I watched Mary's back, saw Christine smile to her and felt jealousy so sharp that I shuddered with the shock. The great eagles circled us, and Lorna gasped her relief that we were all safe after the perilous crossing. I heard the whirr of wings and looked up to see the eagles attack again, two huge birds with hooked beaks and talons extended, ready to rip and rend. Lorna ducked in anticipation, but the eagles ignored her and struck Mary. She turned to face them, threw a round-house punch, overbalanced and staggered on the edge of the ridge.*

I was closest to her. Dropping my rucksack, I rushed forward, slipping on the loose stones. 'Mary!' I saw the panic in her eyes and stretched out my hand to help.

'Take my hand, Mary!'

I reached out to pull her back, took hold of her sleeve and… And? Did I try and pull her back? Or did I push her over?

'Mary!' I yelled as she fell, with her eyes anguished and her mouth forming one word: why?

I had pushed her over. I had killed my companion.

'Why would I want to kill Mary?' I stared at the strange woman who put such terrible images into my head. 'Why would I do that?'

'Mary was friendly with Christine,' the strange woman, my co-walker said.

'Oh dear God! Did I kill her? Did I push her over the edge?'

'We did,' my co-walker said. 'We killed Mary like we killed Kate.'

'Kate fell into the lochan,' I said. 'She drowned.'

'Remember again.' My co-walker woman said. 'Remember what really happened.'

'We found her in the morning,' I shook my head, hoping to chase this terrible version of me away with her vile thoughts and awful accusations.

'Think back,' my co-walker said. 'Think of the night before when you were all under the Shelter Stone.'

I tried not to think. I did not wish to face the terrible possibility. I felt myself sinking further into the rock, so I became firmly embedded in An Cailleach. We were fused now, this great hill and I.

'Think back,' my co-walker said.

It was night. We lay under the Shelter Stone, some of us slumped in exhausted slumber, and others awake, staring at the carvings on the rock.

'Are you awake, Christine?' Kate whispered.

Lying across the entrance, Christine whistled softly in her sleep. I watched as Kate rose up and stepped carefully over the sleeping bodies. Stooping, she kissed Christine on the ear. 'Do you fancy a moonlight dip?'

Christine stirred in her sleep, murmured something and fell back to sleep. Her legs kicked out slightly, catching me on the knee. That strange woman was with us. I saw her come towards me and we merged as one.

'I'll come if you wish.' I whispered to Kate.

'Oh,' Kate looked disappointed and then surprised. 'All right then, Brenda. I did not think you would wish to. You're such a shy person.'

I rose. 'Come on then, Kate.'

As we stepped over Christine, Kate looked fondly down at her. I felt an immediate stab of jealousy for I had never had a friend who looked at me in that manner.

'We'll have to keep quiet,' I said. 'Or we'll wake the others.'

We negotiated the steep slope, sliding on the shingle, slithering sideways to avoid the sharp rocks until we arrived at the shore of the lochan. Moonlight gleamed on the water, showing it as clear and inviting, with long tendrils of green weed at the bottom and a bed of smooth white stones.

'Have you done this sort of thing before?' I asked.

'Oh, many times,' Kate said. 'Chrissy and I often swim in the moonlight. There is St Margaret's Loch beside Arthur's Seat in Edinburgh we go to when we're in town. If I am at home at Carnbrora, I take her to our private beach.'

I pictured them together, laughing and capering in the silver surf, splashing each other in friendship.

'That must be lovely,' I said.

'It is.' Kate was stripping off, so she stood naked by the water. I admired her perfect body, slim and elegant, slightly tanned by the sun and with fashionably small breasts. Kate was everything I was not, rich, clever, confident and successful. 'Come on if you're coming.'

'I'm coming.' I dropped my clothes on the white shingle and stepped into the water. I knew that Kate was watching me, inwardly mocking my cheap clothes, laughing at my broad hips and matronly breasts. I

could not match her in anything, not in wealth, health or body. It was no wonder she could attract a friend like Christine.

The water was biting cold as we waded out. Kate reached waist-level and dipped her head under. She swam as expertly as she did everything else, with a grace and power that I could never hope to emulate. I followed her with my clumsy breaststroke, wallowing in her wake.

'Come on, Bren,' Kate called cheerfully over her shoulder. She was like a water-nymph or a mermaid with these smooth lines, those slim hips and energetic legs.

We swam out as far as I could. I turned back as Kate continued, reaching the far bank where the outlet cascaded to the dark depths below. I watched her, knowing I could never manage to swim that far, knowing Kate was better than me at everything. I understood why Christine obeyed her like a puppy following her mistress and I hated Kate for being such a success.

The moon was waxing when Kate returned with the water slicking her hair to her head and her face masked with concentration. 'Are you ready to return to the Shelter Stone?' She asked. 'Or shall we swim out again.'

'Let's swim out again.' I could see that she was tiring. Her breathing was deep. 'How fast can you swim, Kate?'

'I used to be the school champion,' Kate sounded proud. 'The water was not as cold then.'

'I bet you couldn't swim all the way around this loch,' I said.

Kate laughed. 'That's easy when I'm fresh. Not at this time of night. I'm ready to sleep now.'

'Any excuses,' I played with her ego, her only weakness.

'Oh, all right then,' Kate's smile was broad as she plunged back in and kicked off on her circuit of the lochan. I watched and waited. After ten minutes Kate had reached the outlet and was still going strong. Another five minutes and she was nearly back. She stopped suddenly.

'Cramp!' She raised a hand. 'I've got cramp!'

The combination of cold and tiredness had taken its toll. I waded in and swam toward Kate, splashing water with my clumsy stroke.

'Brenda!' Kate surfaced again, looking at me as I swam toward her.

'I'm coming, Kate,' I said. I realised that the water here was shallow and stood on the bed of the loch.

'Brenda!' Kate was panicking, thrashing around as the pain of her cramped limbs chased away her powers of reason.

'I'm here!' Taking told of her head, I pushed her under the water, holding her until her frantic struggled slowed and then stopped. If she had been fresh, I could not have held her. I shoved her under the water and walked away. Kate's clothes were folded in a neat little bundle. I lifted them and hid them under a large boulder, dressed and returned to the Shelter Stone. The moon was down now, and everybody was still asleep. I kissed Christine on the head, returned to my space and closed my eyes, smiling as my co-walker seeped from my body.

'I did not do that,' I denied my memory.

'We did,' my co-walker said. 'We killed Kate, and we killed Mary.'

I was thigh-high in rock now, sinking slowly and feeling some of the power of the mountain surging through me. 'I would not do such a thing.'

'Oh, we would,' my co-walker said. 'Think of poor Charlie.'

'Charlie drowned in the peat-bog,' I denied any involvement in Charlie's death. 'I saw her drown.' I could recall every detail of that horrible event.

'You helped her choke to death.' My co-walker was sinking every bit as fast as I was. She still held my hands while her gaze remained locked with mine.

'I did no such thing,' I shook my head violently. I did not want to have murdered Charlie.

'Let us remember together,' my co-walker encouraged. 'Let me inside your head.'

'No!' I tried to fight her off.

I was back in that fearsome bog with the mist rolling around us and the causeway soft under my feet. Charlie was in front, hurrying to escape from the three men. 'Hurry, Charlie,' I said. 'I can see them. They're catching up.'

Charlie looked behind her, eyes wide. Mud smeared her face from her forehead to her chin. She was panting with fear, limping, with the laces of her left boot trailing in the dirt. 'I can't see them.'

I stopped to listen, hearing only Charlie's harsh breathing and the distant call of a curlew, eerie in the mist. 'Maybe they've gone,' I said. 'Three men, you said?'

'Three men.' Charlie confirmed.

'Maybe I was wrong,' I put doubt on my own words. 'You know how the mist distorts things.'

I heard Lorna's voice behind us, high-pitched.

'That's Lorna,' Charlie said. 'I hope Christine is safe as well.' She forced a smile, her teeth surprisingly white in her peat-stained face. She had lost her hat somewhere and her hair, cropped as short as a boy, was smeared and filthy. The confident, thrusting reporter of last week had long gone.

'Do you like Christine that much?' I thought of that sweet young creature with this dedicated, tenacious woman, shy Christine with Charlie who stepped boldly in a man's world and who faced down any opposition of either gender.

'She's so vulnerable,' Charlie said. 'And so petite. I don't like to think of her out there in the wild world. She should be sitting on velvet cushions, eating strawberries and cream and drinking out of fine bone china tea-cups.'

That image slid into my mind. Christine was purring like a cat, lounging in a basket chair within a rose garden with blackbirds singing and a short-cropped lawn stretching to a Scottish Baronial mansion. She lay languidly back, stretching her legs as she tipped her straw sun-hat over her face. Her eyes were smiling as she waited for me, and only me. With the image came raw anger that Charlie should wish the same thing as I did.

'Did you hear that?' Charlie asked. 'I heard something.'

'It was only a bird,' I said, adding 'I think' to maintain Charlie's fear. At that minute I hated Charlie with unreasoning bile I did not fully understand.

'No, I'm sure it was a man.' Charlie said. 'He was whistling to his friend. They are surrounding us.'

'If we hurry they won't catch us,' I said.

'It's me they want,' Charlie said. 'They know I was an active suffragette. They know I write articles to advance the cause of women.'

'You go first then,' I gave her a little push. 'I'll stay here. If the men come, I'll delay them.'

Charlie ran ahead, her boots splashing on the causeway. I followed, with the mist drifting in and out and the little patches of bog cotton bobbing fluffy white heads as we passed.

'The path's stopped!' Charlie poked Lorna's staff into the ground. 'There's no bottom here.'

'It's over there,' I said. 'We put the table down, remember?'

'Yes, yes. I forgot.' Charlie thrust the staff into the mud, searching for our temporary bridge. 'Here it is.'

'Hurry,' I said. 'The men are coming.' I gave Charlie another shove, sufficient to send her into a panic, so she plunged off the causeway and into the bog. Waiting until she had blundered a good fifteen yards away, too far to return, I shouted: 'Charlie!' and stepped gingerly after her. I knew that Lorna and Christine were not far behind and would rescue me if I were not too far out.

'Charlie,' I repeated when I was sure the peat bog held her firm. Charlie turned toward me, and with a mixed feeling of satisfaction and pleasure, I watched her slowly sink. Good, I thought, she won't come between my young friend and me again. I saw Lorna emerge from the mist with Christine at her back.

'Help her!' I shouted. 'Charlie's sinking in the bog!' I waved my arms to attract attention. 'Somebody help Charlie!'

'Brenda!' I realised that Christine was reaching for me, her eyes liquid with anxiety.

'No,' I said, 'help Charlie!'

'Charlie's gone,' Christine said.

That strange woman left me, and I mourned the death of Charlie, my friend.

I felt the tears burning my eyes as I thought of Charlie. I tried to shake away the memories as I sunk deeper into the granite of An Cailleach. I was up to my hips, with my co-walker still opposite me, still holding my gaze.

'What's happening?'

'You're going home,' my co-walker said.

'Where's home?'

'Where you belong,' my co-walker said.

'I don't belong anywhere,' I said.

'Everyone belongs somewhere,' my co-walker told me. 'You just have to find that place. I will guide you.'

The granite was friendly, warm and enduring, as constant as a home should be. I slid into it, merging as my flesh petrified and my mind focussed on my past of solitariness and isolation. I recalled the orphanage of dozens of children, of comings and goings, with different faces every few weeks and no constant. The staff had been formal but friendly, the food and accommodation adequate. Was that the home where I belonged?

Eventually, an elderly couple had taken me in. Decent enough people, they cared for me with sympathy but without love, and I paid for my accommodation by working morning, noon and night. Was that the home to which I belonged?

I remembered school days when I had been 'that motherless girl' to the teachers who treated me as if my situation had been my fault, and encouraged my fellow pupils to act as if I were some kind of leper. I had been the solitary girl watching from the sidelines, the one always last to be picked for team games or companionship, the girl not invited to parties. Was that the home to which I belonged?

I remembered leaving school after an undistinguished academic career. I was thirteen years old, and nobody noticed that I no longer attended school. Nobody cared if I were there or not. I found a job in a shop, working twelve and fourteen hour days on my feet to pay the rent for my one-roomed flat in a nearby tenement. One of the other girls knew me from school days and soon spread the word that I was an orphan. Naturally, the shop owners gave me the jobs nobody else wanted, and I swept up and cleaned up and survived to return to my attic room with the leaking roof and creeping insects in the cracks of the floorboards. Was that the home where I belonged?

I remembered making the nerve-wracking trip to the capital and searching for work and accommodation in Edinburgh. The size of the city awed me, with the bustling streets, the trams and omnibuses, the khaki-clad soldiers on leave from the front, the great frowning castle and the long-nosed ladies parading along Princes Street and George Street who would not give shop-girls such as me the time of day. I had found a small flat in Stockbridge, a mile from the city centre and lived a quiet life working, walking around the Botanical Garden and Inverleith Park and occasional trips to the Pentland Hills. Living my solitary life in the city was the happiest I had ever been. Was that the home where I belonged?

I had met Lorna there. She had been in the Botanical Garden, outside the magnificent glasshouses and had spoken to me. Lorna had been my key to the Edinburgh Ladies Mountaineer Club where I had discovered women with an even greater affinity with the hills and mountains than I had. I smiled at my memories of Lorna.

'She was a good woman,' my co-walker said. 'What a pity you killed her.'

'I did not kill her.' I denied the accusation in something like panic. 'Lorna killed herself.'

'Remember again.' My co-walker's intense eyes fixed on me, dragging me from the peace of the Botanical Garden to that more stern time of much more recent date.

'No,' I tried to back away, but there was nowhere to go.

Christine was sleeping, her breathing steady and slow. The fire was long dead, and the wick of the candle burned away. The smell of hot wax was vaguely pleasant or at least familiar in that room. I fidgeted on my uncomfortable chair, wondering if it were better to continue dozing there or to stretch out on the floor.

Lorna was stirring in her sleep as the nightmares returned. Creeping, so as not to wake Christine, I stepped beside Lorna. She was mumbling, twitching her hands as though fending off some invisible enemy. That other woman was in the room, observing me as if judging what I was doing.

'It's all right.' I crouched at Lorna's side. 'You're all right.'

Although Lorna's eyes jerked open, I knew that her mind was still in France, driving her ambulance from the butchery of the battlefield to the horror of the hospital.

'They've broken through,' Lorna spoke coherently, as though living through the events. 'There are hundreds of casualties, maybe thousands.'

'That was years ago. You're safe now.'

'They came in the fog,' Lorna sat up. 'They broke through our lines and came on and on.'

'We drove them back.' I guessed that Lorna was referring to the German offensive of March 1918. 'We won the war, or at least forced them to an armistice.'

Lorna continued as if I had never spoken. 'We have to withdraw. We have to leave the casualties and withdraw before the Germans reach us.'

When Lorna spoke, Christine gave a little moan and moved in her chair. 'Lorna,' she said. I felt the jealousy twist within me. What right did Lorna have to be in Christine's mind?

'Do we have to withdraw?' I asked. 'Can we not stay and look after them?'

'No, no,' Lorna said. 'If we stay the Germans will capture us, and we won't be able to help anybody ever again. We must leave.'

I saw an opening. 'If we withdraw we will be leaving all these poor boys to the mercy of the Huns.'

'I know. We have no choice. Too many casualties depend on us.'

'We'll run then,' I said. 'We'll leave the wounded behind. The Huns will appreciate the gift.'

'Don't say that,' Lorna said. 'Please don't say that.'

'We left them behind,' I said, deliberately jumping through time. 'All these poor wounded boys that needed us so badly. You left them behind, Lorna.'

'I had to,' Lorna's voice broke as she spoke. 'I had no choice.'

'They died,' I lied, twisting the knife. 'The Huns killed them all. The Huns murdered the boys you left behind, Lorna. They bayoneted them one by one while you ran away.'

I worked on Lorna's guilt, bruising her tender heart, knowing that the calluses of war overlaid genuine sympathy. 'They died screaming, Lorna, while you ran away.'

'No, please don't say that!' Lorna covered her ears, trying to escape my barbed, agonising words.

'You killed them, Lorna. You were the cause of these poor wounded boys' deaths.' I waited until my words sank in before I continued. 'Now you are living while half your friends are dead. Is that right? Is that how it should be?'

'No,' Lorna shook her head as the tears flowed hot down her cheeks. 'No, it's not right that I should live and they should have died. The best of us died, and the rest only live because of their sacrifice.'

'What should you do, Lorna? What is the only proper thing to do?' I was ruthless, pushing Lorna past her limits of endurance.

'I don't know. I killed those poor wounded boys. I murdered them when I ran away.'

'What happens to murderers, Lorna? What is the only proper thing to do with murderers?'

'We hang murderers,' Lorna said. 'We take a life for a life.'

'That is right, Lorna,' I said. 'A life for a life. What are you going to do, Lorna?' I heard Christine stir and knew I had to settle things before she awoke. Christine was such a lovely little thing that she would not allow Lorna to employ natural justice.

'I must do the right and proper thing,' Lorna said.

'That's right, Lorna,' I glanced towards Christine, lying there with her innocent, elfin face and her need for a particular friend. I must pro-

tect Christine from all others and care for her myself. I must remove all threats to her. 'What is the right and proper thing, Lorna?'

'I have to hang the murderer,' Lorna said.

'That's right, Lorna. That's what you have to do.' I urged her. 'Do it now, Lorna, before you forget, or the guilt will eat at you all your life. If you hang the murderer, all these young boys you condemned to death will find peace.'

'Peace.' Lorna said. 'Will there ever be peace?'

'These boys are not at peace,' I whispered. 'Only you can help them, Lorna. Only you can give them peace. You can join them now.'

I was not sure if Lorna was awake or asleep. I only knew that she responded to my words. Rising from her bed, she lifted her last rope, left the room and climbed to the top of the stairs. I was with her, moving without effort, whispering in her ear.

'That's right, Lorna. That is the only proper thing to do.'

Two of the beams that held the attic floor were exposed. Lorna passed the rope over one and tied a secure knot before forming a simple loop at the opposite end. 'Those poor boys,' she said. 'If I had remained behind I could have saved them.'

'You can save them now,' I said. 'The boys are waiting for you, Lorna. You can give them peace.'

'It's all my fault.' Lorna's guilt was evident. 'If I had stayed, I could have saved them.'

Pulling herself to the top of the bannister, Lorna looked down the stairwell. 'They're waiting for me,' she spoke in a conversational tone. 'I'm coming boys. Don't fret, I'm coming to help. Hold on now, and I'll be with you in a jiffy.'

She stepped off the bannister and landed with a jerk. I saw the rope tighten around her neck. Lorna convulsed, tried to speak and slowly choked to death inside Tigh-na-Beiste. I watched, knowing that Christine only had me, now.

Leaving Lorna to hang, I returned to my chair, pausing only to kiss the top of Christine's head as I passed. That strange woman slid free of my body as I sat, and watched me from the other side of the room.

'No!' I denied. 'I did not kill Lorna.'

'You did not kill Lorna,' my co-walker agreed. 'You only persuaded her to kill herself.'

Breast high in the granite, I stared at this co-walker who was so like me yet so different, my identical opposite, and at last, I could see her features. They matched mine in every respect, from the shape of my nose to the cynical twist of my mouth, a contortion created by a lifetime of rejection and humiliation. I no longer feared repudiation by those who could pretend friendship; instead, I sought it. Aware of its inevitability I pursued denial to justify my bitterness, thrust away overtures of friendship to find the solace of loneliness. I allowed only a very few people close to me and held them secure while expecting betrayal. Now the result of my actions stared me in the face.

Above us, two eagles circled closer and closer until I could see the substance of every feather and the glint of their eyes. Trapped in the granite, I could not fend them off. I only watched, waiting for the rending of claws on my face and the ripping of sharp beaks in my eyes. I blinked, and they were beside us, standing and I was no longer afraid. Why should one fear oneself? Or perhaps oneself is the greatest threat of all? I did not know. I do not know. The eagles came close, two witches from Badenoch stepping toward me and then I felt the power of flight and saw everything in the most amazing clarity. The past and the present were as one, a kaleidoscope of events, one following another in a sequence that contained a pattern of inevitability and repeated itself like an actress performing the same play forever. The only thing that altered was the audience and the face of the actress, who aged with each appearance.

'It is time to go home.' The voice came from inside me.

'Where is home?' I asked as An Cailleach claimed us all.

There was nobody to ask. My co-walker had disappeared. I was within the body of An Cailleach, with a host of people around me. There was laughter and music, smiling faces with hazel eyes and small ears, light without a source and a feeling of belonging such as I had never experienced before.

As the light strengthened, I could see more clearly, as if a veil had been withdrawn. I remembered something that Mary had once told me. An Cailleach was said to mean 'old woman' or 'old hag', but the literal meaning was 'veiled one,' somebody who belonged to a hidden world. I was within An Cailleach now, within her hidden world, her veil was dropped, her secrets revealed and the recesses as open to me as a garden on a bright spring morning.

'Where am I?'

'You already know the answer.' The words came unbidden to my head. I was home. I was inside An Cailleach, I was An Cailleach, I was mistress of all I surveyed, and I was home. When I looked around at all the dancing, happy people I knew them as friends. Rather than being barely tolerated in a hostile world I was part of a community, accepted, welcomed, loved for who I was; I was wanted.

The feeling of peace grew so strongly within me that I felt I could burst.

What was this place called? Different people gave it different names. Was I dead and a spiritual soul in heaven, or was I a nymph in Arcadia? Was I in Elfhame, or Fairyland or was I within the body of An Cailleach, she who dominated this part of the world, the great queen, the goddess of winter and summer, the woman who revived every year at the first caress of the sun and the kiss of love from humanity?

The music was within me, and the People of Peace were dancing. They were neither human nor spiritual; they were both. They were peace of mind and the peace of belonging; they were everything that mattered, not wealth or conquest, not power or domination. They were acceptance and equality, presided over by An Cailleach, the veiled one, the one with a secret, the queen of the Daoine Sidhe.

'Welcome,' the words said.

'Welcome,' the People of Peace echoed.

'Welcome home to acceptance and peace.'

I saw her sitting on a throne of glittering granite, smiling to me through hazel eyes with her small ears slightly pointed and her hand extended in welcome. I stepped forward, gliding through the People as the music rose to a crescendo within my mind.

'Welcome,' Christine said.

The man with the kindly eyes stood at Christine's back. Dressed in ecclesiastical garb from the past, if such a term was correct in such a timeless environment, he appeared relaxed and content. We were of the same blood and bore the same name.

'Welcome to my kin,' said the Reverend Robert Kirk.

'Welcome to my most particular friend' said the Queen of the People of Peace.

'I am home,' I said and I did not wish to be anywhere else in the whole world. I allowed the music and love and sense of belonging to flow around me and enter in me. 'I am home,' I repeated.

The granite began to shake. The whole foundation of my world altered as something dragged me away from that magical place. I struggled and fought to return, reaching out to grasp the Queen's welcoming hand. The music faded, the light died, the warmth dissipated, the acceptance vanished, the sense of belonging altered to one of familiar cold alienation. I was back in Tigh-na-Beiste with the rain smearing the grimy windows and the chair hard under my unfashionably ample backside.

'Brenda!' Christine's voice was in my ears. 'Brenda! Come back!'

I opened my eyes. 'Christine? Where am I?'

Concern filled Christine's eyes. 'I thought I had lost you!' Christine did not relinquish my shoulder. I took hold of her hand, grasping at hope, trying to retain some memory of that place of hope.

'You were right,' I said, still confused. 'You were right about the Reverend Kirk.'

'Never mind that now. We have to get out of here.'

'Why?' Only then did I smell the smoke. 'What's happening?'

'The house is on fire. Either a spark from the fire hit the wooden floor, or a draught knocked down the candle. Come on, Brenda.' Christine's voice was urgent.

I struggled to return to sordid reality and fastened on one fact. 'You came to save me.'

'Of course, I did. You're my friend. Come on, Brenda!'

Clinging to Christine's hand, I staggered across the room, with my mind fastening onto her words. 'You're my friend'. The floorboards were ablaze, with smoke choking my throat and stinging my eyes. Breathing was difficult. I coughed and slipped, with Christine hauling me along. The door of the doom was on fire, orange-yellow flames licking around the handle and the hinges.

I coughed, choking, remembering Lorna's death struggle. Would we die in here? Would this be the end? I preferred the languid dream of the Reverend Kirk's world to this nightmare of substance.

'Take a step back,' Christine was in control. 'The fire is weakening the door.' She coughed and continued with tears streaming from her eyes. 'If we both charge at it we might break it down.'

I nodded, unable to speak, unwilling to accept this world after my brief visit to the other.

'On three.' Christine looked at me and, amazingly, she smiled. 'We'll do it together, Brenda!'

'Together,' I said.

'One, two and three!'

We jumped forward, hitting the door with a mighty wallop. Either Christine was correct, and the fire had damaged the door, or age had weakened the wood, but we crashed through and into the landing outside. Smoke and flames greeted us down the stairs and in the lobby.

'Rescue the rucksacks,' Christine croaked, for we had piled the rucksacks outside the living room. Opening the front door, we threw all we could outside until the heat and smoke grew too intense and forced us away. We staggered, gasping as the flames roared around Tigh-na-Beiste, burning the body of Lorna, consuming the evil of that fearful place.

We lay together, side by side on the damp earth with the heat of the burning building behind us. Stretching out my arm, I touched Christine's hand. She gripped my fingers, wordless.

'What now?' I looked toward An Cailleach. The first glow of dawn touched her face, lighting her summit like a beacon. 'Christine,' I said, and stopped. I was not sure what I wished to say.

'I'm here.' Christine said.

I touched her arm, relieved to find that she was flesh and blood. In this terrible peninsula of deceptions and nightmares, I was unsure what to believe and what to discard.

'We're not alone.' Christine said.

I felt the sick slide of dread. 'What is it this time, Christine? What horror has that house devised next?'

'It's all right, Brenda,' Christine reassured me. 'Look out to sea.'

I saw the lights offshore. 'A fishing boat,' I said.

'We'll see.' Standing up, Christina stepped away from the burning building and sat on the drystane dyke that surrounded the garden. Even smoke-blackened and with her hair a tangle around her head, she seemed quite composed. I joined her, coughing in the smoke as the fire consumed the evil that had been Tigh-na- Beiste.

We sat side-by-side as the sun gradually slid up the sky, bringing light, warmth and colour to the world. I said nothing. My mind was busy with what had happened the previous night. Had I murdered all these women? What had it all meant? I did not know. I only knew that I ached to return to that place where I had felt so welcome.

'Here she comes.' Christina said. 'She's a yacht, not a fishing boat.'

'A yacht? That's unusual.' I looked up as the sun caught the brilliant white paintwork of the one-masted sloop. She slipped close inshore with a dinghy towing behind her and her name in simple black letters painted on her bow. *Luceo non Uro.*

'*Luceo non Uro*,' I said. 'That's a strange name.'

'I shine not burn,' Christine said. 'It's the motto of Clan Mackenzie.'

'Trust you to know that,' I tried to smile.

'Did Major Mackenzie not say that his wife was sailing around the coast?'

I said nothing to that. I could not remember.

'Ahoy ashore!' The woman at the wheel was about thirty, blonde, and tanned with wind and weather. 'Do you need help? I'm Catriona Mackenzie, and I saw your fire.'

I felt the tears burning my eyes as Christine answered. 'Yes, please! Could you take us to the mainland?'

And then I collapsed.

Chapter Seventeen

I awoke with the scent of clean sheets and the bustle of busy nurses. A brusque sister hurried over to me. 'You're awake then, Miss Smith.'

I nodded. 'Yes. Where am I?'

'Belford Hospital,' the sister spoke as if she disapproved of the entire world. 'That's in Fort William, in case you did not know.'

'How did I get here?' I looked around me. The ward was scrupulously clean, with the smell of disinfectant prevailing. 'Where's Christine?'

'Miss Brown is two beds down from you,' the sister said.

'What happened?' I asked. I lay on my back with the crisp linen tucked so tightly around me that it was nearly impossible to move, let alone to sit up and look for Christine.

'Here comes the doctor,' the sister said. 'He'll tell you all you need to know. Dr Ferguson! Miss Smith is awake.'

Dr Ferguson was about 40, with sandy hair and a pale complexion. He marched towards me with military precision that his neatly clipped moustache only emphasised. 'Good afternoon, Miss Smith. How are you feeling?'

'I'm fine doctor, thank you.' I tried to sit up. 'Why am I here?'

'When you came in you were semi-conscious and rambling.' Dr Ferguson sat on the edge of my bed. 'We thought it best to give you a thorough examination.'

'An examination for what, doctor?' I tried to see past him, to see Christine.

'You were semi-conscious,' Dr Ferguson repeated, 'with some convulsions and a high fever. What you were saying made no sense, no sense at all and I suspected that you were experiencing hallucinations.'

I felt the colour rush to my cheeks. 'What was I saying, doctor?'

'Oh, all sorts of rubbish,' Dr Ferguson said. 'You were mumbling some nonsense about a living mountain and people of peace and other things.' He shook his head, smiling. 'My nurses thought they were dealing a mad woman, but I had seen the symptoms before.'

'How is Christine?'

'Christine Brown is recovering.' Dr Ferguson said. 'She had the identical symptoms you had, which alerted me to a possible cause. Now I have some questions for you to see if my diagnosis was correct.'

I braced myself for the searching probe to find out how and why I had murdered Kate, Mary, Lorna and Charlie. 'Yes, Doctor.'

'What have you been eating recently?'

That question took me completely by surprise. 'Eating?' I tried to remember. 'Trout. Potatoes, apples, sandwiches…'

'Stop there,' the doctor held up a hand. 'What kind of sandwiches?'

'Marmalade,' I said. 'Dundee marmalade.'

'And what kind of bread?'

I shrugged. 'I don't know. The bread kind of bread.'

'Try to remember. Was it wheat?'

'No,' I thought back to what the manager of the inn, Maurice Nott had said a week and half a lifetime ago. 'We were told that it was rye. The only rye in Scotland I think Mr Nott said.'

Doctor Ferguson nodded with some satisfaction. 'I thought so. I believe you have both suffered from Ergot poisoning.'

I must have looked as uncomprehending as I felt. 'Ergot poisoning?'

Dr Ferguson looked pleased to elaborate. 'Precisely. Rye bread is prone to a fungus called ergot. When people eat infected rye, they can experience a number of symptoms such as nausea, increased heartbeat and vision problems, then hallucinations and eventually death.'

I stared at him. 'Hallucinations?' I repeated. 'Can it make you imagine seeing things that don't make sense and think things that are not possible?'

Dr Ferguson gave a slow nod. 'That's exactly what may happen,' he agreed.

I clutched at this saving straw. 'Do you think that's what happened to me, Doctor? I had the strangest of visions.'

The doctor nodded again. 'I am certain you suffered from ergot poisoning, which leads to hallucinations.'

I closed my eyes. *Oh, thank God.* There was no witch-mountain, no co-walker, no Washerwoman at the Ford. All these things had been hallucinations. I had not murdered Mary or Kate, I had not enticed Charlie or Lorna to their deaths. I felt the slow tears burning my eyes.

'You are safe now,' the doctor said. 'We'll keep you in hospital for a few days to allow the ergot to clear from your system and you'll be right as rain.'

I shook my head. 'No, doctor,' I said. 'You don't understand. Most of our party died. Kate Gordon, Lorna Menzies, Charlotte Gunn and Mary Ablach. They're all dead.'

'Miss Brown gave me a full account of your terrible experiences. I was sorry to hear about the deaths of course,' Dr Ferguson said, 'if not surprised. They will also have endured their own hallucinations.' He stood up. 'Well, Miss Smith, at least you're safe in hospital. I hear that there is a party going across to recover the bodies of your friends.'

'Thank you, doctor.' I lay back in the bed. Ergot poisoning. All that happened had been due to hallucinations caused by a fungus on the rye bread. The delusions must have affected us in different ways so that we saw or imagined that we saw things that were important to us personally. Such a little thing, a fungus in bread given to us by the Inn as a peace offering, yet it had caused the deaths of four good women. Did that mean I had not murdered my colleagues? Did that mean I had never visited that place of incredible peace where I had felt so much at home?

I did not know. It had seemed so real at the time. I felt the tears burn my eyes at the thought of my companions being dead, yet I was also immensely relieved that I had not killed them. I was not a monster.

Looking sideways, I saw Christine lying quietly on her bed. When she smiled at me, I knew that everything would be all right. I watched her for a few moments as the light from the tall windows fell on her slightly pointed ears.

Christine stuck out her tongue. 'It's all right, Brenda,' she said. 'You'll never be alone again. Whatever happens, we'll always be together.'

Comfortable warmth spread over me as I lay back in bed. When I looked out of the window, I saw a pair of eagles spiralling upwards into the sky; my guardian eagles, looking after me as they had been for millennia. Everything was right with the world; I would never be alone again.

Notes

Much of the background to this story is based on Scottish folklore and legend, with slices of factual history where required. Scottish folklore has the Washerwoman at the Ford and the *Caoineag*, as well as mermaids and witches. The story of the Badenoch witches was taken from folklore, although I added the part where the witches, as eagles turned into mountains. However, there are many hills with the name of *An Cailleach*, meaning old woman or hag throughout the Scottish Highlands including one in Badenoch.

The name *An Cailleach* may also mean 'veiled one' and could refer to somebody from a different world, the world of the supernatural. In old Gaelic tales, the *Cailleach* was often *Cailleach Bheur*, the blue-faced hag or the goddess of winter. She appeared, or was reborn at Samhain, now Halloween, and brought snow, until Brigit, the spirit of spring removed her. In Ireland, *Cailleach Bheare* was the home of the dead, where the Cailleach wore out a succession of husbands while she enjoyed eternal life.

The use of rowan wood and rowan berries to protect against evil was a common practice in old Scotland, and many old farm steadings, clachans and cottages have a rowan tree planted nearby. The Moray cottage in which I spent many years has a rowan tree in the back garden.

The Reverend Robert Kirk was a real person, a late 17th-century intellectual who translated the Bible into Gaelic. His beliefs and actions are as described in the book, while his book about fairies is often regarded as a classic in the genre.

The Highland Clearances were one of the darkest episodes in Scottish History. It was a time that included forced evictions when the landowners, often clan chiefs, removed their tenants to make way for sheep, which made more money. Some of the mass evictions involved extreme violence, with entire communities forced onto ships and sent abroad. Many people even today, are still bitter about events that emptied many inland glens.

Finally, there is the cave in the hidden corrie and the accounts of human sacrifice. Although that particular cave is fictional, it is based on the Sculptor's Cave on the Moray coast where children's heads were placed on posts. Sacrifice to water spirits seems to have happened in various places in the Celtic world, including, perhaps at the Dour Water at Aberdour, where there are legends of human sacrifice near a fairy hill.

Helen Susan Swift, Moray, Aberdeen and Sutherland, Scotland, 2018

Glossary

Bein – mountain, hill
Burn – stream, often fast flowing down a hill
Caoineag - Scottish version of the banshee
Clach – stone
Clachan – a small settlement in the Highlands
Clach gorm – blue stone
Deisil – sunwise, right handed and lucky
Drizzle- fine persistent rain, common in Scotland
Drystane dyke – wall fashioned from stones without mortar. Making these walls is a rare skill and thousands of miles of them cross the hills and fields of Scotland.
Gaelic – the language of Highland Scotland. One of the most ancient languages of Europe, it was once spoken over much of the country but is now confined to the Outer Hebrides, although the present Scottish government are making efforts for its preservation.
Gabhar adhaire – snipe, literally air goat
Ghlo – mist
Gin ye daur – 'if you dare' or 'go on, I dare you'. The motto of the most ancient and noble Order of the Thistle and also of 603 City of Edinburgh squadron Royal Auxiliary Air Force which helped shoot down the first German bomber over Britain when the Luftwaffe raided the Firth of Forth in September 1939.

Glaistig - or green lady, often the guardian spirit of the family. Usually a long-dead ancestress.
Kisimuil's Galley – 16th century song from the isle of Barra. It celebrates MacNeil of Barra, who was a famous or infamous pirate.
Loch – Lake
Lochan – small loch
Lum- flue of a chimney
Munro –Scottish mountain over 3000 feet high
Peat bog – area of ground composed largely of liquid peat. It is not advisable to try and walk across, especially after rain.
Tuaithiuil – opposite of deisil, also known as widdershins, the way of evil, unlucky.
Whaup – Scottish name for the curlew

Dear reader,

We hope you enjoyed reading *Dark Mountain.* Please take a moment to leave a review, even if it's a short one. Your opinion is important to us.

Discover more books by Helen Susan Swift at https://www.nextchapter.pub/authors/helen-susan-swift

Want to know when one of our books is free or discounted? Join the newsletter at http://eepurl.com/bqqB3H

Best regards,

Helen Susan Swift and the Next Chapter Team

You might also like:

Saucy Jacky by Doug Lamoreux

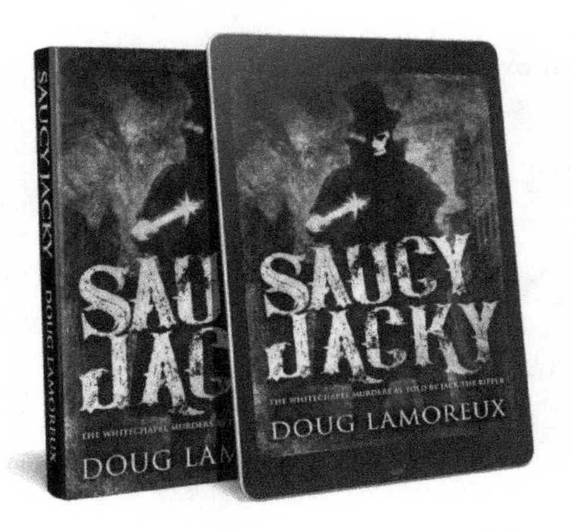

To read the first chapter for free, please head to:
https://www.nextchapter.pub/books/saucy-jacky-whitechapel-murders-told-by-jack-the-ripper

Books by the Author

- **Tales of the Dark Past**
  - Dark Voyage
  - Dark Mountain
- **Lowland Romance**
  - The Handfasters
  - The Tweedie Passion
  - A Turn of Cards
  - The Name of Love
- The Malvern Mystery
- Sarah's Story
- Women of Scotland

Dark Mountain
ISBN: 978-4-86745-714-6

Published by
Next Chapter
1-60-20 Minami-Otsuka
170-0005 Toshima-Ku, Tokyo
+818035793528
29th April 2021

CPSIA information can be obtained
at www.ICGtesting.com
Printed in the USA
BVHW080444120521
607042BV00004B/469